LOVING YASMINE

BEYOND GRANITE FALLS - BOOK 1

ANA E ROSS

CEDAR TREES PUBLISHERS

LOVING YASMINE

Copyright © 2015 by Ana E Ross
ISBN: 9780986339929
Cedar Trees Publishers

Edited by Crazy Diamond Editing
Cover Design by Najla Qamber Designs
Cedar Trees Publishers

ISBN: 9780986339929
ISBN-13: 978-0-9863399-2-9

www.anaeross.com

To my loyal fans, my family, and my friends who believe in me. I love you, guys.

To my editor, Jane, who lets me know when I need to make a change.

Blessings!

CHAPTER ONE

"You want to stay over tonight?" Yasmine gazed up at Robert as he stood hesitantly at the door of her condo with one foot in and one out.

"I don't know, Yas." He set her suitcase on the floor and dropped her keys into a bamboo bowl on a table near the door. "Should I?" he asked, his entrancing chocolate eyes level under dark bushy brows.

Untangling her gaze from his, Yasmine removed her Valentino crossbody bag and placed it on the chair next to the table. As much as she would love to rip off their clothes and writhe under Robert for an hour or so before falling asleep snuggled up to his hard muscular body, she wasn't one to beg—not even for the best sex of her life.

Lifting her gaze again, she watched his mouth tighten with irritation as he stared down at her. Her desire to reach up and kiss the softness back into his smooth sexy lips was strong, but Yasmine squelched it. She was so good at controlling her desires—sometimes. "Can you close my door? All my cool air is escaping to the outside."

"You want me on the inside or the outside of your door when it's closed?"

Yasmine shrugged indifferently. She'd already posed the question, and that was all the invitation he was getting tonight. "That's up to you, Robert. I'll be upstairs while you decide." Before he could reply, she wheeled her suitcase toward the flight of stairs that led to the second floor.

"Let me help you with that," Robert said behind her, his footsteps following in the wake of his deep baritone voice.

"No, I got it."

"Why do you always have to be so—so…independent, Yas? Let a brother help you once in a while."

Because that's how a lot of women get lassoed.

Yasmine lifted the suitcase and ascended the steps as quickly as she could, carrying about thirty pounds of clothes, shoes, handbags, makeup, and toiletries with her. A smile briefly braced her lips as she felt the heat from Robert's stare burning a hole in the back of her bare legs and thighs left visible from her white shorts. She put a little more effort into wriggling her buttocks under the cotton material.

She knew he hated her independence and wished she would lean on him more, but that wasn't Yasmine's style anymore. Like a lot of women, she used to think that she needed a man to perform certain tasks and solve certain problems. She'd kicked that philosophy to the curb when she became a divorce attorney, and realized how one woman after another got sucked into a relationship she shouldn't have been in, merely because a man flexed his muscles at her.

After her first few cases, Irina Dunn's famous catchphrase, "A woman needs a man like a fish needs a bicycle," had become Yasmine's mantra. When she needed a plumber, she called a professional, paid him, and sent him on his way. No expectations. No obligations. When she wanted a man and his sweet loving, she called Robert. They gave and they took equally, enjoying each other to the max.

As she walked down the hall, Yasmine heard Robert's footsteps retreating across the floor, followed by the firm thud of her door closing behind him. *So he decided to go home to his Beacon Hill townhouse after all.*

She flipped a switch as she entered her master suite, and blinked as all thirty bulbs from the crystal chandelier hanging over her bed flooded the bedroom with light—too much light. With a sigh, she dimmed the bulbs, placed her suitcase on the luggage stand, and unzipped it. As she proceeded to unpack, she heard the engine of Robert's silver Ferrari roar to life.

He'd been moody on the ride back from Granite Falls—a bustling little town in the foothills of the White Mountains in northern New Hampshire—where they'd spent the last three days. Yesterday, they'd attended the most magnificent wedding she'd ever witnessed in real life, or even seen on TV. Yasmine hadn't even imagined weddings could be so grandiose.

Four billionaire friends and their wives had renewed their vows of love and commitment to each other and their families. Michelle Carter—Yasmine's best friend since childhood, and Robert's younger sister—was one of the bride wives.

Yesterday, Robert had given his sister away for the second time to Dr. Erik LaCrosse. Yasmine had had the pleasure of being Michelle's matron of honor at her first wedding four years ago, but yesterday she'd sat at the front of the church among the honored guests.

Robert, Michelle, and Yasmine had all grown up together in one of the toughest neighborhoods in Manchester, New Hampshire, but they'd all made it out of the hood to a more affluent lifestyle.

Eighteen years ago when Yasmine was eleven, Robert had packed up twelve-year-old Michelle and rented an apartment in a better area of town to get her away from their abusive alcoholic father. Although they weren't living next door to each other, she and Michelle were able to attend the same middle and high schools, graduate together, and maintain their BFF relationship.

Robert never returned to that neighborhood, but a series of unfortunate events that had almost totally destroyed Michelle had sent her back to live with Yasmine for a while. She'd eventually left it for good four year ago when she married the sexy, widower, billionaire doctor, Erik LaCrosse, father of her charge when she worked as a nanny in the LaCrosses' Amherst home. And last but not least, Yasmine had said goodbye to their rundown neighborhood, three years ago.

It had taken Yasmine a bit longer to leave her origins because unlike Robert and Michelle, she still had family ties in Manchester: her parents, Luke and Marie Reynolds, her brother, Luke Jr., her sister, Naomi, Naomi's husband, Felix, and Yasmine's thirteen-year-old nephew, Peter—Naomi and Felix's son—on whom she shamelessly doted.

And besides, she hadn't had the fortune of meeting, falling in love with, and then marrying a billionaire. She'd had to work hard and fight for every little bit of luxury she now enjoyed— mainly her high-end, ocean-view, three-bedroom condo in Charlestown, Massachusetts, and her little red Jaguar F-type.

Not that Robert and Michelle hadn't worked hard as well. Robert had been working since he was ten years old to keep him and Michelle from starving when their worthless father continuously neglected and abused them. Robert had singlehandedly put himself through Harvard School of Dental Medicine, graduated top of his class, and established Carter Orthodontics that eventually expanded into the very prosperous Carter, Obryan & Levitt Orthodontics. Robert was one of the best dentists in New England with a clientele that included the wealthiest and most influential people in Boston and the surrounding areas.

He recently became a self-made billionaire through Carter Dental, a company that invented and manufactured dental instruments both domestically and globally. Yasmine was very proud of his accomplishments. As a matter of fact, he had been her inspiration to make something of herself. She'd also admired the way he took care of his little sister, even when he was just a kid himself. He'd had to grow up fast.

As for Michelle, even though she'd married her billionaire soul mate, she was a #1 *New York Times* bestselling author many times over, and a multimillionaire in her own rights from the sales of her books—stories she'd written about the kids from their old neighborhood, kids she used to mentor, and was still mentoring up to this day—many of whom had attended the wedding yesterday.

Those little rascals—Yasmine's nephew, Peter, included— probably thought they were stuck in a dream during their three-day stay at Hotel Andreas, one of the best hotels in the world, eating cuisine they couldn't pronounce much less spell, pampered by private caretakers, and being chauffeured around in tinted limousines. *That was Michelle. Advocate for the underdog.* No matter how rich and famous she got, the girl would never forget where she came from, or those she'd left behind.

Yasmine swallowed back a lump as she thought of her oldest and best friend who now lived three hours north of Boston, and who had since made three new best friends—Kaya, Shaina, and Tashi—wives of Erik's billionaire buddies, Bryce Fontaine, Massimo Andretti, and Adamo Andreas. They were all wonderful, down-to-earth women whom Yasmine had met and, God help her, liked a lot.

But Yasmine missed her Mich something terrible.

With her unpacking complete, Yasmine walked into her en

suite and began removing her makeup. If she were to be honest with herself, she'd have to admit that she was jealous of Michelle's new friends. Not only did the billionaire wives have a lot in common with each other, including hot, handsome husbands, adorable children, and fast, expensive sports cars, but they all lived within a ten-minute drive of each other and saw one another almost daily, while Yasmine was lucky if she saw her best friend four times a year.

They talked on the phone frequently, but it was never the same. It would never be like it used to be when she and Michelle lived next door to each other in Manchester, or even when Michelle lived with her while she was going through the most difficult time of her life. Yasmine had known for sure that things between them were changing the night Michelle had invited her and Robert to dinner at the house in Amherst, five years ago.

Nobody, not even Yasmine and Robert, had known at the time that Michelle and Erik had secretly married, until some stinky shit had hit the fan months later and ripped them apart. Paradoxically, while Michelle's life was on a downward spiral, Yasmine's was flourishing, and as much as she'd longed to share her joy with her best friend, she hadn't. How could she, when her new love interest was Robert? It would have been cruel to flaunt her own happiness in Michelle's face while her best friend's heart was broken up over Erik.

Then, just when Yasmine was about to share her joy, fate threw her a curve ball, turning her own life upside down, forcing her to make some fast and hard decisions about her future. Those decisions, regrettably so, were now Yasmine's deepest, darkest secrets.

Four years later, Yasmine still didn't know if she'd ever confide in Michelle. It might destroy their friendship. Plus, Michelle might feel compelled to tell her brother, which could inadvertently bring Yasmine's relationship with Robert to the ultimate end. She couldn't risk losing her friendship with Michelle, or the love Yasmine and Robert had for each other. She knew she'd have to tell him sometime, but that *sometime* should be at her own choosing.

Expelling a deep breath, Yasmine pinned up her hair, dropped her clothes on the bathroom floor, and stepped into her shower stall. She squeezed her lids together and turned her face toward the warm sprays as tears stung her eyes. She should know better than to dwell on her dark secret, especially after spending so much time with Robert—a man who loved kids, and who'd been voicing his desires to have a family ever since his sister had gotten married and begun popping out babies one after the other.

Robert was always excited about visiting Granite Falls, mainly to spend time with his sister's children—twelve-year-old Precious, four-year-old Erik Jr., three-year-old Tiffany, and seven-month-old Fiona. The kids were always equally excited to see their Uncle Robert, who had no qualms about getting down on the floor or rolling around in the grass with them. The experience of watching them interact always filled Yasmine with conflicting emotions.

Yasmine had been crushing on Robert ever since she was a little girl. She'd dreamed of marrying him and living Happily Ever After in a condo in the north end of Manchester—where the rich people lived. She'd admitted her feelings when she turned fifteen. He'd said she was just a kid and too young to know anything about love. He'd broken her teenage heart, and to hide her hurt, Yasmine had started making fun of his arrogance, calling him boring and a stuffed-shirt, and in turn, he'd called her impertinent and a sassy mouth.

Yasmine smiled at the memories. They used to make Michelle so mad with the name-calling. But when push came to shove, she could always depend on Robert to be there for her, even more than her own brother. After Michelle graduated high school, Robert moved to Boston to start his dental practice, and Yasmine began seeing him less and less. Soon years passed without any contact, until the night of Michelle and Erik's dinner party in Amherst.

The minute she saw him, Yasmine's heart had begun to pound like a jungle drum that could be heard for miles, and she'd begun to quiver inside. And to cover up her reaction to seeing him, Yasmine had done what she always did to hide her feelings: attack his rigid personality.

By the end of the night, neither one of them could resist the strong vibes between them. Robert had spent that night and the next two at her apartment in Manchester, and they'd stayed in bed all weekend, living off of passion, pizza, and water. They'd been hooked on each other since then.

But skeptical Yasmine knew that hot sex, especially hot sex in a new relationship, wasn't enough to build anything on. Jeremy, her first boyfriend, had proven that to her when he too had broken her heart.

Yasmine had given Robert a second chance, then just as she'd begun to feel hopeful about a future with him, he'd discovered the ugly truth about the man he'd called *Dad* for most of his life. It was a difficult and painful time for him as he tried to reevaluate himself as a son, a brother, and a man. But instead of turning to her for comfort and moral support, he'd pulled away at a time when she needed him most.

How could she trust him with her most precious commodity when he'd rejected her twice? How could she believe in love and marriage, and Happily Ever After when her career as a divorce attorney brought her into daily contact with couples who were once in love, but who eventually reached the stage where they ripped each other apart over silverware and chandeliers?

To avoid that kind of turmoil and disappointment in her life,

Yasmine had conditioned herself to believe in *here* and *now*. And right *now*, she wished Rob was *here*.

Yasmine turned off the shower, stepped out of the stall, and wrapped a fluffy towel around her body. It was going to be a lonely night, but at least she had the erotic memories of making love with Rob before they left Granite Falls that afternoon. Those memories would have to suffice until they saw each other again —hopefully tomorrow after he'd had time to cool down and miss her.

In the meantime, she had King George to help her cope with her Robert withdrawal. King George never gave her any grief about anything. He just did his damn job, got out, and left her alone until she summoned him again.

As Yasmine walked into her bedroom and headed for the bureau, she swore that vibrating dildo enjoyed her body just as much as Robert did. She might have to change his name to Sir Rob or Sir Robert. Whichever. One of them.

CHAPTER TWO

I t was a beautiful August night and the sound of soft jazz filtering through the car stereo coupled with the moonlight reflecting off the ocean had Robert in a highly amorous mood as he sat in his Ferrari—still parked in Yasmine's driveway—staring up at the window to her bedroom.

He leaned his head against the headrest and tapped his fingers against the steering wheel, vacillating on whether or not to go home or go back inside. He'd left her house forty-five minutes ago, determined to put some physical distance between them, but five minutes after he'd started his engine, he'd turned it off when he couldn't make himself drive away.

That little wisp of a woman had a hold on him like no one else in this world. He loved her so damned much, his heart hurt every time he thought of her, saw her, heard her voice, and when he touched her, God, his fingertips sizzled from the electricity between them. Making love with her was like swimming through a sea of hot thick honey. She was that sweet and addictive.

Robert groaned and adjusted his position as he felt his cock begin to tighten and strain against his cargo shorts. They'd made love just a few hours ago, yet he yearned for her as if they hadn't seen each other in weeks. His addiction had led him to propose to her twice, and she'd turned him down twice for two different reasons.

Three years had passed, and he hadn't asked her the third time because he knew that when and if he popped the question again, it would be the last time—whether or not she accepted. A smart man would probably have said to hell with her and moved on, but Robert wasn't smart. *He was a fool in love.*

Although Yas hadn't said it—except for that one time—he knew she loved him. He saw it in her eyes, heard it in her voice, and felt it in her tremor every time he touched her. It would be nice if, every once in a while, she would act as if she needed him.

A man needed to feel like a man in areas of a woman's life other than the bedroom. A man needed his ego stroked. Having his ego stroked was just as important to him as having his cock stroked—and Yasmine was the best cock-stroker he'd ever known—a fact he'd discovered when she was way too young to be doing the kinds of things grown men and women did with each other. But liberal Yasmine hadn't thought so.

Robert grimaced as he recalled one particular hot summer night when she'd spent the weekend at his and Michelle's apartment. He'd never taken any of his girlfriends to the home he'd made for him and Michelle, and Michelle was not allowed to have any boys there. As a precaution against potential false accusations of rape and molestation on his part, Yasmine—whom they both knew they could trust—was the only friend who was allowed to sleep over.

Robert's trust was breached that weekend when in the middle of the night, fifteen-year-old Little Miss Yasmine left the one bedroom that Michelle occupied, crept into the living room, and crawled in beside him on the sofa bed where he slept. Robert had been awakened to her warm, near-naked body curled around him, her hand caressing his junk through his boxers, her wet kisses on his lips, and her tantalizing whispers in his ears—telling him that she loved him, and wanted him to be her first and only lover.

He was twenty-one at the time, and horny as a grumpy toad since his then college girlfriend had gone back to Oregon for the summer. Somehow, he'd found the strength and the morals to say *No* to Yasmine's awkward attempts to seduce him. He'd pushed her roughly away, and scolded her for behaving recklessly, just as sternly as he would have scolded Michelle if he'd ever found out she'd pulled such a brazen stunt with a boy her age, much less a grown man.

Yasmine had run back to the bedroom in tears, probably from a mixture of embarrassment and rejection. He knew he'd crushed her ego, and hopefully her infatuation with him, but he couldn't risk her fantasizing about him in any way, shape, or form, or hoping he'd change his mind about making love to her.

She was a minor, not to mention his little sister's best friend, and at that time of his life, Robert's main priority was looking after Michelle, making sure she made it into adulthood without adding to the scars—both emotionally and physically—that their father had already inflicted on her. He would have been of no use to her if he'd been thrown into jail for statutory rape, or had been put six feet under if Mr. Reynolds had gotten to him first.

He would have lost his integrity and his sister's respect, which were far more essential to him than a few minutes of awkward sexual pleasure with an underage virgin. He'd never told Michelle about that night, and he doubted Yasmine ever had either. For his sister's sake, instead of banning Yas from sleeping over again, he'd made her swear that she would never again pull such a stupid stunt with him or any other man. She'd kept her promise—well, to him at least.

That night, their relationship had changed from warm and amicable to almost hostile. It was as if they were both trying too hard not to like each other. Knowing where even the mere thought of his attraction to her could lead, he'd hidden his true feelings by pretending to be unfriendly.

Robert now wondered if Yasmine was punishing him for breaking her teenage heart. He knew her; she didn't forgive easily. Or could it be that her fear of commitment was directly related to her successful career as a divorce lawyer at Hayward & Harley Law? After all, she dealt with failed marriages on a daily basis—spouses whose love for each other had turned into contempt. Maybe it was a combination of both.

Yasmine had initially been interested in criminal law, but she switched to family law after Michelle's first *and* secret marriage to Erik fell apart, and Michelle had ended up living with Yasmine at her apartment in Manchester. That marriage and the ensuing breakup were both a blessing and a curse for Robert. A blessing, because it was Erik and Michelle's dinner invitation that had brought him and Yasmine together again. A curse because their breakup was the catalyst that had changed the course of Yasmine's career, and possibly turned her off from believing in Happily Ever After.

Prior to that night in Amherst, Robert hadn't seen her in years, but when he'd walked into the living room and had seen her sitting there, damn tantalizing in her little black dress, his heart had stopped beating for countless seconds, and the rush of feelings he'd locked away since the night she'd tried to seduce him had come flooding to the surface of his being.

He'd been enchanted with her sexy smile, her glowing smooth caramel complexion, her compelling chestnut brown eyes under dark sweeping lashes, and her rosy lips that made his mouth water. His little Yas had grown up into a gorgeous desirable woman with the tempting body of a goddess. All during dinner, Rob had done nothing but fantasize about stripping her naked and spreading her out under him.

Fortunately for him, those had been Yasmine's thoughts, too.

When they left Amherst, they'd broken every speed limit racing to her apartment in Manchester, where they'd spent the next three days discovering and devouring each other over and over again. Robert had never met a woman as flexible as Yasmine. They'd made love in positions he'd only fantasized about. Up to that point, that night had been the most memorable of Robert's life. He'd found his groove and he'd sworn never to lose it. His only regret was that he wasn't her first and only lover.

Robert sighed as he thought of the flip side of the coin—the collapse of his sister's secret marriage. Yasmine had been so mad at Erik for hurting Michelle that she'd wanted to take him for everything he owned, including his child, and give it all to Michelle. Her best friend's heartache had transformed Yasmine into an advocate for women who'd married into wealth, and whose husbands tried to stick it to them in divorce court.

Not that Erik had tried to railroad Michelle or anything like that. Michelle had placed herself in a very sticky situation by lying to Erik and hiding secrets from him. Although Robert's heart had broken over his sister's pain, he understood Erik's feelings. You can't build a relationship, much less a marriage on lies and secrets. They'd found their way back to each other, and one of the happiest days of Robert's life happened four years ago when he gave away his sister to Erik in a public wedding at their lakeside home in Granite Falls.

Unfortunately for Robert, while Michelle and Erik went on to revel blissfully in their Happily Ever After, his and Yasmine's relationship had taken a downward turn when she rejected his first proposal.

At that painfully embarrassing memory, Robert tapped one hand against his steering wheel, as the first floor of Yasmine's condo and eventually her bedroom plunged into darkness. His other hand hovered over the ignition button of his Ferrari. Should he go or should he stay?

He started as his cell phone rang. Recognizing the ring as Lani Obryan's, one of the two associates he'd brought into his practice, he reached over to the driver's seat and tapped the "phone" and "speaker" icons. "Hey, Lani."

"Hey, Rob. Are you back in Boston?"

Lani wasn't one to beat around the bush. Robert rubbed at the muscles in the sides of his neck. "Yeah. We're back."

"I watched a replay of the wedding on TV last night, but I'm sure it was nothing compared to being there in person. You looked very handsome, by the way." She chuckled.

"Thanks, Lani. It was fabulous. Beautiful. Breathtaking." A smile split his lips as he recalled the joy of walking his sister down the aisle and giving her to Erik for the second time. Michelle was happy. That's all he'd ever wanted for her. He'd sworn to protect and look after her since the day their father brought her home from the hospital without their mom, who'd died giving birth to her baby girl.

Robert had been only five years old, but after listening to his baby sister cry for hours on her first night home while their drunk father slept, he knew that if he himself didn't take care of her, she would have died. All his hard work had paid off. His little sister was a beautiful, intelligent, and kindhearted young woman, a brilliant writer, and a loving and dedicated mother and wife. She'd already accomplished so much in life, much more than he could have ever dreamed for her. She'd exceeded his biggest hopes. He was proud of her.

"Are you on the hill?"

Lani's voice cut into his thoughts. He blinked at the mist in his eyes and cleared the frog from his throat. "No. I'm—I'm at Yasmine's," he said deliberately.

"Oh."

Robert wasn't surprised at her cool response. He'd met Lani during his college senior year. She was a transfer junior, smart and attractive, and they'd quickly begun a friends-with-benefits relationship. When he graduated, they parted as friends, but kept in touch. A year later, when she graduated, he'd asked her to join his practice. Initially, for professional reasons, they'd agreed not to resume their sexual relationship, but as the months and then years slipped by and they both went in and out of relationships, they'd begun flirting with each other, and had one *let's-see-where-this-might-lead* date a week before Michelle's dinner party.

It was possible that if he and Yasmine hadn't hooked up that night, he and Lani might now be in a very serious relationship, perhaps even married, with one kid, at least. But as fate would have it, Lani met John a year after he and Yas began seeing each other. She was now a happily married wife, and mother of a ten-month old baby girl.

"Do you have a moment to talk?" Lani cut into his reverie again.

Robert shifted in his seat and took a quick glance toward Yasmine's house. "Sure. What's on your mind?"

"I checked your schedule and noticed that you're free until eleven thirty tomorrow."

"Right."

"I was wondering if you could take my first two clients in the morning. I have to take Colleen to her pediatrician."

"Is she ill?" he asked of his goddaughter.

"She's been battling a cold for the past few days. I just need her doctor to look at her, make sure she doesn't have an infection or anything serious."

"I get it. Family comes first, especially the little ones. Besides, you covered for me last week while I was up north. What time are your appointments?"

She sighed. "You're gonna hate me."

"Just give it to me."

"I have a brace removal at seven."

Robert groaned. "Seven?"

"I know. I know. Sorry. She has to catch a ten o'clock flight out of Logan to the west coast for a family wedding."

"Yeah, yeah, yeah. When's the next one?"

"I have a consultation for a possible implant at ten. It shouldn't take too long and should give you enough time to make your first appointment. I would have asked Vaughn, but he's booked solid from eight."

"No problem."

"I can take one of your later appointments though."

"No, you—" He stopped. He needed to see his shrink. "As a matter of fact, I would appreciate that."

"Okay, then it's settled. "I'll email you the files in a minute." She paused. "I hope getting out of bed that early doesn't cause a problem for you and Yasmine."

It won't, since I won't be in her bed. His cock throbbed in protest.

Robert pulled his seat into an upright position, pushed the red ignition button, and listened to his Ferrari's engine roar to life. "She understands," he said, as he put the car into reverse.

"Great. Thanks a lot, Rob. And I'll see you around noon tomorrow."

"Night, Lani. Give my regards to John, and a get-well-soon hug to Colleen. Tell her that her godfather loves her and sends her kisses."

"Will do. Bye. Oh, and give my regards to Yasmine. Tell her that she looked absolutely lovely in that white lace dress," she added and then immediately ended her call.

Sure, Robert thought of her patronizing comment about Yasmine looking lovely in a white dress. Lani had helped him pick out the first engagement ring, so she knew all about Yasmine's rejection, and although she had never openly said it, he knew that like Michelle, Lani didn't appreciate Yasmine stringing him along. Michelle, on the other hand, freely and frequently shared her opinions with both of them, as recently as last week. Michelle had even hinted that perhaps he should start dating other women, or give her an ultimatum. That way he'd know once and for all if Yasmine really wanted him. He and Yasmine had done *ultimatum*, and they always found themselves back in each other's arms and beds.

As he backed out of Yasmine's driveway, Robert wondered what his life would be like if he hadn't hooked up with Yasmine in Amherst that night. Would he have married Lani or some other woman? Would he be happy, or would he and his hypothetical wife be staring angrily at each other across a table with their individual attorneys by their sides? Would he have hired Yasmine to represent him?

Robert didn't know. Once thing he was sure of: from the moment he had his first taste of Yasmine, he knew without a shadow of a doubt that he would never be satisfied with any other woman. Back when he was taking care of Michelle, he'd promised to wait until she was married and settled before he got serious with any woman. There was nothing holding him to that oath anymore. He knew women who were willing to commit and give him the children he wanted, but Yasmine Reynolds was his soul mate. He'd known since that night in Amherst, maybe even before then, like the night she'd crawled into his bed, thirteen years ago.

Lord, he'd been tempted, so tempted, not just physically. He'd needed an emotional connection with someone other than his sister. Someone who knew and understood the hurts and the pain inflicted upon him by his father. Yasmine was that someone. Other than Michelle, she had been the one constant in his life. Back then, her perception of love was pure and innocent, albeit premature. Now it was stained with doubts, imperfections, and fears.

As he blended into the Sunday afternoon traffic on Chelsea Street, Robert wondered if his fantasy of having a family with Yasmine Reynolds was an impossible dream.

CHAPTER THREE

"You're rather quiet tonight, Robert. You usually have a lot to say after visiting your sister."

Robert pulled his gaze from the tree branches bobbing in the wind outside the window and brought it back inside his therapist's Dorchester office.

Dr. Doris West, a stout woman with an ultra-white complexion, a rectangular face, and a square, somewhat masculine-looking chin, stared at him from a white wicker chair. Her hair was a cobweb of silvery gold that made her look much older than her fifty-something years. Robert supposed taking on the burdens of the constant stream of broken patients who flocked to her door had robbed her of her youthfulness.

She adjusted the spectacles on her high-bridged nose, brushed back thin bangs of hair from her forehead, and squinted her hazel eyes at him. "What was different this time, Robert?" she asked in a voice, soft and prodding like an adult would use on a distracted child.

"Weddings make me sentimental."

She chuckled softly and shifted on the chair. "They have that effect on me, too."

Robert leaned back into the sofa and studied the labyrinth of deep wrinkles that had taken up permanent residence on her face. He'd started seeing Dr. West four years ago, a year after he'd first discovered that Timmy Gleason, the man who'd raised him and Michelle, was not their biological father, but a homeless imposter who'd stabbed their real father, Dwight Carter, to death in a back ally in Richmond, Virginia, where his family had once lived.

Robert was a malleable four-year-old when the murder occurred, so it was easy for him to believe the fabricated story his mother had drilled into his head the night she'd returned to their Church Hill apartment with a strange man—a man he clearly knew wasn't his father, but whom he'd accepted as such from that night forward.

Through hypnosis, Dr. West had taken him back to his pre-Timmy Gleason years and helped him awaken the memories that had been suppressed for decades. Before long, his personal memory tract began to come back into focus, and he could hear and see his real father—and recall the woody smell of Old Spice tainted with the smell of motor oil on his skin. He'd begun recalling specific events, pleasant time spent with his parents, laughing and playing together as a family. One recurring memory was sitting on his mother's lap at the kitchen table while his father fixed their toaster oven, tinkered with the handle of their fridge, or fixed the hinges on a drawer that had fallen apart. Robert loved to burrow his nose against her neck and breathe in her cocoa butter and lavender scent. They used to be happy. So happy…

Robert smiled as he remembered visiting the garage where his father worked as a mechanic. He used to look forward to hanging out with his dad on weekends while his mother worked as a waitress in a local diner.

"*I would never want to be a mechanic,*" *Robert had said to his father, who'd been working under the hood of an old pickup truck.*

"*Why?*"

"*Because my hands would get greasy and dirty and Mommy would have to clean under my nails with a toothpick, like she cleans yours. That would hurt.*"

His father had chuckled. "As long as your work is honest and you enjoy it, it doesn't matter what you do, my son. I love working on old engines because I love the sound of them roaring back to life. It gives me satisfaction that I brought something back from the dead. What do you want to do when you grow up, my little Robert?"

"*I don't know, Daddy. Maybe I'll be a fireman.*"

"*Why a fireman?*"

"*'Cause I like big red trucks.*"

His father had dropped his greasy rag on the engine and straightened up like a giant. "No, Robert," he'd said, wagging a finger at him. "You should always know why you want to do something. If you know why you want to do something, you'll feel fulfilled as you do it. If you're not certain why you're doing it, it won't bring you satisfaction."

He'd returned to working on the engine for a few minutes, and then paused to glance at Robert again. "That goes for love as much as it goes for work, Robbie. I know you're too young to understand, but I'm going to say it anyway. You must know why you love one woman above all others, why you want to marry her, and make a family with her. I know why I wanted to marry your mother."

"*Why, Daddy?*"

His father had dropped his rag again, came over to the bench where Robert was sitting, touched his greasy finger to Robert's nose, and kissed him warmly on his forehead. "Because she's beautiful, strong, loyal, kind, and loving," he'd said, his black eyes smiling as he stared into Robert's brown ones. "She has a big heart and she makes me happy. But above all, I knew she would give me a sweet little boy just like you. And soon she will give me a——"

"Robert."

Robert jumped at Dr. West's voice. He shook his head, blinked away the pleasant memories, and then frowned as he realized that he was lying on his back on the sofa. When had he become so comfortable and assumed the proverbial position in his counselor's office? He pushed to a sitting position. "Did you just hypnotize me?" he asked.

She wrote something on the pad on her lap. "You know I will never do that without your permission, Robert. You just zoned out. I've been patiently waiting for you to come back." She took a quick glance at the clock on the table beside her chair. "I would have allowed you to remain in your happy place, but I do have another client in fifteen minutes."

Robert was moved by the smile that flitted up her face to her eyes. She always referred to her patients as clients. "I guess this was a wasted trip?" He rubbed at the muscles in his neck.

"I won't say that. Maybe you just needed to come here to relax."

Yeah right. He could have gotten a full body massage, a pedicure, a manicure, and a fancy dinner for a lot less than what he was paying to sit on Dr. West's sofa and zone out.

"What brought you here tonight?" she asked as if she didn't know.

He always saw her immediately following his trips to Granite Falls when his internal dilemma about Yasmine was at its highest peak. Tonight was no different, although he'd been hoping not to see Dr. West at all.

Yasmine had been overly affectionate in Granite Falls, especially when they were in the company of his sister and their friends, giving him hope that she'd been infected with the love and commitment bug. She'd looked stunning at the wedding, and had caught the attention of many eligible bachelors who'd asked her to dance at the reception. Robert had cut in on every one of those dances. And Yasmine had smiled her wickedly teasing smile every time he pulled her out of the arms of another man.

After Michelle and the gang left for their honeymoon, he and Yasmine had hightailed it back to the LaCrosse mansion and had made love into the night and early the next morning. Robert trembled at the steamy memories, but just as quickly his body tensed in frustration.

On their ride back to Boston yesterday, he'd tried to engage Yasmine in conversation about the wedding, the kids, and how happy the couples were in their marriages, but she'd changed the subject every time, until he'd just given up in defeat. If she'd only asked him nicely to stay last night he would have, but she had to go and make it seem as if she didn't care one way or the other. That had pissed him off.

Robert left the sofa and walked over to the window he'd been staring out of earlier. "The usual," he finally said in respond to Dr. West's question.

"Wanting what your sister has, and frustrated that Yasmine is holding out on you."

"She's too liberal. Too independent."

"Those are the things you love about her."

What exactly is she writing? Robert wondered as Dr. West jotted on her notepad.

"You say you love Yasmine and that she loves you, although she's never said it out loud. But, Robert, have you ever stopped to think that maybe she isn't the right woman for you, or that you're not the right man for her? Sometimes love just isn't enough."

Turning his back to Dr. West, Robert shoved his hands into the pockets of his slacks and clenched his fists as her words reverberated around in his head. He didn't want to think of Yasmine as not being the right woman for him. *She was.* "Of course we're right for each other. We've known each other all our lives. She's been in love with me since she was a little girl. I probably loved her when I was younger too. I couldn't dwell on those feelings for obvious reasons."

"She turned down your marriage proposals, Robert. Twice," she added with emphasis.

"Neither one of those times was right for her." He paused. "*Time* seems to be always against us, doesn't it?" His voice was heavy with cynicism. "Time, and Yasmine's commitment issues brought on by her career. Love doesn't last in her line of work. Her skepticism is warranted."

"You defend her, yet you've stopped seeing her several times over the past five years."

"That was just to cope with my frustrations."

"Your frustrations with her, or with yourself?"

Robert walked across the carpet and, resuming his spot on the sofa, he stretched his legs casually before him.

"You once told me that you felt as if you needed to resolve the issue with your past before you can fully commit to any woman," Dr. West continued, looking at him speculatively. "Since you have your own reservations about settling down before the mystery of your past is solved, I can't help but wonder if you're somewhat relieved Yasmine turned down your proposals."

Robert locked his hands together behind his head and pondered on her observation. Could he really be unjustly placing all the blame for their stagnant relationship on Yasmine? Sure, it was always easier to blame the other party when things weren't going the way one wanted.

"Or perhaps you resent Yasmine for voicing her suspicions that the man who raised you wasn't your father," Dr. West continued. "Her theory sent you searching for the truth of your existence and made you relive that horrifying night in your past?"

"No way!" Robert said heatedly to her absurd suggestion. He

pulled his legs up and sat forward, and planting his elbows on his thighs, he clasped his hands tightly together. "If anything at all, I love Yas more for her insightfulness. If it weren't for her, my sister and I would have had to carry the disgrace of that imposter for the rest of our lives. Yasmine gave us the means to eliminate the stain that man had placed on our family name. She gave us the chance to live our lives above reproach. Because of her, I can hold my head high. I can be the man I want to be without feeling undeserving. I can never resent Yasmine for that. She's the reason I can love at all, that I know I will never be like Timmy Gleason because his blood isn't running through my veins."

"Rightly stated, Robert! But is it at all possible that you're confusing gratitude for love?"

"No." He shook his head vigorously. "I love Yasmine. She's smart, sexy, and desirable. I know our love is crazy, but it's genuine. Sex with her is phenomenal, intense, and totally satisfying—the best for both of us. That's not gratitude. That's love. I can't imagine myself with any other woman. She perfects me."

Dr. West dropped her gaze to her notepad. Her fingers toyed with the ruffled collar of her purple blouse as two bright spots appeared on her cheeks.

Robert blinked with bemusement. Dr. West's stalwart outer appearance did not reflect her inner personality at all. She was a kind, gentle soul who instead of marrying and raising a family of her own had made it her lifetime mission to help bring healing to the wounded souls and hearts around her. But watching her reaction now, Robert had to wonder if she was a virgin in addition to being a spinster.

This was the first time he'd ever discussed his sex life with her, and from her uneasiness, he knew it would be the last. No need to get her old engine revving if she had nowhere to go, nor anyone to ride along with her. There was nothing more frustrating than getting all hot and bothered and having no one but *Madam Fist,* or in Dr. West's case, a *King George* to put out the fire.

"Apart from the—um—optimum sex," Dr. West said, meeting his gaze again, "what else about Yasmine attracts you?"

"Yasmine reminds me of my mother—loyal, trustworthy, strong, and independent." A warm glow filtered through his chest as bits of his childhood conversation he'd had with his father at the garage flashed across his mind. "My mother *had* to have been strong in order to protect Michelle and me from Timmy Gleason. That's the kind of mother I want for my children, one who would make sacrifices for them."

"How can you be certain Yasmine would make sacrifices for her children?"

"She took in my destitute sister—twice—when she herself didn't have much. She never asked her to pay rent once, and she fed her." He paused as a dichotomous wave of bliss and betrayal seized him. Bliss, because Yasmine and he had just begun seeing each other, and betrayal because his sister had been at the lowest point in her life when she'd moved back in with Yasmine.

Robert cleared his throat. "I've watched Yasmine with her nephew for years before she became a successful attorney, back when she was temping and waitressing to put herself through school. She used to deny herself to provide for him when his parents were going through hard times. I have no doubt that she would be an excellent mother, like mine was."

As Dr. West scribbled on her pad, Robert stared out the window at the bobbing trees again as he recalled that horrible night his mother had come back from her walk with that strange, mean man. She was crying as the man barked at her to pack her and her little boy's clothes and gather everything of value in the apartment.

His parents didn't have much, but his mom had a few pieces

of jewelry his father had given her over the years. The man had stuffed the jewelry into his pocket, then forced Robert and his mother from the only home they'd ever known. Over a period of weeks, Timmy had made them hop one bus after another until they reached Manchester, New Hampshire, where he ran out of money.

For a while, they'd walked the streets by day while Timmy tried to find work, and by night they'd eaten and slept at a homeless shelter. After Timmy found his first of many menial jobs at a tire shop, they'd lived in a smoky motel room for a few months before moving into their first of many rundown apartments in inner city Manchester.

Those were the facts Robert had remembered as he'd grown into a man. What he'd suppressed, killed, hidden away was the image and identity of his real father—the muscular, tall man with a mop of soft black hair on his head, and a face that seemed to be always smiling—the man who'd been in his life up until that strange night.

During a hypnotherapy session, Robert had recalled lying in bed under an open window with the hum of a box fan pushing cool air around the room. He'd remembered hearing his parents talking and laughing in the alley below. Some nights after putting him to bed, they would leave their second-floor apartment and take a walk around the building to sit directly below his bedroom —their time alone after a hard day's work.

They always stayed within hearing range, and often shouted up at him to go to sleep when he tried to engage them in conversation. They'd shouted up at him that night, and after much coaxing, he'd climbed back into his bed and fallen asleep to the hushed voices of his parents beneath his bedroom window.

It was the last time Robert had heard his father's voice.

Once Robert had recalled his lost memories, he'd been certain that Timmy had forced his parents away from the alley, probably at gun or knifepoint for reasons he would never know. What he did know for a fact was that they would never have wandered away from the building and left their little boy alone. They weren't negligent parents.

"Robert."

Robert turned to find Dr. West had left her seat and was now standing at a corner table, filling a fresh glass with water. "Yes, my time is up."

She smiled at him. "Perhaps we can make another appointment for later this week."

"I'll call your secretary," he said, rising to his feet.

Her eyes twinkled in the lamplight. "You'll figure out the right thing to do about Yasmine, Robert, and about your past. Just follow your heart."

Robert nodded and left her office, his mind still unsettled.

Discovering that neither he nor Michelle was related to that scumbag should have been liberating for him, Robert thought, as he eased his car into the flow of traffic on East Broadway, the first leg of his drive back to Beacon Hill.

Contrarily, it had the reverse effect on him. He'd felt like a failure, for not remembering their real father while he and Michelle were growing up—almost starved and beaten to death, and left alone for days in the winter in an apartment that had no heat, while Timmy was out drinking and gambling his meager paycheck away. He felt guilty for not remembering and speaking up on his father's behalf, for not avenging his murder and making Timmy Gleason pay for what he'd done to him.

That bastard should have been hung upside down by his balls. Instead, he'd had an easy out by dying from cirrhosis of the liver while waiting in jail to be tried for another ghastly crime—a crime that had ended Michelle and Erik's secret marriage, and had almost destroyed his sister's life.

Ironically, it was that second crime that had set Robert and

Michelle on the path to discovering that they weren't related to the man who'd been abusing them all their lives—thanks to Yasmine who'd been privy to a lot of outrageous real-life cases while she'd been studying criminal law. She had posed the possibility that Timmy might not be their father, seeing that neither he nor Michelle looked anything like him. It had set Robert thinking.

Timmy Gleason was short and stocky, while Michelle, Robert, and their mother were all unusually tall. Timmy's nose was so flat, Robert used to wonder if air could pass through it, while, again, his and his sister's were somewhat Grecian—a trait they'd inherited from their biological father, he'd later come to realize. Timmy's eyes were gray while all the members of the Carter family had black and brown eyes.

Those were the divulging details he should have noticed while he was growing up, he thought as he flipped on his signal light and drifted on to Storrow Drive. But as Yasmine had stated, he was too busy taking care of Michelle to suspect anything out of the ordinary. He couldn't see the forest for the trees.

Taking Yasmine's advice, Robert had gone through some boxes of his mother's belongings and found a letter from a woman, warning Timmy not to return to Virginia because the man he'd stabbed had died. The envelope had been addressed to Dwight Carter, but in the letter, she'd called him Timmy. Armed with the evidence, Robert had visited Timmy Gleason in jail, and left with a couple strands of his hair. A DNA test had confirmed that neither he nor Michelle was related to him.

Robert had immediately hired a detective to research his father's death. He'd confirmed that Dwight Carter had died from multiple stab wounds to the chest, and that a woman who'd claimed to be his common-law wife had identified his body as that of Timmy Gleason, and then had him cremated. Robert was sure it was the same woman who'd written the note to

Timmy twenty-five years earlier. Unfortunately she'd also been dead for years. He had no idea if his father's ashes had been buried in a cemetery, scattered across Richmond, dumped into a trashcan, or flushed down a toilet.

And to add to his frustrations, further research revealed that Dwight Carter and his wife Violet had both been raised in foster care, making it damned near impossible for him and Michelle to trace their family heritage.

Robert pulled his car into the deeded parking space outside his front door, killed the engine, and sat staring at the rush of traffic and pedestrians going by. He'd dropped the investigation into his parents' past lives around the time Michelle had given birth to Little Erik so he could concentrate on being there for his sister, and bonding with his new nephew and step-niece, Precious.

He'd meant to continue researching his roots when things settled down again, but it never seemed to be the right time. Or perhaps he'd been making excuses because he was afraid of the unknown. It was time he found out where he came from, whose blood was running through his veins. He needed to test Dr. West's theory that he'd been blaming Yasmine for their dormant relationship. Hopefully once the mystery of his obscured past was revealed, he'd be more optimistic about moving from his latent present, and into a satisfying future with the love of his life.

Loving Yasmine was easy, and fulfilling, and delightful, and he knew in his heart and gut that they were right for each other. But in the meantime he would stay away from her, make her miss him, just a little.

CHAPTER FOUR

"Why are you so edgy today?"

Yasmine glanced up from her laptop on the desk in her office to see Sylvia Harley, one of Hayward & Harley Family Law Firm's personal assistants, leaning against her doorframe. The strap for Sylvia's Versace purse hung from her shoulder. She was obviously done for the day, and Yas wished the woman had headed straight to the garage and her brand new white Porsche. "You want something, Syl?"

Syl walked, uninvited, into the office and stood staring down at Yasmine. "Okay, since you asked, I do want something, an answer to my question. What's eating you? You almost took poor Ned's head off. He's your client. Remember? You'll be lucky if he doesn't start looking for a nicer attorney."

"It's what's not eating me that's getting under my skin." The minute the words left her mouth, she regretted saying them.

Syl's eyes widened into big gray saucers. She flipped her straight blond hair over her shoulders and dropped her skinny frame into one of the two brown leather club chairs on the other side of Yasmine's desk. Planting her elbows on the edge of the desk, she settled her chin into her palms. "Man trouble?"

Yasmine slapped her laptop and the enormous law tome on her desk shut. There went her concentration for the day, like she was having any concentration all week, anyway. It was Friday afternoon, almost five whole days since she'd last seen or even talked to Rob. She'd called him Monday morning to see if he wanted to get together that night. Her call had gone straight to voicemail, and then around noontime, she'd gotten a text: *Real busy today. Have an appointment tonight. Rob.*

She'd balked at *Rob,* his signature that indicated that he didn't want to be bothered. She'd been so hurt and mad, she hadn't responded. They'd never gone this long without even a phone call between them. Even when they were off-again he would call just to see how she was doing. After all, they were friends long before they'd become lovers.

Yasmine had been fuming all week, and today she'd taken out her frustrations on poor Ned Brown, a bumbling but sweet sixty-year-old man whose estranged, cheating, twenty-seven-year-old wife was fighting him for custody of their four-year-old son so she could collect child support to maintain the extravagant lifestyle Ned had provided in the four years of their marriage. Today, Ned had shared some information with Yasmine that proved the child was not his, and that his wife was aware of the paternity of her child when she married him. The wife had been having an affair with the child's biological father all during her marriage to Ned. Definitely a master setup.

Five years ago when Yasmine switched her career from criminal to divorce law, defending women against abusive and vindictive spouses had been her priority. Little did she know that there were a lot of men out there who were victims of mean, nasty, gold-digging bitches, especially the older lonely men who were trying to recapture their youths by taking up with Silicone Barbie doll look-alikes.

Ned had no business with a woman thirty-three years his

junior, but he'd been pussy-whipped, like a lot of men his age, and he now had the unpleasant task of cleaning the nasty cream off his face. Not to mention the hefty legal fees he was paying to do it.

"So are you going to tell me, or what? Are you and Sexy Rob off-again?" Syl leaned back into the chair and tossed Yasmine a critical look. "I don't know what's wrong with you, girl, but if a man looked at me the way he looks at you, his bone would not get a break."

Yasmine pursed her lips and gazed out her North End office window at the bustling Boston city streets below. Yes, she missed Rob's bone, but that wasn't what was bothering her. Her worries had begun Sunday night when he hadn't called to wish her good night. Since they hooked up five years ago—and were *on-again*—every single night that they weren't sleeping next to each other, Rob would call to wish her good night. It didn't matter where he was. Sometimes he would stay on the phone until she fell asleep just to listen to her breathe.

Sunday night, she'd lain in bed, missing the hell out of him. She'd even massaged her body with his favorite scented oil, just in case he came back to her place. He did that sometimes: leave and then come back. But he hadn't returned on Sunday night, and seeing that she'd told him she didn't care whether he stayed or went, pride, and her resolve to be independent had kept Yas from calling him.

In desperation, she'd pulled King George from under the pillow where she'd stashed him while she waited for Rob to appear. King George lived up to his reputation and even made her scream out Rob's name a few times, but since he lacked a pair of strong warm arms and legs to wrap around her body, when she was done with him, she'd tossed him on the floor. He'd gotten his revenge for being used and tossed aside when she'd stumbled over him and almost broken her neck during her midnight trek to the bathroom. Her upper arm was still bruised where she'd bumped it into the side of her dresser.

Was Robert taking his revenge by giving her the silent treatment? Had she pushed him too hard and far this time? Had he finally had it with her fear of commitment? Were they *off-again*?

"Yas!" Sylvia barked.

Yasmine jumped and brought her attention back inside and to her nosy neighbor and work colleague. "What?"

"Are you and Robert off or on?"

Yasmine squinted her eyes. "What's it to you?"

"I tell you about my love life."

"You don't have a love life. You have a sex life."

"Which I share with you."

You share it with everybody. "You do that on your own volition. I don't ask you."

"But you listen."

Yas shrugged, pushed back her chair, and stood up. "I figured you need someone to talk to." She picked up the two heavy tomes and took them back to the built-in bookshelf on the opposite side of her office.

"And you don't? You're always talking about how you miss your girl, Michelle. You said you used to tell each other everything ever since you were kids, but it's hard now that she's married, has kids, and lives so far away."

Yasmine turned around and watched as Sylvia collected a pile of folders from her desk and brought them to the filing cabinet next to the bookshelf and began sliding them into the appropriate drawers.

Syl was pretty, a couple years younger than Yasmine, and had been working at Hayward & Harley since she was eighteen. She was Charles Hayward's niece, the only child of his sister who'd passed away when Syl was nine. After her father died a couple years later, Charles had raised her along with his two daughters. Of the three girls, Syl was the only one who'd shown any interest in joining the family business—but only as an assistant to several of the attorneys. She was intelligent, had earned a Bachelor's degree in Communication from Northeastern University with honors and was efficient and helpful in the mundane matters of a law firm. Yas suspected that she worked at the firm merely to earn her keep without putting out much effort.

"I'm just trying to pick up the slack, you know," Syl said, closing and locking the cabinet. "I can be your new BFF."

Yasmine huffed. "You're just trying to get all up in my business."

Sylvia grinned. "Well, it's juicy business, isn't it? I mean you're dating one of the best orthodontists in the area, not to mention that he's a hot hunk and a billionaire."

Yasmine's lips puckered. *And I'm sure if I turn my back for a minute you'll have no qualms about trying to jump his bones.*

"Well." Sylvia spread her hands.

"It's my juice to drink, not yours." Truth be told, it would be nice to have someone else to talk to about Rob since she couldn't talk to Michelle, who continuously accused her of stringing her brother along. She couldn't talk to her sister, Naomi, either; they weren't that close, not even when they were kids. But gossipy Syl definitely didn't qualify as an alternate confidante.

During her first few months at the firm when she and Rob were *off-again*, Yasmine had made the mistake of mentioning it to Sylvia, who'd stopped by her house on a Saturday afternoon. By the time Yasmine arrived at the office on Monday morning, everybody knew her business.

"Come on, Yas. Every girl needs a girlfriend to talk to."

"Hmm." *Nobody burns me twice.* Yas walked over to a cabinet and retrieved her purse and briefcase. She never talked about her personal affairs at work. The less the senior partners and her colleagues knew about her private life, the more power she would have when it came time for negotiating her partnership in the firm. She was already making backup plans in case they turned her down.

Unfortunately for Yas, Sylvia owned a townhouse four doors down from her end unit on Pier 7 in the Charlestown Navy Yard —a fact neither of them was aware of until after Yasmine had signed on the dotted line of her deed. If she'd known that her assistant lived on Pier 7, Yasmine would have chosen another neighborhood to call her home.

Sylvia was a big party girl. She hopped bars, and clubbed most weekends and even some weeknights if her friends were available. She was very promiscuous, and Yas knew for a fact that she'd slept with most of the single lawyers at the firm. Yas had seen a few entering and leaving Syl's townhouse, but none of them would ever brag about it, because she was the boss's niece.

Yas also suspected that she slept with some of their clients, but she had no proof. Syl probably kept them away from the pier after Yas moved in. If anyone ever found out, the partners of Hayward & Harley would find themselves in a labyrinth of legal mess.

But as Yasmine knew, shit had a way of forcing its way to the surface when it had been compressed for too long—hers included, which was why she presently had no clue whether or not she still had a man.

"A new bar and seafood restaurant just opened in the South End. Why don't you join me and my friends tonight? We can have a wild time," Syl said.

Yasmine placed her laptop and some documents she needed

to read over the weekend into her briefcase. A wild time out on the town with a subordinate was exactly what Yasmine needed to avoid. Especially not with Sylvia, who she knew would eventually get high and or drunk and start talking about her fling with a client or some other unethical incident that Yas might legally have to disclose, consequently causing her to lose a case. It had happened before with a paralegal who knew no boundaries. They'd fired her, but not without paying out a huge hush settlement. Yasmine knew that it was just a matter of time before Sylvia brought them back to the bargaining table for another settlement.

"Thanks for the invitation, Syl," she said, looping her purse strap over her shoulder, and picking up her case. "But I'm spending the weekend in Manchester. I promised to take my nephew to Canobie Lake tomorrow. Maybe next time." She headed toward the door.

"You always have something planned every time I ask you to socialize with me outside of the office," Syl said, disappointment evident in both her face and voice as she fell into step beside Yasmine.

Then why don't you take the hint and stop asking? Yasmine conjured up a sweet smile as they walked along the empty corridor toward the elevators that led directly to the underground garage. Most of the lawyers had already left for the day. She'd stayed late to meet with Ned, who'd asked for an emergency appointment to discuss the evidence against his wife.

"Yas."

Yasmine turned around at the sound of her name. "Hey, Armand," she said with a smile as a man in a dark suit and white shirt hurried to catch up with her and Sylvia.

"Is that a new suit?" he asked, looking her up and down with approval. "It looks fabulous on you. But then again, everything looks fabulous on you."

"Yes, it's new, and thanks for the compliment," she replied, running her palms over the silky material of the gray suit and the baby blue blouse she'd bought at Joanne's Boutique in Granite Falls last week when she'd joined Michele and her friends on a shopping spree. Yasmine had sweetly declined Michelle's offer to put it on the LaCrosses' account. Yas loved her girl, but she refused to be one of her charity cases. To this day, this outfit was the most expensive piece of clothing Yasmine owned, but a girl had to splurge on herself once in a while. "What are you doing here? I thought you were in court all day," she said to Armand.

"I was, but I stopped by to pick up a file." He waved a manila folder in the air. "I'm meeting a client at a golf course in Cambridge in a couple hours." Finally, he turned and acknowledged Sylvia. "Hi, Sylvia," he said on a half smile.

"Hi, Armand." Sylvia threw herself against him, her kiss clearly aimed at his lips, but landing on his cheek when he quickly and astutely turned his head, perhaps from years of practice.

The look in his eyes told Yas that he was very uncomfortable with Sylvia's advances. Armand Hendricks was a thirty-something, handsome, six-foot man of West Indian descent whose parents had moved to the states from St. Lucia when he was three. Armand joined the firm four years before Yasmine, and as far as she knew, he was probably the only single male employee who hadn't slept with Sylvia—not for a lack of trying on her part.

Out of a pool of twenty attorneys, Armand and Yasmine were the only two African-Americans on staff, and like her, he kept his personal life private while most of the others seemed to enjoy sharing their business. Yasmine admired his reticence, but she also knew that he had a big crush on her, one she didn't encourage. She was in love with Robert, and she had no interest in any other man on this planet, not even when she and Rob were *off-again*.

"What are you doing this weekend?" Armand asked Yas as he disengaged Syl's arms from around his neck and pushed her at arm's length away from him. "My parents are having a cookout tomorrow afternoon. I'd love for you and Rob to come."

Yasmine cleared her throat. "I'm—we're heading up to Manchester tonight." Best if she included Rob in her travel plans, even if it was a lie. She didn't want Armand, who'd recently ended a two-year relationship with his girlfriend, to get any ideas about her availability. "We're taking my nephew to Canobie Lake tomorrow."

"I thought you were going to Manchester alone," nosy Syl interjected. "I thought you and Robert were—"

"Because that's what I want you to think," Yasmine said tersely. She wished she could lodge a sock in that girl's mouth. She smiled up at Armand. "Maybe next time."

"Sure." Armand gave her a *don't worry, I got you girl,* wink of the eye over Sylvia's head, for which Yas was grateful.

He knew Syl had a big mouth, and he would never discuss his or her personal matters in front of her, even though the look on his face hinted that he was dying to hear more about the current state of her relationship with Robert.

Like Yasmine, Armand was skeptical about commitment. He wasn't a player; he just wasn't interested in marriage and children. He'd often joked about the two of them making a great noncommittal couple. He'd even gone as far as to admit that he was fine with an open relationship—sharing her with Robert. Yas had playfully socked him in the gut.

Armand's lack of interest in marriage was the number one reason his relationships always ended around the second year when the women finally took him at his word that he wasn't a marrying kind of man.

"What about me, can I come?" Sylvia asked, batting her fake eyelashes at him. "I'm not busy tomorrow afternoon. And since you don't have a girlfriend, I can be your plus one."

"Um, you're allergic to dogs, remember? And my mom has four."

Yasmine snapped her mouth shut to keep from laughing out loud. Armand's mom didn't own any dogs, but from the moment he'd learned that Syl was allergic to dogs, he'd been using her allergy to keep her at bay. Maybe Yas should get a dog.

"I'm parked out front," Armand said. "Tell Rob hi for me."

"Will do, and give your parents our regards."

Armand gave Yas a friendly hug, then turned to Sylvia. "Bye, Syl."

"Bye, Armand," Sylvia answered in a shameless, provocative voice.

Yas smiled as Armand practically ran in the opposite direction, obviously in a hurry to get away from Sylvia.

"Armand likes you, and you lied to him about you and Robert. Armand is so sexy, and I know for a fact that what they say about black men is true," Sylvia added as they continued toward the garage elevator. "But I don't have to convince you, Yasmine. You have one of your own. But if you asked me, I'd say you should give Armand a chance. I mean, I like Robert, but he can be kind of conservative, almost an introvert sometimes, if you know what I mean. Armand is a lot more fun, even if he's not as hot as Rob. He knows how to have a good time, like me. Did I ever tell you about the time I…"

Yasmine rolled her eyes and kept her mouth shut all the way to the garage as Sylvia continued her exhaustive monologue about Robert, Armand, and the myth about black men, not to mention a couple brief details of her experiences with black men —details that made Yasmine wish she could climb into her own brain, armed with an icepick, and gouge out the cells that were now polluted with Sylvia's sexual escapades.

Yasmine breathed a sigh of relief when she saw her car, but because her parking space was right next to Syl's, she was subjected to her unbridled loquacity for a few more minutes. Yasmine unlocked her door and tossed her briefcase and purse on the back seat. "Have a great weekend, Syl," she said, unbuttoning and removing her suit jacket.

Sylvia grinned. "I'm heading straight home, so we'll be pulling into our driveways at the same time. Maybe we can share a beer before you leave for Manchester. I have so many stories to tell you," she said with excitement. "See you on Pier 7, neighbor."

Like hell! Yasmine tossed her jacket into her car, climbed in, slammed her door, and started her engine. She was at the exit gate when she heard the engine of Sylvia's Porsche rev to life. Instead of turning right out of the garage, Yas turned left and headed for the grocery store. By the time she got home, Sylvia should be safe and sound inside her own townhouse.

Ninety minutes later, Yasmine pulled into her driveway and shut off her engine. When she planned right, the drive between her office and her home usually only took between fifteen and twenty minutes. But it was Friday, at the height of Boston's rush hour, and it seemed like the entire state of Massachusetts was headed north for the weekend. Plus, she'd been forced to make an unnecessary stop at the grocery store.

Since she too would be joining the migration later in the evening, Yasmine left her car in the driveway instead of pulling into the garage. She grabbed her purse, lifted her jacket and her small paper bag of groceries from the back seat—leaving her briefcase since she was taking it to Manchester—exited her car, kicked the door shut, and ascended the few steps to her front door. Balancing her load in one hand, she pulled her mail from the box on the side of her building, slid her key into the lock, and pushed her door open.

All the carefully balanced contents in Yasmine's hands went crashing to the floor. She stood numb with shock at the scene she'd walked in on, and the sounds of soft jazz filtering from her surround sound system.

CHAPTER FIVE

A white duvet—surrounded by pillars of red burning candles and four tall crystal vases overflowing with long-stemmed roses and baby's breath—was spread out on her living room floor in front of her gray and white striped couch. A silver tray with a pitcher of water and two glasses were on the floor next to the sofa.

And on that duvet, the dark powerful figure of a naked man lay fully reclined with his head resting on a pillow.

Behind the sofa, on the other side of the French doors of her living room, sailboats and ships glided by in their colorful and astounding glory, and beyond them in the distance, the magnificent views of the Boston skyline glittered in the afternoon sun.

The romantic backdrop, the sexy look in the brown eyes and the devilish grin on the face of the naked man sprawled on her floor made Yasmine's breasts swell to bursting and her nipples tighten under her black lacy bra.

But what sent a dizzying current racing through her entire system was the action going on between his muscular thighs. One hand was wrapped around his engorged shaft, stroking it slowly up and down, while he beckoned her over with his other hand.

Yasmine pressed her fists into her belly as it tightened with raw need, and the warm juices that had instantaneously pooled inside her silk thong when she first stepped into her house began to dribble down the insides of her thighs. The inner walls of her sex vibrated savagely, and her body trembled so hard from carnal hunger that she fell back weakly against the door. "Oh my God," she rasped on a shaky breath.

"A bit premature, don't you think?" Rob's deep sexy voice bounced off the walls and seemed to drum against her wildly beating heart. "Why don't you come on over here and let me give you something that'll make you scream for real?"

His lascivious invitation was a passionate challenge, almost impossible to resist. Yasmine licked her lips at the countless memories of his long legs, brown and firm as tree trunks, entwined with her slender ones. Her heartbeat throbbed in her ears. She was horny. She wanted him, needed him like a fish needed gills, but she'd be damned if she would let him think he could not speak to her for a whole week, then just show up at her house with his fine sexy naked self, expecting her to put on an eager smile, shed her clothes, lie back and spread her legs for him —exactly what she'd been yearning to do all week.

Yasmine pulled herself together, toed off her black Gianvito Rossi heels—a surprise gift from Robert a few weeks ago—and bent down to pick up the mess around her feet, not in the least bit surprised that he hadn't left the duvet to help her—like a gentleman would.

She also noticed that the week-old mess she'd left in her dining area was still there. Robert was a neat freak, and when he came over, he couldn't help himself from cleaning up after her— which always ticked her off—but he hadn't touched a thing today. After all, she was constantly telling him that she didn't need his help. She knew it had been her determination to carry her thirty-pound suitcase up the stairs the other night that had pissed him off and sent him and his hard cock home, and then kept them away for a week.

Yasmine dropped her keys into the bamboo bowl on the table near the door, and stacked her mail beside the bowl where they should have been placed initially if Mr. Hot & Spicy hadn't waylaid her and turned her into a bundle of confusion and jittering nerves.

Placing her purse on the chair next to the table, Yasmine picked up her jacket, stood up, and carefully folding it, she draped it over the back of the chair. Taking a deep breath, she looked at the man on her floor and when she knew her voice wouldn't betray the excitement bubbling inside her, she asked in as nonchalant a tone as possible, "What are you doing here, Robert?"

"What does it look like?" There was a maddening hint of arrogance in his voice.

"Suppose I'd brought someone home with me?" she responded, needing to maintain her sense of indifference toward him.

"I'm not ashamed of my junk. Are you, Miss Independent?"

Miss Independent? He'd never called her that before. Yasmine met his seductive smile with a moping frown. Maybe he'd finally decided to listen and give her what he thought she wanted from him—mind-blowing sex, and nothing more. All the same, she'd missed him, missed his voice, and his.... Her gaze inadvertently dropped to his crotch.

As if reading her thoughts, Robert pointed the broad tip of his shaft, already coated with pre-cum, in her direction, and wagged it at her. "Little Rob missed you."

He's anything but little was the retort on the tip of Yasmine's tongue, but she didn't want to encourage him. Even though he knew he was twice blessed down there, like every man on the planet, he loved to hear the affirmation falling from a woman's lips. "Well, you have a strange way of showing it, Mr. Carter."

"Isn't this the way a man shows his number-one woman how much he needs her?" he asked, waving his free hand around the romantic setting.

"Oh, so after a week of silence, I'm number one? Pffft, so glad I'm not *number two*."

"Come on, Yas. You're going to make me beg?" Huskiness lingered in his eyes and voice, echoing her own longing.

Yasmine plopped her hands on her hips and tilted her head at the sizzling temptation spread out on her floor. He projected an energy and power that she found hard to deny, but deny she must. "I'm not making you do anything."

"I have the jazz going and everything, baby. You know how I love to make love to the sound of jazz."

Yasmine glanced at his hands working at his groin. "And you're already enjoying it, it seems. I don't have time for you, Robert. I'm heading up to Manchester in a while. My family is expecting me."

"Yes, I know you're going to Manchester."

"And that's how you were able to surprise me with this." She waved one hand around. "You parked your car in my garage, knowing that I always leave mine in the driveway when I'm heading north after work. Tricky, Rob."

"Come over here, baby, and let me park *this* car in your *garage*," he said slyly, as he wagged his cock at her again and rolled the foreskin up and down his length, the way she loved to roll it before taking him into her mouth. "It's been almost a week, Yas. I just want to give you a little something before you leave for the weekend."

Again, there's nothing "little" about your "something," she thought, following his gaze to her nipples, hardening even more and poking out like little pebbles against her blouse.

"And whose fault is that?" Yasmine picked up her bag of groceries that consisted of a sourdough baguette, a box of pasta, a chunk of Brie cheese, and a bunch of scallions, and walked toward her kitchen.

She should have known better than to turn her back on him, because halfway into the dining room, Robert's muscular arms were about her, the tight muscles of his six-pack stomach was pressed into the curve of her back, and the ridge of his cock was lodged against her buttocks.

When his hands cupped her breasts, her grocery bag fell to the floor for the second time in less than ten minutes. Before Yasmine could react, he lifted her off the floor and headed back to the living room.

"Put me down, Robert!" Yasmine hissed, struggling against him without success.

"I will in a minute. On your back," he whispered, his breath hot on her neck. "I need to teach you how to appreciate your man's thoughtfulness."

"I thought you were too busy for me."

"Not as busy as we'll be together, soon."

"I'm not having sex with you," she said in a winded voice, more for her own conviction than for his.

He turned her in his arms and gently placed her on the duvet —on her back as he'd threatened. "We don't have sex, baby. We make love."

Giving her no time or space to escape, he planted his knees between her legs, prodding them as wide as her pencil skirt would allow. Then he settled his hard naked body on top of her, pressing his groin into hers and stationing his elbows on either side of her head. He leaned close to her face, his lips drawn into a firm, yet sensual line, his eyes glittering with love-filled combat.

Dismayed at the magnitude of her own desire, Yasmine pushed at his forearms, but her attempt to move him failed. "If you think for one minute that I'll enjoy—" Her rush of harsh words were locked inside her throat as Rob's warm, smooth lips came down hard on hers. He opened his mouth over hers, nibbling on her lips, and nudging the tip of his tongue against her clenched teeth, until she could do nothing but moan and open up for him.

With a groan, he cupped her chin to hold her steady and slid his tongue deep into the sweetness of her mouth. His kiss was more persuasive than she cared to admit as he began to strum the roof of her mouth and suck on her tongue, slowly and intimately, intensifying her need to be taken by him.

Yasmine's defensive hold on Robert's bulging biceps softened and before long she was rubbing her palms frantically up and down his arms, across his broad shoulders, and thrusting her hips upward trying to increase the pressure of his male hardness against the softness of her feminine sex.

The smooth melodies from "Endless Summer," one of their favorite lovemaking jazz compilations, romanticized the air indicating that her man was in the mood for some serious loving. It might be a while before she made it out the door to New Hampshire, if at all tonight.

Robert confirmed her thoughts when he reached up and tugged the elastic from her hair, freeing her natural curls from their bun. He spread them out above her head on the pillow and, in the next instant, his hand crawled over her neck and breasts, down her chest to her heaving stomach. He tugged the tail of her blouse from the waist of her skirt and, breaking their kiss briefly, he pulled her blouse up her body, over her head and tossed it on the floor. Bare skin to bare skin, they sizzled. He recaptured her mouth as his trembling fingers unsnapped the front clasp of her bra.

Yasmine sighed into his mouth when his fingers curled around the mounds of her swollen breasts, squeezing and molding her flesh, massaging her nipples until her heart jolted and her pulse pounded out of control. "Rob," she breathed his name into his mouth.

He dragged his mouth from hers and grazed his wet lips against her cheek. "Hike up your skirt," he whispered hotly in her ears as he drew his lower body back to give her room.

"Rob, I just paid a fortune for this outfit. Let me take off my skirt."

He brushed gentle kisses across her forehead, her eyes, her cheeks, and her lips. "Hike up your skirt," he repeated as if she hadn't even spoken. His mouth moved over her throat and chest, and then he encircled one hard nipple, suckling so earnestly, it sent a bolt of electricity blazing down Yasmine's body to her sex. "Do it, Yas."

With trembling fingers, Yasmine reached down, grabbed the hem of her very expensive skirt and pulled it up past her buttocks and hips, high above her waist, out of the path of the river of bodily fluids she knew would be flowing from inside her shortly.

"Ease your panties aside," he commanded in a husky voice. "Take me in your hand and put me inside you."

"Rob—"

"Yas, if I'm not inside you in a second, you will have my cum all over your beautiful expensive skirt."

Yasmine didn't have to be told twice. It was better to have him come inside her than on her skirt. She couldn't believe she was thinking logically enough to make that kind of decision, but her rationality turned into full-fledged lust as her desire for Robert overrode everything else. With one hand, she pulled the silky strip of her thong aside while with the other she clasped the smooth hot hardness of Robert Carter's enormous cock, and began to pump him.

He stiffened above her and groaned out her name.

She couldn't wrap her hand all the way around it—no woman could—but Yasmine remembered very well the lusciousness of that beautiful love machine fitting snugly inside the hot cavern of her sex.

A little wriggling around by both of them and soon his broad head was wedged against her tight opening.

"Oh God, you're already so wet, and slick, and hot," he whispered on a sturdy downward thrust.

"Robert!" Yasmine stiffened and screamed as she felt the engorged veins running the length of him pulsing with life and vigor as he pushed himself inside her. She opened her mouth and panted at the sensation of being filled to completion even though only half of him was encased inside her. They'd barely been joined for a minute and even though he hadn't yet begun to thrust, she was already trembling violently on the verge of an orgasm. But then again, this intensity had been building up for five lonely nights.

"Oh yes, baby, that's it. Come for me. Come for me, my sweet little darling. Show me how you appreciate me. Show Little Rob how much you love him." Rob pulled back and thrust, again, burrowing deeper.

Yasmine curled her legs about his and locking her arms around his neck, she braced herself as he pulled back and launched like a rocket to the hilt inside her, choking her, filling her to ultimate completion. He captured her mouth with his, stifling her screams of ecstasy and sending them cascading like a waterfall back down to her belly, spreading like wildfire through every inch of her being as he began to push back and forth inside her.

I'm coming. I'm coming, Oh, God, I'm coming, she shrieked inside as her body began to quiver and buck under the weight of the powerful man on top of her, hitting bottom each time he lunged.

The fiery friction of his shaft grating against the walls of her sex sent Yasmine's heart shattering. Her eyes rolled back into their sockets, her mouth opened in a silent scream, and her body tightened like a bowstring before disintegrating into a pile of ash.

As she smoldered in the flames of her orgasm, Robert lifted his mouth from Yasmine's and gazed down at her writhing under him. Hypnotized by the vision of unadulterated passion she presented, he slid his hands down her body and cupped her buttocks in his palms, pulling her closer still. He locked their pelvises together and ground his hips against hers, side to side, up and down, round and round, until he felt the walls of her vagina tighten around his cock again, gnawing like an insatiable predator demanding more from him, all of him.

His release would be just as quick. He'd been holding out on her for five days, and it damn near killed him. He loved her. And when a man loved a woman, no matter how much he tried to resist her, he would always come back to *this*. *This* right here, with his woman coming under him, screaming his name and massaging their sexes with her hot love juice.

As she shuddered on the aftermath of her orgasm, Robert held her close and dropped his head in the sweet hollow of her neck. "Wrap them chocolate legs around me, baby."

He groaned when she did, locking him in place. The feel of her smooth dainty heels pressing into the hard muscles of his buttocks was as erotic and sensational as any touch could be. She moaned weakly when he began thrusting again, going deeper and faster and harder until the fire shot up and down his spine and his entire body began to vibrate with the intensity of his own passion.

"Yasmine!" He collapsed on her and spewed his hot cum

deep into the recesses of her womb. "Oh God. Oh my God," he groaned as he felt her hot flesh convulsing around his shaft as she surrendered to yet another ground-shaking climax. Her convulsing sex clung to his erection, sealing his cum inside her, melding them together in the most intimate way a man and a woman could be joined.

When he regained consciousness, Robert gathered Yasmine into his arms and rolled over on to his back, bringing her to a straddling position on top of him—their sexes still joined together. He eased her bra off her shoulders and dropped it on the duvet, before arranging her damp, limp body on his. She nestled her cheek against his neck and sighed deeply as he began to caress the delicate curve of her back, lulling her into her customary post-sex catnap—well, when she was truly satisfied. Their ride had been short and intense.

The aftermath was always sweet and relaxing, he thought as he savored the silky dampness of her skin under his palms and the tight grip of her sex on his cock. He wanted her again. He wanted her all night, every night for the rest of his life, but as they basked quietly together, Robert's thoughts wandered back to his most recent conversation with Dr. West.

Her advice about revisiting his past had been gnawing at him all week. He'd picked up the phone several times to call the detective he'd hired previously, but each time his gut had tied up into knots at the thought of reopening old wounds, turning the lights on the darkness of his past, knowing the unknown.

Both of his parents had been raised in foster care, a fact that made him wonder about their parents—his grandparents. Why weren't they around? Had they been abandoned, neglected, given up for adoption, or taken away by the state? Were they born and raised in Virginia, or had they moved there from some other place? His father was a mechanic, his mother a waitress.

Were they educated, or had they even finished high school? What if they were living a double life and were criminals themselves? *What if…. What if…*

Did he really want to know the truth? Was it important that he knew? Those latter questions were the two that bothered Robert most. Perhaps the answers were buried in his sister's happiness. She knew as much as he did about their past, and yes, she was curious, but it hadn't stopped her from moving on with her life.

It hadn't really stopped him either, not professionally, Dr. West had pointed out on Wednesday night when he'd returned to see her. It had brought them back to the topic of whether or not his desire to marry Yasmine and his fear of the unknown were entwined. Maybe subconsciously he was content with the nature of their relationship. Maybe he hadn't proposed the third time because he knew things between them would change regardless of her response.

If her response was negative, it would really be over between them—*off* for good. Why go on when their major goals in life were so different? He wanted a wife and children. If Yasmine was really opposed to marriage, it would be pointless to keep pursuing her. He didn't even know if she wanted children.

Robert's brows pulled together pensively as he recalled part of a phone conversation he'd overheard between Yasmine and her sister, Naomi, shortly after Little Erik was born.

"I don't know how any woman can put herself through so much pain just to bring a baby into the world," Yasmine had said. "Yeah, but it's a crapshoot," she'd continued, apparently in response to her sister's argument. "Look how many kids turn out bad. How many parents have we heard tell their kids they wish they never had them? Look how many women die giving birth."

Could the fear of childbirth labor and death be the real reasons Yasmine was opposed to marriage? After the second proposal, she'd made a comment that she wasn't "wifely material." She didn't cook, she hardly did laundry, and she only tidied up when she was expecting company.

And company didn't include him, Robert thought, glancing at three uneven stacks of books on the floor in the dining area of her open-concept first floor. Dishes from the previous nights' takeout dinners, along with two used coffee mugs and wine glasses, one still half full of her favorite Pinot Noir, sat on her dining table. Four opened law tomes and some magazines took up the rest of the free space on the table. Two of the four chairs were facing away from the table; two were pushed under it in their rightful places, with a shawl draped over the back of one. Used dishes were scattered on her granite countertop—no pots or pans—he noted, but her floor was clean, shiny, and polished.

She wasn't a slob by any means; she just got to stuff when she got to stuff—which was usually on the weekends—when she set aside time to tidy up, unlike him who had to get things done immediately. For him, everything had, and should be in its place when not in use. Even his toss-in drawer was organized. It was the only way he could keep sane and balanced. His maid constantly complained that she'd like to do other chores besides just clean his bathroom during her weekly visits to his townhouse.

Robert smiled. Yasmine Reynolds definitely was not "wifely material" when it came to the general consensus of "wifely material," but Robert wasn't looking for a woman to cook for him, do his laundry, nor tidy his house. He did all those things for himself. His years of practice taking care of Michelle had turned him into a neat freak.

Robert didn't need a maid. He wanted a partner who matched him in intelligence, ethics, integrity, loyalty, and sexual passion, a woman who made him laugh and curse, happy and mad in the same breath, one he yearned for every single minute of the day, whether he was near her, lying with her as he was at the moment, or if he was hundreds of miles across the ocean from her. Yasmine Reynolds wasn't perfect, but she was perfect for him.

The thought of Yasmine being perfect for him made Robert pause and catch his breath. Had he really not popped the question the third time because he was afraid she would say *yes* this time? Monday night, Dr. West had mentioned his concern about not being able to commit to any woman until his past was resolved. But that was shortly after he'd learned that he had a buried past, and long before his first proposal to Yasmine. Plus, he'd never thought of Yasmine as *any woman*. She was *the woman*.

Dr. West had often pointed out that his sister had moved on with her life even with the mystery about their parents' background hanging over her head. *Well, of course it was easier for Michelle.* She never knew either of their parents. Their father died before she was born and their mother died giving birth to her. He, on the other hand, had known them, even if it was just for a few years of his life. He'd known his parents, and that was the difference between him and his sister.

His need to know was compulsory, and for his own peace of mind, pivotal. He had to find out who he was before he asked Yasmine to marry him again. His feelings for her would never change, no matter what he discovered. With that thought, Robert made a mental note to contact Detective Gilbert and put him back on the case before the night was over.

It didn't mean he was letting Yasmine off the hook while he awaited the results. On the contrary, he was keeping the conversation of their stagnant relationship open to make sure she was aware of the incompleteness of them.

Yasmine stirred, and not a minute too soon, he thought. He shuddered as her long lashes fluttered against his neck, and his now flaccid shaft slipped out of her, sending a puddle of warm sticky moisture—the evidence of their undeniable desire for each other—pooling around their groins. Love backed up into Robert's throat.

"What was that you said about not enjoying it?" he asked, slapping her lightly on the buttocks to bring her fully awake.

CHAPTER SIX

Yasmine jumped at the playful tap on her backside. She opened her eyes fully and stretched her body like a contented kitten before raising her head to gaze at Rob. He always patiently waited for her to sleep off the effects of his loving. Her lips spread on a lazy smile as she drank in the comfort of his nearness, reveling in the dreamy aftermath of their intimacies, relishing the possessiveness of his hold on her. She'd missed him, so damn much. "I was just faking it," she said, her lips trembling with the effort of containing her humor.

He trailed his knuckles across her cheekbones, her chin, and the bridge of her nose, his chocolate eyes misty with love and contentment. "Sure you were, baby. You fake it every time. And you fake it so well, too." He dropped his hand to her ass and slapped her again, a little harder this time.

"Ow!" Yasmine yelled and retaliated by slapping his bulging biceps. "What the hell was that for?"

"For being so damn sweet, and addictive. There should be law against you."

Yasmine chuckled so hard, she would have fallen off him if he wasn't holding her tightly. "Well, there is, but seeing you have your prescription filled on a timely basis, you're not breaking it." Laughter lingered in her voice as she ran her fingers through the soft mat of black hair on his chest, still damp from their passion.

He studied her for a moment. "I saw Dr. West on Monday night, and Wednesday, too."

So that's where he'd been instead of with her, and doing what they'd just done together. Yasmine dipped her head to one side. "And what, she advised you to whip me into submission?"

His chest rose and fell on a heavy sigh. "I was looking for a reason to stay away from you."

"She must have given you a good one. You stayed away for four days."

"She told me to follow my heart. And this is where my heart led me—to you. It will always lead me to you, Yas."

"Oh Rob, that's so— Oh, my God, my skirt," Yasmine cried as her gaze drifted to her hips where her skirt was now bunched in a damp mess. "It's soaked, Robert, and stained, and ripped at the seams. I told you I should have taken it off."

"After what we just shared, your biggest concern right now is your skirt? Really, Yas? I can replace your skirt a hundred times over without breaking a sweat."

"What else is there to be concerned about? You proved to me that you can treat me however you want, but when you show up, I'll lift my thousand dollar skirt for you."

His lips twisted into a smile as he held her hair back from her face. "It's called love, darling."

"Yeah, yeah, yeah," Yasmine murmured, resolving not to brood over her ruined skirt. What was done was done. And truth be told, she didn't regret what she and Robert just shared. That kind of intense loving was rare, and she was lucky enough to have it. The fact that she'd obeyed his order to hike up her skirt instead of insisting that he let her take it off, said it all. She loved him. *Then why can't you tell him?*

"You may not be able to say it again, but I know it," he said as if reading her mind. "I feel it even when we're not together, but even more when we're like this. Wouldn't it be nice to come home to this every day, Yas?"

Yasmine broke her gaze and glanced around her living room at the candles and flowers Rob had set out to entice her, a huge contrast from the mess in her dining area. It was nice, romantic and thoughtful, but she didn't need any of it to make love to Rob. All he had to do was show up.

His gaze followed hers, and then a strange faintly eager look flashed across his face. "Why did you buy this condo, Yasmine?"

"Because I wanted my own place," she said, meeting Robert's disparaging gaze. "I love being on the water," she added, as the mass of a sailboat passing a few hundred yards away came into view. "Where else can you enjoy the excitement of city life and the quiet calm of the ocean in one place?"

"You know that's not what I mean." His hands dropped to the duvet with a soft unified thud.

The splendor of their aftermath was over, Yasmine thought as she slid off his rock-hard body. She really didn't want to have this conversation with Rob tonight because it always left her feeling drained and guilty. She wanted, needed to be in a good mood while in Manchester. Her sister was like a human stress radar, and the last thing Yas needed was Nurse Naomi insisting on taking her emotional temperature and diagnosing her state of mind.

As Robert lay stiff, unyielding, and quiet—his *I'm upset with you* persona, she unzipped her skirt, and with a regretful moan, pushed it off her hips along with her thong and tossed them off to the side of the duvet. Completely naked, she snuggled up to Robert's warm frame and rested her cheek on his chest.

He remained unresponsive for a few breathless seconds, and then, slowly, his arms draped about her as if he had no choice.

Yasmine smiled as he began to caress her shoulders and back. Her man was still tender even though he was frustrated to the hilt with her. *That was love.* She trailed her fingers up and down the rigid muscles of his stomach, smiling as he trembled under her fingertips. "I know that's not what you mean, Rob. It's just that—"

"It's just what, Yas?" he interrupted. "I asked you to move in with me when you came to Boston, but you went behind my back and bought this condo. It's a waste. You could have put that money aside for your retirement. I never intended to ask you to pay me rent."

"I know you wouldn't have asked me to pay rent. I just needed to do this for me."

"Your thoughts, your future plans should be about us. I want to share my life with you, Yasmine Reynolds. I want kids. I want them hanging off me, jumping up and down on me, riding me like a pony. I want to see my child staring back at me through your eyes."

That last statement hit Yasmine hard, but she swallowed back her reaction. "I'm only three years into my career, Rob. There are so many things I still want to accomplish before I settle down into marriage and kids."

"Like what? You're already successful. Clients are taking numbers, waiting in line for your services. It's depressing, given the nature of your work, but that's the reality. It doesn't mean we will end up in the same boat. In fact, I know we won't. I wouldn't allow it," he added, his voice resonating with assertion.

Yasmine closed her eyes as guilt rippled in her gut. She wanted the same things Rob wanted. Any child she gave birth to would be Robert's. She could never picture herself sharing such an important and intimate part of herself with any other man. But she could neither dwell on that fantasy, nor share it with him.

Not while Yasmine also longed for the things she desired.

She'd worked so hard to get to where she was, and she just wanted a little taste of being at the top. Her *top* meant making partnership at Hayward & Harley. She was already one of most lucrative lawyers at the firm, and she believed she deserved partnership.

She wanted to accomplish her goals while she was still single, so no one could assume she'd hitched a ride up on her husband's elevator, especially if that husband was Dr. Robert Javier Carter, a self-made millionaire who was revered and admired by many in his field.

Yes, her future plans should be about *them*, but it was imperative she did this one thing on her own. She needed to be able to say that *she* had made it to a place where no one could discredit her, put her down, or make her feel inadequate. And just in case partnership at Hayward & Harley didn't work out, Yasmine had a backup plan—one that might require leaving Boston and Rob behind.

She prayed to God that it didn't come to that, because deep down inside, she knew she wouldn't be able to leave Robert, and consequently, years from now, she might end up still feeling inadequate as far as her professional life was concerned. And then *they* would have been right about her. She needed to show *them* that they were dead wrong.

"Maybe someday," she said softly, her voice a bit shakier than she liked.

"You're twenty-eight. How much longer do you expect to wait? Michelle's only one year older than you and she already has three kids," he stated matter-of-factly.

"Michelle's crazy," Yasmine said, as she recalled the honor of being present for Little Erik's birth. Michelle had asked her to be present for the other two, but Yasmine had been forced to say no. She couldn't bear the thought of watching another woman give birth when she…

"Don't you hear your biological clock ticking away?" Robert said, breaking into her thoughts. "*Tick, tock, tick, tock...*"

"That's the woman's argument."

"That's blasphemy coming from the mouth of a liberal woman. But with all due respect, it is the truth. Your biological clock is ticking. Your eggs won't remain viable forever."

Yasmine's stomach contracted, but she sucked in her breath to contain her pain and her guilt as Robert's last statement reminded her of her secret—the main reason she'd turned down his proposal the second time. As Robert's girlfriend, she wasn't compelled to confess, but if she agreed to marry him, she would definitely have to spill her guts before she said, "I do." If he was going to leave her over it, she would rather he left before they pledged themselves to each other. She didn't want to end up like many of her clients, fighting over who got the primary residence, the vacation home, or custody of the children.

But on the other hand, Rob was right. She was twenty-eight, and with each passing year, her eggs became less and less viable. Her forehead furrowed. What if she gave Robert half of what he desired—a child? Maybe that would be enough for him until she arrived at the place where she would be more self-confident and more emotionally equipped to handle losing him—if it came to that—when she told him her secret.

Having Robert's baby would bring her much joy and fulfillment, and it would be risk-free for the time being. Yas couldn't believe she was thinking along those terms, but she was in a jam. She raised her head and smiled at Robert. "Say I am worried about my biological clock. I don't have to be married to my kid's father," she said in a noncommittal way, even as she tried to breathe through the pain in her chest.

He glared at her through lowered lashes. "If it's my kid, you will be married to me. I'm not having kids out of wedlock."

"That's so old-fashioned, Rob. Nobody needs to be married

these days to have kids. As long as the parents are committed to taking care of the child, then—"

"It's all or nothing, Yasmine. No in-between with me. I don't intent to be anyone's baby-daddy. I will be married to my child's mother." He paused. "Maybe I'm being foolish in thinking you want a family, or that you want it with me. I'm thirty-five. I want to have my kids while I can still play ball with them, romp with them on the floor without being afraid my back will give out." He shrugged. "We don't even know if we are fertile, if we can reproduce, but I don't want to wait until I'm fifty to find out."

We're fertile, Robert. We can reproduce. Yasmine squeezed her eyes as her stomach clenched up in tight little knots. She swallowed compulsively as if a hand had closed around her throat, cutting off her circulation. She hadn't realized that she was trembling until Robert's hands tightened about her.

"Yas, baby. Why are you shaking? Does the thought of giving birth scare you this much? God, you're cold." He tightened his hold on her and, struggling to a sitting position, he pulled a cream knitted throw from the back of the sofa and spread it over them. He reached for the tray he'd set out earlier, filled two glasses with water and handed one to her.

Yasmine sipped her water slowly as she watched Robert gulp his down eagerly, pour himself another, and finish that off while she was still halfway through hers. As she felt the tension in her body loosen, she gave him her glass.

"Feeling better?" he asked, placing it on the tray before wrapping his arms around her again.

Yasmine nodded, and relaxed into his embrace. She touched her fingers to his cheek, caressing him softly. He was so wonderful to her. She wanted so much to trust him with the secrets of her heart, tell him why she'd reacted so emotionally to his statement about their fertility a few minutes ago, why she fought to control her emotions in public whenever she saw a newborn baby or saw him interact with his nieces and nephews, why she fell apart at home when she saw mothers interact with their babies on TV. She wanted to tell him.

"I have a confession to make," he said, stroking his fingers through her hair.

"About what?"

"A conversation I overheard between you and Naomi a while back."

"Concerning?" she asked quietly.

"Kids."

Yasmine stiffened as the uneasiness began to creep back into her system. Oh God, please don't let it be *that* conversation. Her hand that was caressing his face felt increasingly heavy and fell listlessly on to her lap. "What—what conversation was that?" she asked in a squeaky voice.

"You were telling her you don't understand how women put themselves through the pain of childbirth. It was right after you watched Michelle give birth to Little Erik. And the fact that you declined her invitations to be present for Tiffany and Fiona's births makes me wonder."

Yasmine sent up a prayer of thanks that it wasn't *that* conversation. It had been scary to watch Michelle go through the labor of childbirth, but the pure rapture on her friend's face when she held her newborn son in her arms for the first time told Yasmine that it was worth it. It was a labor of love. "Well, yes. It's not a pretty sight. But, that's not it," she added, not wanting Rob to think that her fear of labor was the reason she'd turned down Michelle's invitation, but wishing that it was nevertheless. It would make their relationship much less complicated if it was.

"Then what? You don't think I'm good enough, that I would make a good husband and father?" He placed a finger under her chin and forced her to meet his gaze.

Yasmine attempted to smile, but her lips just trembled.

Robert would make the best father and husband. He'd raised Michelle, and look how wonderful she'd turned out. Any woman would be blessed and proud to have him father her children. And the fact that he'd chosen her for that honor was tearing Yasmine apart. She swallowed the lump in her throat. "You're the best, Robert," she said in a tremulous voice. "Sometimes I wonder if I'm good enough for you."

He inclined his head. "Are you kidding me?"

"There are things you don't know about me."

"I know everything I need to know about you, Yasmine Reynolds. I've known you since you were toothless, and running around in diapers. We were like family growing up."

"Yeah, but you left, and we lost touch for so many years. A lot happened during the years we didn't see each other."

"But once we reconnected, it was like we were never separated. At least, that's the way it was for me."

"Me, too. But we'd changed. We'd gone through different life experiences, experiences that changed us from the people we once were."

His eyes narrowed considerably. "Are you talking about your previous lovers?"

Yasmine rolled her eyes at him. "Lovers! I was with one man before you. One!" She held up a finger, just in case he didn't understand the concept of *one*.

He gave her a measured look. "Only one?"

"What kind of girl do you think I am?"

"Well you did try to seduce me when you were fifteen, you little hussy. You crawled into my bed in the middle of the night, and began stroking my—"

She smacked him in the gut, making him grunt. "I was dumb, immature, and horny," she said, her defense mechanism snapping into gear at his affectionate teasing. Robert had broken her heart that night when she'd told him she loved him. Her pride, and some of her confidence had been seriously bruised by his harsh scolding, and then seven years later, she'd been crushed again by another man.

"Now you're smart, mature, and still horny. Hornier," he added, unaware of her paralyzing stroll down memory lane. "And the best cock-stroker ever." He kissed her on the lips, lingeringly and tenderly, until her awakening desires chased away her brooding thoughts. "So, who was it?" he asked, raising his head, his gaze hard and relentless.

"Who was what?" She'd already forgotten what they were talking about.

"Your first lover."

In spite of the wild fluttering of her heart in her chest, Yasmine was happy that the topic of conversation had changed from family, kids, and her deep dark secret. "I'm not telling you that. I don't want you looking at him cross-eyed," she said, lying about the true reason she didn't want to reveal the identity of her first lover. Just thinking about Jeremy and his family caused her inner turmoil and embarrassment at her poor choice. They were the *they* she needed to prove herself to.

"I don't watch people cross-eyed. This is my natural look." Robert rolled his eyeballs around until both his irises were pointing toward his nose.

Yasmine giggled at his comical expression. That's one thing she loved about Robert. In spite of his conservative demeanor, he made her laugh—something Jeremy was never able to do. She'd always felt as if she were under a microscope when she was around him and his parents. They'd made her feel small and self-conscious. "You keep doing that and your eyes might get stuck in that position one day," she told Robert.

"And if that doesn't work, maybe I'll do a little tic with my head, like this," he said, snapping his head and shoulders erratically as he held his cross-eyed expression. "Guys would think I'm crazy and wouldn't even give you a second look. You know I'm-sayin'?"

Yasmine doubled over with laughter until tears stung her eyes. "They'd be like 'Girl, what you doin' with that crazy-ass man? You can do better.' You know I'm sayin'?" she said, when she was sober enough to speak.

"Yeah, and I'd be like, 'Git!'" he said, following it up with another tic.

"You're a jealous man, Robert Carter," Yasmine said, laughter lingering in her voice. "I see the way you look at other men when you think they're checking me out. You cut in on every man who tried to dance with me at the wedding reception last week."

"I think it's rude for other men to be drooling over you in my presence," he said, returning his eyes to their natural state and stretching his legs out in front of him. "That's just disrespectful to me, and to you. As for the wedding reception, most of those old farts have a lot more money than me. Didn't want to give you any ideas about sailing around the world in three-hundred-foot luxury yachts and flying off on equally luxurious private jets to secluded island paradises. I was just making it known that you were mine. Staking my claim. You know I'm sayin'?"

"Mmmm."

Flinging the throw aside, he entwined the fingers of his right hand with her left ones. "This is what I'm saying," he said, pointing to his shaft, growing full and long again.

Yasmine swallowed and licked her lips.

"So what's his name?"

A hysteria of delight stirred inside Yasmine as he raised their hands to his lips and kissed the inside of her wrist. "Are you willing to name every woman you've been with?" she asked.

"If you want me to."

Except for Lani, she knew nothing about Robert's former

lovers. When they'd started dating, Robert had felt the need to tell her about his past with Lani, and had even offered to let Lani go if she felt threatened by their working together. She'd told him not to be stupid in dissolving his partnership with a brilliant orthodontist, just as long as he had no residual feelings for her. He'd promised he had none. "I don't care about the women you've been with, Robert. Just as long as you haven't been with any since we've been together," she added, looking at him speculatively.

"I haven't. And I'm pleased to know that you haven't been with anyone besides Mr. Cherry Snatcher." He cocked his head to one side. "Why did you guys break up, anyway?"

Yasmine dropped her gaze. "I don't want to talk about it."

"Did you love him?"

"I thought I did at the time. I wouldn't have slept with him otherwise."

"Are you still in love with him? Is that why you keep rejecting me? You're holding out for something better, for him?"

"Don't be ridiculous, Robert. You know how I feel about you."

"Do I really? You haven't said it lately, so maybe your feelings for me have changed. Did you tell *him* that you loved him?"

"See, there you go being jealous about the only other person I've slept with." She sucked in her breath as he kissed his way up her arm.

"I'm just curious. I can't be jealous when I've picked a few cherries in my time. Some guys are probably looking at me cross-eyed and I don't even know it. But if you had been my first, you would have been my only, Yasmine." The hot tip of his tongue collided with the tender area of her skin between her arm and forearm.

"How—how could you know that?" she asked on a shiver and a moan.

"Something happened to me the first time we made love, something I've never felt with any other woman. You gave me that *Uh Oh* feeling Brian McKnight sings about. You complete me. Period."

"Oh, Rob, you are the most romantic man I know, and that's why I—" Yasmine caught herself as the forbidden words almost spilled from her lips. "I got that *Uh Oh* feeling too," she said. "From the first moment we touched, I felt as if my body was made for you, and you alone to enjoy." *And I tried to tell you thirteen years ago, but you shut me down.*

"Yas." His hands were on her breasts molding her as his head ascended to her neck. He continued licking at her, delicately and intimately. "How old were you when Mr. Cherry Snatcher wandered into your orchard?"

A burst of laughter escaped Yasmine's throat, but it quickly faded as Robert continued his information diving in the form of masterful seduction. "Twenty—twenty-one," she stuttered.

"The same age I was when you tried to seduce me. Did you specifically wait for twenty-one to give it up? Was twenty-one associated with that hot Sunday night in Manchester when you crawled into my bed and began fondling me?" His mouth dropped to her chest and his tongue lashed at her swelling breasts.

Yasmine swallowed the saliva that backed up in her throat. "Get over yourself," she managed weakly, even as her hands reached up to guide Roberts's mouth to her quickly hardening nipple.

"Was he a college sweetheart?"

"No. He was a cop and we—"

His head sprang up and his mouth that had been about to suck on her nipple, twisted wryly. "A Manchester cop?"

Yasmine buried her face against his throat and groaned, both from his leaving her high and dry, and from the fact that she'd let him trick her into giving up valuable information. She should know better than to play his cat-and-mouse games when they were both naked. She usually ended up being the mouse, manipulated into saying anything he wanted her to say—most times.

"So every time I see a Manchester cop, I have to wonder if he's the one who picked your cherry," he said, lifting her head and gazing at her quizzically.

"Well, he's a state trooper now."

"Even worse." He grimaced. "That sucker might be stalking me on the highway, just waiting for me to mess up. Now I have to watch my speed and be extra careful while driving around in New Hampshire."

"That's what you get for probing into my past sex life," she said silkily, poking a finger into his chest.

"Oh yeah? Let's see what Little Rob gets for probing."

"There ain't nothing little about *Little Rob*."

He responded with a deep husky chuckle, and then, wrapping his hands around her midriff, he lifted and sat her on his lap, facing away from him.

"Oh God. Rob…" Yasmine hissed as she felt the ridge of his hard length pressing along the outer regions of her feminine folds. She rocked from side to side with him, relishing the subtle movements that were sending sharp shards of pleasure shooting from her core to her thighs, her legs, up into her tingling belly. God, and he wasn't even inside her yet.

A moan of ecstasy slipped through her lips when Robert's arms wrapped about her and his hands closed over her breasts, squeezing the swelling flesh, twirling the dark hard nipples between his forefingers and thumbs. Desire edged through her veins as his mouth trailed kisses up and down her back and across her shoulders.

Aching to be connected with him in every way possible,

Yasmine straightened her legs out between his, cradling his shaft in the soft wet place between her thighs. She leaned back into his embrace and, reaching up, she wound her arms around his neck and buried her fingers into the soft mat of curls on his head. Tilting her upper body and head to the side, she pulled his mouth down over hers. Her amazing flexibility made many sex positions possible for them.

His kiss was scorching, ravishing, as he plunged deeper and deeper into her, moaning and sucking on her lips and her tongue, as if she was a sweet piece of chocolate. His pressure on her breasts increased, as did the thrusting of his hips, and soon the grating of his hard smooth cock against her now hot and soaked love trough had her whirling in pleasure. Yasmine squeezed her thighs together to contain her desire, keep it locked inside the core of her womanhood, but it was beyond her. It spiraled up inside like a twisting coil, sending her into a series of erratic tremors.

With a groan, he lifted his mouth from hers, trailed his lips down her heaving chest, and took one aching breast into his mouth, swallowing it whole and sucking so greedily, she felt her nipple hit the back of his throat. When one of his hands dropped to her groin and his finger began to play with her swollen clitoris, Yasmine came, holding on to Robert as if she were bereft at sea, and he were her lifejacket, the only tangible item on an ocean of boisterous rolling waves.

He waited until she stopped shivering before he trailed his mouth over to her other breast, leaving a wet tingling sensation in his wake. "Assume the position," he whispered, before his mouth devoured her mound.

Weak from her orgasm, Yasmine managed to pull her legs up and plant her feet on the duvet on each side of Robert's thighs. She raised her buttocks off his lap, giving him space to position the tip of his shaft against her tight opening. Blood pounded in her veins as he simultaneously pressed her back down and pushed upward into her, burying at least half of his thick hot column of flesh inside her. Yasmine gasped aloud from the burst of fiery flames that arched through her.

Without giving her time to catch her breath, he wrapped his arms around her, one hand tight against her belly, holding her in place, while the fingers of the other wreaked havoc on the sensitive little knob of her clitoris.

Yasmine danced on Robert's shaft as with each thrust he buried more and more of himself inside her until he'd given her all, stretching her and filling her to completion. The turbulence of his passion swirled about her, raw and raunchy, pushing her to heights of passion she'd grown accustomed to every time they made love, and soon she felt him buckling wildly, calling out her name as he yielded to the burning sweetness of her.

They came together, groaning and moaning so hard, Yasmine swore their neighbors could hear them. They collapsed into each other, and then on the duvet, quivering as they both tried to savor the lingering heat of their passion for as long as possible.

CHAPTER SEVEN

Yasmine was savoring the afterglow of Robert's loving as she drove along Route 93 North toward Manchester. The featured love songs on Heart & Soul, her favorite XM radio channel, intensified the warm memories.

She'd started out a lot later than she'd anticipated. But considering the reason, she felt no guilt or regret at cutting her time short with her family. Besides, if she'd left earlier, she would have been stuck in heavy traffic anyway. It was almost seven p.m. yet there were still quite a few vehicles traveling north. Her family would have lost time with her one way or the other. A few hours wasn't going to kill any of them.

She turned up the volume on her radio as Erik Benet's "Chocolate Legs" came over the airwaves. As she sang along with him, her legs began shaking as she recalled Rob huskily commanding her to wrap her chocolate legs around him during their first round of lovemaking. God, that was so damn sexy. She loved him talking to her while they made love. The echo of his voice resonating deep inside her was like an audible aphrodisiac, making her blood boil in her veins and setting her skin on fire.

After their second round of lovemaking on the floor, she and

Robert had been famished, but the only food in her house was the baguette and cheese she'd picked up from the supermarket in her attempt to avoid running into Sylvia. It was faster than ordering takeout. It was also very romantic to just sit on the floor surrounded by burning candles and vases of red roses and enjoy their meager supper while they watched sailboats and mini yachts go by in her backyard.

With their hunger somewhat appeased, they'd taken a shower together. After lathering up and washing each other, Rob had sat her on the bench in the stall, knelt in front of her, and insisted on eating her out—to make sure she was spanking clean for her trip up north, he'd said. Yasmine hadn't argued with him. Instead, she'd just lain back against the tiles and let him do his thing. And oh boy, did he do his thing…

Going down on her had turned him on again, and while she was still coming from his tongue-lashing, he'd lifted her up, settled her on top of him, and taken her hard and fast while they stood under the warm shower sprays.

He would have cleaned her again if her ringing phone hadn't interrupted them. Naomi wanted to know when Yasmine was leaving Boston so she could plan the pizza pickup to coincide with her estimated time of arrival into Manchester. It was with a great deal of regret that Yasmine had gotten dressed, packed her weekend bag, and left her house, and a still naked, horny Robert on her bed.

"Watch your speed," he'd said as she'd draped the strap of her bag over her shoulder. "You don't want Officer Cherry Snatcher pulling you over."

"Maybe, I do," Yasmine had retorted, even as she dreaded the possibility of running into Jeremy on the highway or anywhere else. She hadn't seen him since their breakup five years ago, and that suited her just perfectly. "He might want to catch up, see how I'm doing," she'd added, unable to resist the urge to tease Robert.

"Then maybe I shouldn't have cleaned you up, sent you off smelling all

fresh and sweet. Next time, I'll leave my scent on you to ward him off—him and all the other men who might think they have a chance with you."

"Who says they don't? I don't see any ring on my finger," Yasmine had tossed back as she walked out of her bedroom, grinning.

"And whose fault is that? I'm not gonna wait for you forever, Yasmine Reynolds."

Yasmine turned down the volume as the significance of Robert's words pounded against the walls of her brain. His statement had caused her to falter as she'd descended the steps, but once she'd gotten downstairs and seen the evidence of their sweet afternoon together, she'd shaken off the ominous feeling. Surely, he was just kidding.

But was he really kidding? Was he getting tired of waiting on her? Four years was a long time to ask anyone to wait for anything. Yet, Robert had been waiting dutifully, loyally, and patiently.

Yasmine had never thought about Robert not being in her life, neither as a friend nor a lover. Like he'd pointed out earlier, he'd known her since she was in diapers, long before she was old enough to understand the meaning and significance of knowing anyone.

Even though their most recent conversation had been peppered with humor and laughter, the topics were nonetheless poignant. Marriage, children, and career choices were the most important subjects for any couple to discuss. They were the frameworks, the backbones of any serious relationship. And she and Robert were as serious as they came.

She'd known that for sure when, even after she'd turned down his proposals, he'd asked her to move in with him. And now she wasn't even enjoying her townhouse as much as she'd anticipated. It was lonely when Rob wasn't there. Plus, having Sylvia for a neighbor was growing more annoying by the day. It would be nice not to be filled with anxiety each time her doorbell rang. Sylvia came by way too often for her taste—her reason, "We single girls have to keep each other company." Yasmine wasn't married, but she definitely wasn't single either.

Which brought her back to Robert's threat. *I'm not gonna wait for you forever, Yasmine Reynolds.*

And as if the universe were siding with him, Meghan Trainor and John Legend began singing "Like I'm Gonna Lose You."

As she listened to the words of the song, a deep unaccustomed pain settled in Yasmine's chest, and visions of a lightless future without Robert flashed across her mind. She didn't want to lose him. *Ever.* And for that to happen, she needed to forgive him for hurting her as a teenager, and then pulling away from her four years ago.

"I forgive you, Robert. I love you, and I forgive you."

As Yasmine heard the words falling from her lips, she realized that she didn't need to forgive Robert for anything. As a matter of fact, she should be asking his forgiveness for putting him in a compromising position—and on top of that, thanking him for not giving in to his lust.

Butterflies fluttered around inside Yasmine's stomach as she thought of the pressure Robert must have been under that night. He'd gotten mad and scolded her because he was looking out for her like a little sister, the way he looked out for Michelle. How would she feel about him and herself now as adults if he'd granted her request? Yasmine wondered.

They'd never really talked about that incident, except in jest, like they'd done this afternoon. But as cars whipped past her on the highway, one bad scenario after another about that night flashed across Yasmine's mind—scenarios she'd overlooked over the years because she'd been too deeply in love with Robert to see them.

What if Michelle had caught them? What if she'd gotten pregnant? From what she knew now, she was certain that if they'd done it that night, they would have been sneaking around to do it again, and again. What if her parents had found out? Robert would have been in a hell of a lot of trouble with her father who'd been very protective of her and Naomi when they were little girls.

Dear Lord, she'd mistaken Robert's concern for rejection—the worst kind. And that night she'd sworn in her teenage heart that she would never put herself in a place to feel that kind of pain again.

But she'd grown up, and time had dulled her hurt enough for her to make herself vulnerable to Jeremy after he flexed his muscles at her by fixing her flat tire when she'd broken down on the side of the road, and giving her rides to and from school and work when her car was in the shop. And when she got her own apartment, he'd fixed the leaky kitchen faucet, installed her air-conditioning unit in her bedroom window, chipped away the ice on her back patio, and performed many other "manly" duties around her house. Yep, Yasmine had been lassoed, and then when she'd told Jeremy that she loved him, he'd dropped her like she had the plague, and had even moved out of town to get away from her.

After that, Yasmine had sworn to keep her promise to her broken heart, and when she and Robert began seeing each other, she'd added a few extra padlocks to the chamber where she kept it out of harm's reach.

She'd learned to play the game, and had taken away the opportunity for Robert to hurt her again. He'd only screwed up once—after he began seeing his hypnotherapist and his memories about his real father began to surface. Those harrowing memories had plunged him into a period of grave depression for months. Yasmine had expected him to turn to her for comfort, but instead he'd pulled away, and the more she'd reached out to him, the more he'd withdrawn into his own private world, and at a time when she had been going through the most difficult time of her life.

She had needed Robert more then than she'd ever needed him, or anyone else. Michelle was preoccupied with her new family. Naomi and Felix had been going through a rough time in their marriage, so Yasmine couldn't even talk to her best friend or her sister about what was going on in her life. She'd felt alone. *She'd been alone.* And so she'd had to make critical decisions about her life—*alone.* That was the first, worst, and longest *off-again* period she and Rob ever had.

Yasmine sighed. Months later, when Robert proposed to her the second time, she'd turned him down. How could she trust him with her heart when he couldn't trust her with his emotions? Her refusal did not deter him, though. In fact, over the years, he seemed more determined to prove his love and his commitment to her. And when he pulled stunts like the one today, the pressure on Yasmine's heart not to trust him again eased up tremendously.

She did want to marry Robert and have his babies before they were both too old to enjoy them, but dealing with divorcing couples on a daily basis had taught her that there were so many things that could derail plans and keep dreams from coming true.

Yasmine sighed again as she flipped her signals and took the exit for Manchester. Even though she missed Rob already, she was looking forward to spending time with her family. Perhaps being around them would take her mind off the negative aspects of married life and couples who hadn't made it, and instead help her focus on those who had made it work, those who had learned how to love and trust, and how to bare their hearts to each other —even with the knowledge that it could be broken beyond repair.

She personally knew of those kinds of couples: Michelle and Erik, and their friends, her brother, her sister, and her parents—

especially her parents, whose thirty-eighth wedding anniversary was just around the corner. Those were couples who valued their marriages. All for the sake of love.

Their commitment to each other and the sacrifices they'd made for their children gave Yasmine hope.

❧

The moment he'd made his, *"I'm not gonna wait for you forever, Yasmine Reynolds,"* threat, Robert had regretted it. But after a short reflection on their afternoon together, he'd tossed his remorse aside and smiled as he heard her drive away.

He would wait for her forever if he had to, simply because he knew there wasn't a woman out there who could make him even slightly as happy as Yasmine made him. She knew that he loved her, but maybe it was time she began to wonder if that unrequited love would always be around. He hadn't meant to scare her, but then, maybe she needed to be scared of losing him. She didn't believe in Happily Ever After, so perhaps the reality of *Lonely Ever After* would shake her up a bit.

Before she left, she'd told him not to clean her house, that she would do it when she returned from Manchester. He'd tried to obey her wishes by reaching for her house phone and calling Detective Gilbert to put him back on the case of researching his parent's past. And the minute he'd hung up the phone, Robert had hopped out of bed and was now standing butt naked in Yasmine's kitchen, stacking a week's supply of dirty dishes into her dishwasher.

Love had made him start the four loads of laundry she had sitting around for the past weeks, and tidy up her living and dining room areas, stack her books on the bookshelf in her office, and sweep her floor.

Yasmine's proclivity for disorder might have put off another man a long time ago, but Robert didn't mind it in the least. In fact, he enjoyed cleaning up her messes and doing her laundry, he thought on a smile as he started up the dishwasher and wiped down her countertop. It made him feel closer to her, loving her in spite of her imperfections.

Robert had dated women who weren't even marginally as untidy as Yas, yet he couldn't tolerate being in their homes. He'd never felt the desire to clean up after any of them. Instead the neat freak trait in him had been irritated by their lack of good house maintenance. He'd ended those relationships quickly.

Not Yasmine, though. He'd accepted and even embraced the fact that her housekeeping habits were different from his. He would compromise for her in a minute. He would wash her dishes and scrub her floor every day if he had to, because once the sun dipped behind the horizon, he knew he'd be richly rewarded when she wrapped her silky chocolate legs around him in the dark of night.

Robert trembled as a hot shiver rushed up and down his spine. Little Rob jumped to life and banged his head against the cabinet, sending a sharp pain into Robert's groin. "Down boy," he said, dropping the paper towel into the garbage bin under the sink. "You have to make do with what you just had until Sunday. She'll be back on Sunday."

He groaned as he walked toward Yasmine's office that doubled as a lounge overlooking the ocean. He picked out a pair of jeans and briefs from the piles of clean laundry he'd dumped on her sofa earlier. Half dressed, he sat down, flipped on the TV, and skipped to his favorite sports channel.

Yasmine compromised for him, too, he thought as he reached for one of her T-shirts from the pile of clothes, and began folding it. He was allergic to certain chemicals in her favorite laundry detergent and softener, but once they got together, she'd stopped using them for him, without him even asking her.

She wasn't into sports, yet she accompanied him to pro baseball, football, and basketball games at Fenway Park, and even as far as Yankee Stadium in New York when the Red Sox played there. And when he came over, she gave him the freedom to enjoy his favorite sports channels on her sixty-inch, flat-screen TV. She never complained once, not even when her favorite shows ran opposite something he wanted to watch. Sometimes she would cuddle up to him and read one of her law books or work on briefs while he listened to Bryant Gumbel or any other sports broadcaster of his choice.

She gave up the favorite side of her bed for him when he slept over, although it never really mattered since they always ended up tangled up together in the middle. Nonetheless, he appreciated that she was considerate of the fact that he could only fall asleep on his left side and only facing the door. A habit he'd developed from his abusive childhood. He'd learned not to turn his back on Timmy Gleason, especially after his mother died and he himself had to assume the role of protector for his newborn baby sister.

Yes, Yasmine loved him, but he wished she would say it, just once. He knew it wasn't because of what happened between them all those years ago. They'd talked about it, and she'd said that she understood why he'd rejected her. Was she lying to protect her ego, her heart? Robert wondered now. Or was it something that Office Cherry Snatcher had done to her? Had he hurt her so badly that she was afraid to love again? Robert hoped *he* wasn't paying for another man's iniquities.

He was halfway through folding the pile of laundry when his cell alerted him to a text message. He picked it up off the coffee table and smiled when the most recent picture of Yas in the dress she'd worn to Michelle's wedding flashed on the screen. With eager fingers, he pressed the *text* icon.

I love YOU!

Robert stared at the words, his heart thundering in his chest, and his mind jumping ahead that maybe she'd meant to send that text to someone else, like Officer Cherry Snatcher. Could talking about him this afternoon have evoked memories and feelings for her? He'd known a few women who never got over their first love. Could Yasmine be one of them?

No. "No!" Robert said vehemently and, pushing the preposterous possibility aside, he clasped his cell phone between his palms, pressed his hands against his chest, and squeezed his lids as tears stung his eyes.

The words hadn't spilled from her lips, and he didn't have the pleasure of hearing them echo in his heart and mind over and over again, nor did he have the thrill of gazing into her eyes as she spoke them. But reading them on his cell phone's screen, knowing that it must have taken a lot for Yas to write them, and then hit *send*, filled Rob with unutterable happiness. Maybe it was better that she'd written the words because now he could read them whenever he was overcome with doubt. She'd given him hard proof that she loved him.

In the past, when he'd expressed his love for her, she would respond with: *I know. Yeah? You better. What's not to love?* Superficial responses that always frustrated the hell out of him. But, today Yasmine Marie Reynolds had admitted, albeit by text, that she loved him, Robert Javier Carter. She'd spoken from her heart. They were making progress. Maybe his threat of not waiting around for her forever had gotten to her. It was about time.

Swiping the back of his hand across his eyes, Robert set his cell phone aside and resumed his laundry-folding chore. But no sooner had he picked up a towel, his phone went off again. This time he recognized the ringtone as Michelle, and a smile broke over his face when the photo of her in her wedding dress flashed on the screen. His two favorite women were thinking of him at the same time. He was a very lucky man. He set the towel aside and picked up his phone again.

"Hey, Michelle." He cleared the catch from his throat.

"Hey, Rob. Are you okay? You sound like…shaken."

Robert's smile widened. Michelle had the uncanny ability to read him, even from miles away. He longed to share his good news, but knowing she would probably downplay the fact that Yas had admitted that she loved him in a text and not in person, he kept it to himself. For the moment it was enough for Robert, and he didn't want anyone, not even his darling sister, stamping on his modicum of bliss. "I'm fine," he said. "You must be back home because I'm sure you wouldn't be calling me from *Baia degli Amanti*," he added to keep her from prying further.

"Wait, you knew where we were going?"

"Yeah, I knew."

She giggled. "Well, you always knew how to keep a secret."

Yes, years of practice, he thought sullenly. "How was the island?"

"Fabulous."

"You're back early though."

"Unfortunately, yes. We came back yesterday."

"Why? I thought you'd want to stay away a day longer." He turned down the volume on the TV.

She sighed. "We wanted to, but Fiona wasn't feeling well."

Robert sat up straight and muted the TV. "What's wrong with my niece? Why didn't her grandparents call me?"

"It's okay, Rob. She's fine now. I'm trying to wean her off nursing, but I left a supply before I went away and asked Mom to interchange her feedings with the same formula I gave to Little Erik and Tiffany, but she had an allergic reaction to it."

"Poor baby. Philippe and Felicia should have called me," he said, referring to Michelle's father and mother-in-law. "I want to come up and hold her, let her know her Uncle Rob loves her." He took a swift glance at his Rolex. "If I leave now, I could be at your place in three hours, maybe two and a half if I speed, and Fi can fall asleep on my chest like you used to when you were a baby. Remember?" he asked with a tender smile and a catch in his voice.

Michelle chuckled. "I remember. I was falling asleep on your chest until I was around three. You kept the big bad monsters away."

"That's what big brothers are for." Too bad their big bad monster was their father.

"Anyway, Fi is already asleep," Michelle said, pulling him back from his trip down memory lane, tinged with both pleasant and painful images. "But first thing in the morning, I'll tell her that her Uncle Rob loves her."

"You better, and give her lots of kisses and hugs, too. If she's still not feeling well tomorrow, call me and I'll be there." It wasn't like he had anything else to do. Yasmine was gone until Sunday afternoon, and unfortunately, he had no buddy-buddies to hang out with, except Vaughn, who'd gone to Martha's Vineyard for the weekend.

"You know, for a man who doesn't have kids of his own, you're very sensitive to their needs. You have a natural instinct for fatherhood, Robert. I'm sure it's because you spent most of your life taking care of me, being a father and mother to me, and it makes me sad to think that..."

Robert pushed to his feet and walked out on to the balcony. The pleasantly cool August night air, making contact with the bare skin of his upper body, made Robert shiver a little, but he held his ground, unable to take his eyes off the magnificent views of the Boston skyline, and the chain of twinkling white and amber lights of traffic traveled back and forth across the Zakim Bridge in the distance. Much closer, the gentle sound of the ocean lapping against the pier and the boats below added a degree of magic and tranquility to the night.

As much as he gave Yas a hard time for purchasing this condo, Robert understood her fascination for living on Constellation Wharf. It was simply beautiful, like her, but not a place to raise children—the children his sister was presently berating him about not yet producing.

"I'd love to have a couple nieces and nephews to adore, the way you adore my children," Michelle continued. "I love Yasmine like a sister, but I love you more, Rob. You're my brother, my flesh and blood. I'm worried about you. I'm worried that you might end up alone with no family, no children, and—" She paused, then added, "I mean this tenderly—specifically no Yasmine. It's been three years, and —"

"Well, five," Rob said, as he recalled the day, three years ago when Michelle had stopped by his brownstone a day early to surprise him while she was in Boston for a book signing event. She had instead gotten a shock when Yasmine answered the door, wearing one of his shirts. The three of them had engaged in a long heated debate during which time Michelle had expressed her feelings of hurt and betrayal that they'd kept something so important from her.

"You remember how upset you were when you found out that Yasmine and I were seeing each other behind your back?" Robert leaned against the steel railing of the balcony and gazed into the glimmering water below. "I think you were more pissed off that she was wearing an insanely expensive shirt you'd just given me more than anything else. You tried to rip it off her until you realized it was all she was wearing." He chuckled.

"This is no laughing matter, Robert," Michelle stated in a disapproving voice. "It wasn't nice of you to hide your relationship from me. But that's water under the bridge. You two can't go on like this forever, moving in and out of love when a situation changes. You know it. Yasmine knows it. Everybody knows it."

"Michelle, I—"

"You're a catch, Robert..." Her voice cracked. "You're handsome, charming, loyal, and you have the biggest, kindest heart of any man out there."

"You're my sister. You have to say that," he teased her.

"I'm not saying it because I'm your sister. I'm saying it because it's the truth. You sacrificed your life to raise me and make me into the woman I am today, a woman who's blessed beyond my own imaginations. And Yas, I couldn't have chosen better for you. I love both of you with all my heart and I want you to be as happy as me. You would make such a wonderful dad, and Yas would make a great mom, I know she would."

Robert pressed his fist into his chest as a strange numb comfort swept through him. It was uplifting to hear his sister speak so kindly of the woman he loved even though she was aggravated with Yasmine's indecision about marrying him. "I know Yas would be a great wife and mother, but I feel like there's something keeping her from following her heart." He was surprised at the ease with which he was confiding in Michelle. This was the first constructive conversation they'd had about Yasmine in a long while.

"Like what?" Michelle asked, just as the horn of a tugboat passing by blasted three times. "Are you at Yasmine's?" she added in a high-pitched voice. "She's been listening to me criticize her behavior toward you? Oh Robert—"

"Relax, relax," he said with a grin. "Yas isn't here. She's visiting her family in Manchester."

"You weren't invited?"

He grimaced. "She's taking Peter to Canobie Lake tomorrow."

"Oh yeah, you're afraid of heights." There was concern, not ridicule in her voice.

"Don't remind me." Robert pushed off the railing and

walked back inside, shaking off the ominous sensation of being dangled upside down from a great height. It was strange that he wasn't afraid of being on balconies or even hiking to the top of a mountain, standing at the edge, and looking down on the world. It was just the thought of being catapulted through the air or being dropped suddenly that scared the skin off his back.

"I think you should try to figure out why," Michelle said. "Dr. West should be able to help you dig a little deeper. Have you discussed it with her?"

She'd offered but the thought of discovering the source of his fears scared Robert just as much. He'd discovered his acrophobic tendency when he was nine and had gone on an end-of-year school trip to Whales Tales. He'd thrown up after the first ride, and had spent the rest of the day cowering under a table, too afraid to even watch his friends ride. To rub salt into his wounds, when he got home, Timmy Gleason had called him a sissy. Robert shook the images away with a deft shake of his head and headed for the kitchen. He was getting hungry, and was hoping that Yas had some leftover takeout that he could stick in the microwave. He didn't feel like getting dressed and going out.

"Speaking of the past," he said, bringing the conversation back to Yasmine, "maybe someone hurt Yas." He opened the refrigerator and stared at a few containers of yogurt, a loaf of sliced bread, a carton of eggs, an assortment of aged fruits, and a load of condiments that dared him to be inventive and whip up something appetizing. "Maybe she's afraid to make herself vulnerable again," he added, slamming the door and walking over to the drawer where Yas kept her collection of restaurant menus.

"Well, I know the feeling of being hurt and being afraid to put yourself out there again. But I also know that you can't let past experiences stop you from living, from going after your heart's desires. If I had let my pain control me, I would not have my beautiful family today. You have to let go of the past, Robert," she said, her voice uncompromisingly gentle.

First he had to find his past—his and Michelle's—and then decide if it was worth remembering or best forgetting. He would clue Michelle in when he heard from Detective Gilbert, that is, if there was something concrete to report. He pulled out a handful of menus and spread them on the countertop. "Speaking of the past," he said, "do you know anything about the guy Yas dated before me?"

"Jeremy Arsenault?"

Robert flinched. "That rich little North End snob who used to visit his cousins who lived down the street from the Reynolds? He stole my bike when we were like ten and dismantled it, just to be a jerk. What the hell was Yasmine thinking hooking up with him?" Robert refused to dwell on the fact that according to Yasmine, *Little Arsie* had turned from his wicked ways and was now enforcing the law.

"Uh-oh." Michelle groaned. "You didn't know."

"Nope," he said, trying to contain the rippling in his gut, not sure if it was jealousy or hunger. He opted for hunger. "She refused to give up his name when I asked. Why didn't I know that? I grew up in that neighborhood. I should have heard something."

"Maybe you didn't want to know. Plus, you haven't spent a lot of time in Manchester since you left years ago, Robert." She paused on a deep sigh. "Yas is going to kill me if she finds out I spilled."

"I'm not going to tell her. But since you already spilled, why did they break up?"

"Why don't you ask Yasmine?"

"I did. Said she didn't want to talk about it. Was it something big? Did he hurt her? Did she tell you?"

"I feel like I'm on trial here," Michelle said with a chuckle.

"It wasn't big, according to Yas. He got a promotion in another town and they grew apart. She was busy with school and work; he was busy with learning the ropes of his new job. They weren't meant to be, Robert, no more than Ryan and I were."

"You believe her?"

"I don't have a reason not to."

"From the way she acted when I asked, I believe there's more."

"Well, that's the story she told me."

Story, being the operative word. Yasmine's *I don't want to talk about it,* and what she'd told Michelle just didn't add up. There was more to the *story* behind her breakup with Arsie, and he was going to find out what it was. Knowing what he knew about him, Robert was sure that jerk had done something really awful to her, and that he himself was paying for it.

"Is that Uncle Robert?"

Robert would be lying if he said he wasn't grateful for the interruption. He needed to distance his mind from the facts he'd just learned. He would much rather dwell in the pleasant moments following the *I love YOU* text message from Yasmine.

"Yes, Precious," his sister said, "and we're having an important discussion."

As his stomach made a loud growl, Robert walked back to the lounge. He put his cell phone on *speaker* and sat it on the coffee table before hoisting one of his shirts from the pile of clothes he'd recently folded. He would have to go out after all. He quickly pulled it on as he listened to the conversation between his sister and his twelve-year-old step-niece.

"Can I talk to him? Please, Mom, just for a minute," he heard Precious say.

"Okay. One minute, but I need—"

"Hi, Uncle Robert."

"Hey, Precious. How's my favorite niece?" Phone in hand, Robert made his way upstairs and into Yasmine's closet.

"I know I'm not your favorite niece, Uncle Robert, because you say the same thing to Tiffany and Fiona."

"You're all my favorites. I love you all equally." And that was the honest truth. Robert couldn't love Precious any more if they were blood related. He shoved his feet into a pair of sandals and grabbed his keys and his wallet from the dresser before retracing his steps to the first floor. "What's up with you, young lady? I still can't believe how fast you're growing up, and beautifully so. Before we know it, you'll be off to college."

Precious giggled. "I have to get through high school first. And I hear it's really tough."

"I'm sure you can handle it, kiddo. You're a smart girl. The smartest twelve-year-old I know."

"You must not know a lot of twelve-year-old girls, Uncle Robert," Precious chided him. "When are you coming back up to visit? I miss you already. Or maybe I can come down to Boston for a weekend. Please, Uncle Robert. I need to get out of this house. My brother and my sisters are driving me crazy. It's even worse when Aunt Kaya and Aunt Shaina's kids come over. They're always following me around."

Robert laughed out loud. "It stinks to be the oldest. I know. Your mom used to drive me crazy when she was a kid. She, and Aunt Yasmine," he added.

"See, you get it. So, you'll rescue me? I like spending time with you and Aunt Yasmine."

Back in the lounge, Robert turned off the TV and closed the doors to the balcony. "I'll tell you what, kid. I'll check with Aunt Yasmine, and see what her schedule is like for the next couple weeks. If she's available, we'll plan something fun. You check with your parents in the meantime."

"Thanks, Uncle Robert. I love you. I love you. I love you.

You're the best uncle in the whole entire world," Precious shouted with excitement.

Robert chuckled on his way to the kitchen and the door that led to the garage. "I'm looking forward to it, Precious. Now, is your mom still around?"

"She had to go break up a fight between Tiffany and Little Erik over his LEGO Spider Car that Daddy just bought him. See what I mean?"

"I see what you mean. So, your brother is no longer JP? He's back to Little Erik?" Robert asked. "I mean, it was just a few weeks ago he decided that he wanted to be called JP instead of Little Erik."

Precious' sigh was deep. "Yeah. He decided to change back when Mom and Dad were on their honeymoon. He can't make up his mind what he wants to be called."

Robert laughed. "Well, he'll always be Little Erik, no matter what he calls himself. Where's your dad?"

"At the hospital."

"On a Friday night?"

"He had an emergency."

That's what Robert liked about Erik. He was dedicated to his cause. It was one of the reasons Robert hadn't punched the doctor out when he and Michelle had been separated. He knew Erik would never intentionally hurt anyone, much less the woman he loved. It was just as well that Erik wasn't around anyway. They always ended up talking for long periods of time, and tonight, Robert was too hungry to talk anymore. "I have to go, sweetie. I love you. Say hi to your dad, okay?"

"I will, Uncle Robert. See you next week."

Robert sat behind the wheel of his Ferrari staring at his phone. He'd meant to ask Michelle to order a replacement skirt from Joanne's for Yasmine, and have it special delivered by

Monday morning to Yasmine's office. Before starting up the engine, he texted her.

A few moments later she responded: *What's wrong with the one she just bought?*

It got ruined. And don't ask how.

I wasn't about to. I'll put in the order tomorrow.

Thanks. Are any of the kids bleeding?

No. But when Tiffany sets her heart on something, she fights for it.

Reminds me of you when you were growing up. (Smiley Face) Like mother like daughter.

Whatever. Gotta go. Erik just got home. Good night, Bro.

Good night, Sis. I love you.

Love you, too. Talk to you soon.

Before he put his phone away, Robert read Yasmine's text again. His heart was hammering wildly against his chest, and his face was split into a wide silly grin as he backed his car out of the garage.

Yasmine loved him. His world was all right for the moment.

CHAPTER EIGHT

Yasmine pulled her car into the empty space at the side of the duplex where her sister lived, and was instantly shoved into her past when the television noise from the neighboring houses drowned out the music that had kept her company on her ride north. She cut her engine, and then looked out her side window when canine growls caught her attention.

So her sister had new neighbors, she thought, eyeing the three pit bulls staring her down from the porch of the house next door, as if she was trespassing on their turf. *Well, Boo Hoo. I was here first.*

As if reading and challenging her thoughts, the dogs raced down the steps and flew across the yard toward the fence, their growls growing stronger and meaner. As she watched them, somewhat amused, Yasmine was taken back to when she and Michelle used to tease the neighborhood dogs on their way from school—but only those behind tall fences like the three now barking so ferociously that blobs of white foam dripped from their mouths.

She shifted her attention as the screen door to the house opened, and a fortyish-looking man appeared on the porch and whistled for the dogs. They immediately ceased their barking and ran back to the porch.

"Welcome back, Yasmine Reynolds," she muttered as the screen door slapped shut behind the man and his dogs, and the sounds of male laughter immediately picked up where the canines' uproar had left off.

Yasmine gazed through her rearview mirror at three middle-aged men, sitting in rickety folding chairs around a card table in the yard across the street. A sawed-down tin can—acting as an ashtray—a depleted deck of cards, and a pool of cash were stationed in the middle of the table, while beer cans and dealt hands were in front of each of the men. The cloud of smoke around them was so thick, Yas was sure she could write her name in it and drive around the block and back before it dissipated.

It was another old familiar neighborhood scene that Yasmine didn't miss one bit. She was hardly in town for five minutes and already she longed for her condo and the tranquility of her ocean-view backyard, especially with dogs barking at her, she thought, as the pit bulls resumed their growling, this time from a window inside their house.

Maybe the dogs were trying to tell her that she didn't belong here—not anymore. She didn't feel superior to the people around here, the people she'd grown up with, many of whom she still admired and loved. She just felt blessed to have had the ambition, the courage, and the opportunity to get out. And she did give back to her community. And why not? These people had helped shape her into the woman she'd become. After she'd taken on a couple of cases, pro bono, the president of the youth center that Michelle had built had offered Yasmine a room to set up a local office. And three times a month, Yasmine drove to Manchester to meet and consult with her underprivileged clients.

It might be the last weekend she would spend here since Naomi and her husband, Felix, had recently bought a three-bedroom, two-bathroom house in a nicer area of Manchester. Felix, a construction worker, was in the process of remodeling the kitchen and the bathrooms, but it was taking forever since he was going it alone, and could only work on the house a couple nights out of the week and on weekends.

All the other members of the Reynolds family had already left. Her parents were living in a fifty-plus community in Nashua, and eight years ago her brother Luke and his wife, Christine, had moved to the North End of Manchester—the area where Yas used to fantasize about living with Rob when she was a kid.

Being a stay-at-home mom—cooking, cleaning, and raising Robert's children while he worked as a used car salesman—had been the scope of Yasmine's big dreams. It was her parents' life, and it was all she knew. At nine years of age, she couldn't imagine a world outside of Manchester, nor did she imagine she would reach a place in her life where she could never be content staying at home, cooking, cleaning, or raising anybody's children.

She still dreamed of having Robert's children, but she wasn't staying home with them. Robert might want to consider that fact before they moved forward with their relationship. Well, *if* they moved forward, after they'd had the heart-to-heart discussion about her secret.

Brushing away her childish memories, Yasmine grabbed her overnight bag and briefcase, and hopped out of her car. She locked and double locked it, and then tried all the doors, just to make sure. Her car was fully insured and she hadn't left anything of value inside, but she dreaded the inconvenience and time it would take if she had to replace or fix it in the event of a theft or break-in. It had taken three vehicular break-ins for Felix and Naomi to finally realize that they needed to move.

"Hey, Yas," a voice called as Yasmine got to the sidewalk.

"Hi, Mr. George, Mr. Kendall, and Mr. Jackson." She waved back at the three grinning, smoking, drinking gamblers with gray heads, and jiggling potbellies hanging over the waists of their cut-off shorts. She'd gone to school with their children, so she knew them well. One of the chairs was empty, but a hand of cards and a bottle of beer in front of it indicated that a fourth man was missing, probably on a bathroom break inside the house.

"Did you tease those dogs?" Mr. George, who still lived in the house next to the one where Yasmine grew up, asked.

"I swear I did not," Yasmine said, raising her hand like a witness about to testify.

"Hmmm," Mr. Jackson, the widower who owned the house, said. "We're just messing with you. Those dogs are a pain in the ass, but it reminds me of when you and Michelle were kids. Everybody knew school was out when the dogs began barking. You two were trouble together." He chuckled.

Yasmine grimaced with shame and humor. "I'll be lying if I said I wasn't tempted. But I'm too old for that. I've grown up."

"Yes, you have," Mr. George said, nodding.

Yasmine narrowed her eyes. "Aren't gambling and opened bottles of alcohol in public illegal?" she asked, sending them a mock look of disapproval.

"Not on this street," Mr. Kendall, who lived two doors down, responded.

"Don't know about this street, but not in this yard." Mr. Jackson reached into a cooler on the ground and pulled out another can of beer, before glancing over at Yasmine again. "You looking fine, girl. Makes me wish I was young again."

Yasmine took his comment in jest. She was glad she'd let Robert talk her into wearing the low-cut V-neck, colorful print sundress instead of the shorts and T-shirt she'd intended to wear. Robert had insisted that his woman would look like a queen when she visited their old neighborhood. Feeling confident, Yasmine slapped a hand on her hip, dropped a shoulder, and tilted her head to the side like a Coochie Mama. "You couldn't handle me, Mr. Jackson. Not even in your youth. I'm too fine for you."

"I guess she told you," Mr. George yelled above the roar of laughter from his friends. "She always had a sassy mouth. You gotta love her for it." He paused. "Hey, Yas," he continued, his tone now serious and grateful, "thanks for helping my grandson with that problem he had. We don't know what we would have done without your help. God knows we didn't have the money to hire a lawyer, and he would probably be sitting in jail right now, paying for a crime he didn't commit."

"No problem, Mr. George. I'm happy I could help. Just tell him to choose his friends wisely next time," she said, referring to Mr. George's sixteen-year-old grandson who'd been at the wrong place at the wrong time and had had a break-in pinned on him. "Well, you all get back to your game now." Yas ascended the steps leading to the front door. It was hot outside, and she was starting to sweat under her rayon dress.

"Rushing off so soon?"

At the sound of *that* voice, Yasmine grabbed the wooden railing to keep from falling on the concrete steps. What was Carl Arsenault doing in Manchester, and most specifically, why this weekend at the house across the street?

When Jeremy had hightailed it out of town, his parents had followed him. Yasmine had no idea if they knew why he'd broken up with her, but she didn't care, seeing that she'd overheard Mr. and Mrs. Arsenault saying that she wasn't good enough for their son. They wanted better for him, never realizing that she had ambitions to get out of the ghetto one day.

She'd never told Jeremy about that conversation because she didn't want to cause conflict between him and his parents. But as she thought about it now, she realized that he probably knew all along, and that it might have been his parents' decision to move him out of town, far away from her before she got pregnant, saddled him with an unwanted child, and trapped him in an unwanted marriage. Boy, she was so young and clueless back then.

"Hello, Yasmine. How are you?" Mr. Arsenault asked.

Taking a deep breath of composure, Yasmine turned around, forcing a smile as he walked to the sidewalk, his attempt to cross the street halted by a line of cars going by. "I'm fine, thank you." She wasn't going to ask how he was, because frankly she didn't care. Plus, she didn't want to engage in any conversations about his son. She backed up the steps as if she were inching away from trouble.

Where the heck was Felix? He was supposed to be home to let her in while Naomi and Peter were out picking up their dinner. Yas wished she had called or texted him when she pulled up beside his truck a few minutes ago. Damn it. She should have guessed he wasn't home. He would have come outside when the dogs began to bark. She should have stayed in her car.

Her anxiety increased when Mr. Arsenault took advantage of the break in the traffic and dashed over to her side of the street. "So, I heard you're a high-powered lawyer now," he said, his blue eyes staring at her and his thin lips spilt in a grin that reminded her of the shifty wolf who had eaten Little Red Riding Hood's grandmother. "Hayward and Harley is one of the best law firms on the east coast. Arsenault Insurance has done business with them in the past."

Tell me something I don't know. Yasmine was grateful that she never had to deal with any of Arsenault Insurance claims that had ended up at Hayward & Harley. She wanted to tell Mr. Arsenault to piss off, but her father would be disappointed if he found out she'd been rude to one of his old friends. They might have grown up poor, but her parents had raised her to be respectful to her elders, even if she didn't like them. "Yes," Yasmine simply said as her back collided with the screen door.

"That's very impressive, Yasmine. I always thought you'd make something of yourself."

Liar!

Mr. Arsenault planted a foot on the first step. "You're still not married, I see." His gaze landed on her left hand that was grasping the handle of her briefcase.

The tone of his voice aroused old fears of inadequacy in Yasmine. He made it sound as if she wasn't good enough for any man to make a permanent fixture in his life. Nothing could be further from the truth. Instinctively, she moved her hand behind her, wishing she'd brought Robert along for the weekend, and wishing that she was wearing one of the rings he'd been trying to put on her finger for three years now.

"Have you spoken to Jeremy lately?" Mr. Arsenault asked.

Yasmine frowned, wondering where his line of questions was leading. "No. Why would I? We broke up five years ago. I've moved on, and so has he."

He brought his other foot up and gave her an animated smile. "Well, he did try to move on, but I'm sure you're aware that he's been separated. He's going through a divorce."

Yasmine made no comment. She knew, and she didn't give a flying fig, especially since…

"The only good thing that came out of it was our lovely granddaughter, Skyler," Mr. Arsenault continued, his eyes overcast with affection as he said his granddaughter's name. "You say you've moved on, Yasmine, but you're not wearing a ring."

Yasmine closed her eyes briefly as she recalled saying those exact words to Robert a little over an hour ago. It was in jest, and Robert had taken it as such, but Mr. Arsenault's words left her with a humiliated, deflated feeling. "That doesn't mean I'm not involved with anyone, Mr. Arsenault. I have a boyfriend." To her dismay her voice shook slightly.

"You and Jeremy were young back then, you know. He made a mistake by marrying someone else. But that will be behind him soon." He paused and dropped his gaze before looking up again. "You were Jeremy's first love, and since you're still single, maybe there's a chance you can get back together," he said, clearly refusing to acknowledge her claim to having a boyfriend. "I caught him looking at some old photos of the two of you the other day. He looked sad, Yasmine."

"Mr. Arsenault, I really don't—"

"What are the odds that you would be visiting your sister at the same time I'm here visiting my old buddies?" he said cutting her off. "Maybe it's a sign that I ran into you today." Before Yasmine could spit out a vicious response to his insulting assumption, he reached into his back pocket, pulled out his wallet, flipped it open, and was standing on the platform beside her. "Here's a picture of Jeremy and Skyler. Isn't she adorable? She's almost two. She looks like her daddy. Don't you think? And Jeremy's older, but still charming. You guys were so cute together."

Yasmine silently agreed that the blue-eyed, curly-blond-haired little girl was cute. As for Jeremy, *charming* was not the word she was thinking of as she stared at the picture of her ex. *Bastard? Snake?* Definitely. Yasmine's first instinct was to snap the photo from Mr. Arsenault's hands, rip it down the middle and toss it over the side of the railing into the bushes below. But that would have made her seem petty, bitter, and regretful—emotions she certainly did not feel at the moment.

What had she ever seen in Jeremy? Yasmine wondered as she stared at his picture. Must have been his police uniform and the fact that she had been interested in criminal law at the time. Or maybe it was that he lived in the North End of Manchester. Had she been trying to live out her childish dreams of living in that upper-class environment with Robert?

Yasmine suddenly felt a rush of anger at herself for allowing Jeremy's conduct keep her from opening up her heart to Robert —a devoted, loyal, stuck-to-her-like-gum-to-braids kind of man. A man who she now realized never rejected her, but had been protecting her from growing up too fast and losing her innocence at a time when she wasn't emotionally ready to deal with adult issues.

Yasmine knew that sleeping with Jeremy had been the worst mistake of her life. But she also knew she would be making an even bigger one if she continued to make Robert pay for Jeremy's bad behavior. Robert didn't deserve to be treated like that. He deserved the best. Given her association with a jerk like Jeremy, and her past unwise decisions, Yasmine didn't think she was the best, but it was enough that Robert thought so—had always thought so.

Her mind was no longer congested with doubts and fears. She would not remain in the prison of inadequacies Jeremy and his parents had locked her into. She didn't need to accomplish any more professional goals to prove her self-worth to anyone, especially the Arsenaults. It was time she stopped hiding the truth, swallowed her wounded pride, and let everyone know how poorly they'd treated her.

The truth would surely set her free. In fact it was already setting her free.

Strengthened by her new emotional and psychological objectivity, Yasmine straightened up to her full five-foot, six-inch height, plus the three extra inches her sandals gave her, happy that she'd taken Robert's advice and dressed like a queen. She flipped her hair behind her shoulders and stared Mr. Arsenault fully in the eyes. "I have no interest in your spoiled, despicable son. I would rather die an old, shriveled-up spinster than go back to him. When I told him that I loved him, he split, which was a good thing for me, since I later found out he'd been cheating on me the whole time we were together—with the woman he married and is now divorcing."

Mr. Arsenault's mouth opened in shock. "I didn't know, Yasmine. I'm sorry."

"I doubt that, when neither you nor your wife thought I was good enough for him. You thought I was beneath him, so I'm sure you encouraged him to pursue the governor's daughter, a woman from an upper class family with good breeding and money to her name."

"Yasmine, we never said—"

"Don't stand here and lie to my face, Mr. Arsenault. I heard you one day when I was waiting in the basement of your house for Jeremy to come home. You didn't know I was there. You thought I was too outspoken for a woman and you had a lot to say about my family's socioeconomic status, which had surprised the heck out of me seeing that your sister was in the same societal boat. She lived down the street from us. But maybe you thought the same way about her and her children." *You pompous jackass.*

His gaze dropped and embarrassment colored his leathery face. "Yasmine—"

Empowered by her ability to make him hang his head, Yasmine seized the opportunity to get it all off her chest. "You didn't say it that day, but maybe it was also a color thing with you. I don't know. You thought I would never finish school and have a career. Well guess what? I did! And I want to thank you and your wife for devaluing me to your son, because if you hadn't, he and I would probably have gotten married, had a couple kids, and be hating each other's guts right now.

"I still probably wouldn't have had a career, because Jeremy is the kind of man who would not have been able to handle his wife being more successful than him. But worst of all, I would have had you and Mrs. Arsenault as in-laws." She shivered outwardly at the thought of creating a child with Jeremy and sharing birthdays and holidays with that snooty family. "Thank you for saving me from a life of misery and regrets, Mr. Arsenault," she finished with a toss of her head.

"Aunt Yasmine! You're here. You made it."

Right on time. Yasmine let out her breath as her sister's Honda pulled into the yard behind her Jaguar. An excited Peter was out of the car before his mother killed the engine. *So that's where Felix was*, she thought, as he grinned at her from the front passenger side.

Yasmine dropped her bag and her briefcase and rushed down the steps. "Hey, you." She squeezed Peter tightly and kissed him on both cheeks. "You're getting so big. I swear you grew since I saw you at the wedding last week."

"Maybe you're getting shorter, Aunt Yasmine. I hear that happens to women as they get older."

"Boy, watch your mouth." Yasmine gave him a playful slug on his chubby cheek and ruffled the dark curls on his head. "You never talk to a woman about her age, not even if she's your doting auntie."

Yasmine kept her arms around Peter as she watched Mr. Arsenault descend the steps and, without even looking at her, slink back across the street. She'd handled the big, bad, urban wolf and faced her demon, only to realize that he'd been powerless all along. She need never fear him again. If she never saw another member of that family in twenty lifetimes, it would still be too soon.

She breathed deeply and freely, not even caring that the air was pungent with the bite of rotting garbage from the trash cans at the sides of the house.

"Since when did you and Mr. Arsenault become friends?" Naomi asked, coming to stand beside Yasmine.

"In the year next-to-never." Yasmine hugged her sister, who was an older, slightly taller image of herself. Both she and Naomi resembled their mother—slender with dainty facial features—while their big brother Luke was a colossal chip off their father's block. All the Reynolds children had their father's chestnut eyes. Her mother used to tell their father that he could never deny that they were his. Yasmine always wondered why she used to say that to him.

"Hmmm." She took one of the bags Naomi was carrying, opened it, and shoved her nose into it. Her mouth immediately watered at the delicious mixed aroma of curried fries, garlic onion rings, spicy buffalo wings, and sesame mozzarella sticks. "God, I missed these."

"You mean they don't have pizza joints in Boston?" Felix joined them, carrying two large boxes of pizzas, a big smile on his handsome face. "No wonder Rob eats so much when he visits. Poor guy has to stock up." He kissed her on the cheek.

"Stop making fun of the fact that Aunt Yasmine can't cook, Daddy," Peter said. "Even I can cook a meal."

"Won't cook. Not can't." Yasmine gave him a mean frown. "And preparing boxed macaroni and cheese is not cooking."

"Case in point, Auntie." He charged up the steps, picked up her briefcase and her bag, and opened the door. "I'll take these to my bedroom," he said, disappearing down the hall.

"The boy's got a point," Felix said, as Yasmine and Naomi followed him into the kitchen. "Every man should be able to come home to a hot, home-cooked meal after a hard day at work, even if it's takeout." He winked at his wife as he put the pizzas on the countertop.

"You keep it up, and a hot meal, takeout or not, isn't the only thing you won't be getting for a while, Mr. Chavez." Naomi slapped her bag of food down beside the pizza.

"Is that a threat, Mrs. Chavez?" Felix stared down at her.

"Naomi!" Yasmine glanced from Felix to Naomi, trying to figure out if they were serious or just joking around.

"Yasmine!" Naomi shifted her stare from her husband to her sister.

"Are you guys going to start fighting already?" Peter asked, joining them in the kitchen. He frowned at his mother, then his aunt.

"No, we're not." Yasmine gave her sister a dubious slant of the eye. The family, and probably the whole neighborhood knew that she and Naomi didn't see eye-to-eye on a lot of issues, and that most of their visits ended with one of them storming out of the other's house.

Yasmine hoped that wouldn't be the case today because she was in a really good mood, and wanted to stay and take Peter to the park tomorrow, after which Luke and Christine were meeting them for dinner at her parents' place in Nashua. Yasmine needed the weekend to end on a pleasant note for once, especially since she had to prepare herself for her talk with Robert—the most important talk of their relationship perhaps.

"You boys go wash up. I need to talk to Yas," Naomi said, and then to Yasmine's relief, she smiled at her husband, reached up on her tiptoes and kissed him on the lips.

"Yes, ma'am," Felix said. He had a big grin on his face as he followed his son out of the kitchen.

"You know, just because Felix is younger than you, it doesn't mean you can treat him like a child, even if it's in jest. And you shouldn't do it in front of company." Yas chastised her sister as they both stood at the sink washing their hands.

Naomi snorted. "Well, first of all, you're not company. And second of all, I know Felix Chavez is not a child. He proved it the first time I went out with him." She handed Yasmine the towel she'd used to dry her hands.

"You gave it up on your first date? He was barely legal back then."

"It was a hot summer night. The moon was bright; the stars were out, and he was whispering Portuguese into my ear. I couldn't help myself."

"You cradle-robbing cougar!"

"Hey, at least I was older than you were when you gave it up."

Yasmine flung the towel at Naomi and it landed on her head of black natural corkscrew curls that spiraled from her scalp in a chic short style. Naomi's hair was once much longer than Yasmine's shoulder-length tresses, but last October Naomi and a few other nurses at Catholic Medical Center shaved their heads in honor of Breast Cancer Awareness and donated their manes to Locks of Love. Yeah, her sister came off strong, but she had a soft heart.

With a chuckle, Naomi folded the towel and draped it over a cabinet doorknob. "Felix and I are good," she said. "He's just a little peeved because my shift changed and I haven't been home to cook his dinners. I spoiled him during the first years of our marriage, and now he expects certain things." She shook her head and opened a cupboard. "Anyway, I sent them away so we can talk about Mr. Arsenault. You two looked rather chummy when we drove up. What's up with that?"

Yasmine helped Naomi pull dishes from the cabinets and utensils from the drawers and set them out on the table. "Yeah, that. He was congratulating me on my successful career."

"Well that was very big and nice of him."

"That's what I thought until he whipped out a picture of Jeremy. He suggested that since his marriage didn't work out and I was still single, we were meant to be together. Said he caught

Jeremy staring at old photos of the two of us, and that he looked sad. I'm surprised he kept any photos of me. I tossed all of his."

Naomi emptied the container of Greek salad into a plastic bowl and put it on the table. "He's just looking for a mommy for his granddaughter."

"Or maybe they're looking for a lawyer to keep him from being taken to the cleaners and to increase his custody rights," Yasmine said, just now realizing that it wasn't beneath the Arsenaults to try to use her for their benefit. She knew they were opportunistic. "He probably knows I would have told him to go to hell, so he tried to take a roundabout way by suggesting that Jeremy and I should get back together. A kind of fight-for-your-man approach."

"Girl, could be," Naomi murmured. "He must have heard you've yet to lose a case," she added with a hint of pride in her voice. "Jeremy will probably lose custody of his daughter, seeing he was screwing around on his wife. Serves her ass right since she was screwing around with him when he was with you."

"Actually, he might have been screwing around on her with me. I don't know, and frankly, I don't care, just as long as they all stay the hell away from me."

"Amen. When you were a nobody, you weren't good enough for them. Now you're worth his attention?"

Yasmine began unloading the food and drinks from the paper bags and taking them over to the table. Naomi was the only person she'd told how the Arsenaults had treated her. At the time of the breakup, Michelle was in South Carolina with her then boyfriend Ryan, so Yas had confided in her sister. By the time Michelle got back to Manchester, it was old news, so Yas hadn't bothered saying anything. She'd just told Michelle that Jeremy's new job in another town, and her concentration on school had put a damper on their relationship.

"What did you tell Mr. A.?" Naomi asked, as she placed the pizza slices on two serving trays and took them to the table.

"I told him to kiss my beautiful, successful ass."

"Good for you!" Naomi gave her sister a butt bump. "You know he's going to tell Daddy you were rude to him."

"I'm a grown woman, Naomi. Daddy can't take a switch to me anymore."

Naomi's head whipped around. "What are you talking about, Yas? Daddy never took a switch to any of us."

Yasmine burst out laughing. "I know. It just sounds so good to say it. Makes me feel emancipated. And that shocked look on your face is priceless." She bit off the end of a fry and threw the other half at Naomi.

Catching the fry, Naomi popped it into her mouth, her annoyance immediately turning into a moan of satisfaction as she chewed on the curried fry.

"Besides, when Daddy hears why Jeremy and I really broke up, he's gonna kick both Jeremy's and Carl's asses," Yasmine said, snatching an onion ring from a bowl.

"You got that right, sis. Nobody messes with Luke Reynolds's little girls." Naomi high-fived her before walking to the door that opened up into the living room where the men were watching TV. "Felix! Peter! Dinner is ready."

"Finally," Peter growled. "Come on Dad, the general is letting us back on the base."

"I'm gonna sew that boy's lips together one day." Naomi narrowed her eyes at Yas. "He got that mouth from you. You know that, right? Maybe I should begin limiting the time he spends with you. He's picking up all your bad habits."

Yasmine chuckled as the men burst into the kitchen and took their places at the table, turning the small cramped space into a beehive of action.

"Not all of them, Mom. At least I keep my room clean. And

I made it extra clean today, just for you, Aunt Yasmine," Peter said, grinning at her.

"Maybe she *should* sew your lips together. Yeah, I think it's a good idea," Yas retorted as she spooned some fries and onion rings next to the two slices of pepperoni pizza on her plate.

"So, Yas. How's Rob? Is he getting us season tickets again?" Felix asked, serving himself a generous portion of salad.

As they ate and chatted about old times, new developments, future plans, and the details of the billionaire wedding they'd all attended last week, and especially about their girl Michelle who, in spite of her fame, was still as humble as they remembered, Yasmine's heart filled with warm memories of her days growing up in inner city Manchester.

It was good to be with her family, even though it was in their old run-down neighborhood. Strangely, she felt a sense of loss, knowing that it might be the last time she would have any reason to come here.

Mr. Arsenault had said that it was a sign that they'd run into each other today. Yas agreed. It was a sign that it was time she told Robert that she loved him, that she wanted to marry him and have his babies. It was time for her to stop taking him for granted, and love him like she *could* lose him, because she could lose him.

"Excuse me for a minute, guys." Yasmine dropped her half-eaten slice of pizza on the plate. "There's something I have to do."

Ignoring the questioning stares from her family, Yasmine left the table and, retrieving her purse from the top of the fridge, she left the kitchen and headed for the bathroom and some privacy.

CHAPTER NINE

Yasmine was holding a place in the Sky Ride line at Canobie Lake Park while Naomi, Peter, and his girlfriend, Jessica, were on a bathroom run, finally giving her alone time to reflect on last night.

After dinner, Felix had left to work on the new house and Peter had locked himself in his bedroom to Face Time with Jessica—one of Michelle's former Manchester mentees. Yasmine was surprised that Felix and Naomi let Peter date at fourteen years of age. But they thought it best to give their consent and monitor his and Jessica's relationship, rather than forbid him from seeing her, and risk the chance of them sneaking around behind their backs.

Yasmine's heart hammered against her chest as she recalled being head-over-heels in love with Robert at about that age, and crawling into his bed in the middle of the night to seduce him. She remembered how her skin would tingle and she'd break out into a sweat every time she saw him. Even the sound of his voice used to make her tremble. So intense were her feelings, she used to think she would burst into flames if she didn't have sex with him. Even after all those years, he still had that effect on her. He'd proved her weakness for him yesterday afternoon.

It was the conversation about Peter and Jessica's blossoming infatuation that had sent Yasmine running from the dinner table last night. She'd been so overwhelmed with love for Robert that she'd wanted to tell him. She'd been shaking so hard that when she pulled her phone from her purse to call him, it had slipped from her hands and almost fallen into the toilet.

That near accident was a blessing in disguise, because after she'd calmed down, Yasmine realized that there were two good reasons why she shouldn't call Robert. The most important being that when she said those words out loud, she wanted to be standing in front of him, holding his hands, and gazing into his eyes. She wanted to see the joy and excitement, and relief on his face that she had finally come around to giving him what he'd been asking from her for four long years.

The other reason was that she knew how Robert's mind worked. He would want to know why she was calling from Manchester to tell him that she loved him. Since they'd been talking about her unnamed ex earlier, he would ask if she'd seen him, and if *he* was the reason behind her call. Although the answer would have been *No, I haven't run into my ex*, she would have felt compelled to disclose her run-in with his father, and she didn't want to go into the detail of that conversation over the phone.

She had done the next safest thing, and texted Robert a simple message: *I love YOU*. Then to save herself from anxiety waiting for his response, she'd shut her phone off, and rejoined her family at the dinner table.

She and Naomi had spent the night cruising down memory lane in between watching TV and topping off the two bottles of wine Yas had brought up with her. Yasmine couldn't remember the last time they'd visited without fighting. Naomi's stress radar had been turned off, or maybe it was that Yas had ceased sending out signals after she'd told off Mr. Arsenault, and had texted her declaration of love to Robert.

Yasmine had gone to bed with the happy feeling that everything in her life was falling into place. This morning, she'd awakened with a splitting headache and had immediately turned on her phone. There were no missed calls or texts from Robert. Yasmine would be lying if she said she wasn't disappointed that he hadn't responded, but she knew it must have been a shock for him to receive a text like that out of the blue. Besides, there was no need for him to respond. He'd been telling her that he loved her for the past four years, and as recently as yesterday before she left her house.

"Aunt Yasmine!"

Yasmine turned around and scanned the crowd behind her. "Up here!" she yelled, waving as she saw Peter and Jessica bobbing up and down trying to catch a glimpse of her. Finally, they spotted her and began weaving their way through the thick crowd, with Naomi taking her time behind them.

"Wow, you got far, Aunt Yasmine," Peter said, looping his arm around her waist.

"Yeah, Miss Yasmine. If you hadn't stayed, we would have had a long wait. Thanks for persuading my mom to let me come, and for buying my ticket," she added, her blue eyes shining with warmth and gratitude.

"You're welcome, Jess." Yasmine smiled at the thirteen-year-old girl whose negligent father—a prominent New Hampshire businessman—Yas had taken to court and forced to pay eleven years of back child support. Jessica and her mother, Gina, were finally able to live without scrimping and scraping and begging, but the best thing of all was that Yasmine had gotten the court to make Jessica's father set up a college fund for her, like he'd done for his legitimate kids. Jessica now had the chance to attend college and make something of herself. It had been a difficult trial, because Mr. Plaistow had hired the best attorneys, but in the end, justice had won out. *She* was surprised she'd won, seeing it was her first family law case.

"You sure you don't have to go?"

Yas tucked away her memories of that trial, and turned to her sister who'd just joined them. "Yep." She handed Naomi her purse that she'd been holding for her. "Even if I needed to go, it's too late," she said as the attendee opened the gate that led to the ride.

"How many?" he asked, after the folks ahead of them had gone through.

"Four," Peter answered.

The attendant turned his back, scanned the lifts, then faced them again. "Okay. There are two chairlifts left. You're the last ones for this round."

Peter and Jessica ran ahead of them and climbed into the lift on the far end, while Yasmine and Naomi took one near the front. "I can't remember when I last had so much fun," Yasmine told Naomi as they settled in, and the attendant checked to make sure that they were secured.

"To tell you the truth, me neither, sis." Naomi touched her arm. "The kids are having a blast, too." She turned and waved at Peter and Jessica who were about five lifts behind them. "Just like when Dad and Mom used to bring us when we were little." She chuckled.

"Yeah, and Michelle," Yasmine said, her voice catching with fond memories. While she had been hopping the rides with Peter and Jessica, she had been thinking of Robert, and what it would be like to bring their children to the park, watch them stuff themselves on cotton candy and fried dough, and lick at ice cream as it dripped down their arms. Her fantasies had been a little tainted by Robert's fear of heights. She hoped he would be over it by the time their kids were old enough to visit amusement parks.

Their kids. Yasmine loved the sound of that.

"I'm glad I took a personal day." Naomi cut into Yasmine's daydreams as the chair began to ascend. "I've been doing double shifts at the hospital, trying to make some extra money to buy furniture for our new place. I just want it to be nice, you know?"

Yasmine smiled. "I know. When you buy a place, especially your first, you want it to be perfect." As the chair got higher and they began to sail along, she glanced off, taking in the spectacular views of the amusement park and the lake. It was breathtaking, reminding her of her all-year-round water view from her townhouse.

"Right. It won't be near as sophisticated as your waterfront pad, but it's better than what we have now," Naomi said, following Yasmine's gaze. "We can build equity in our home instead of paying off someone else's mortgage like we've been doing since we got married. It's a good thing all around. I've already met our neighbors and they're wonderful. I don't have to worry so much about Peter being home alone after school until Felix and I get out of work."

Yasmine sighed deeply and turned to her sister. "Is that enough for you?" she asked, watching her closely. "I mean when we were kids we used to talk about you being a doctor, maybe even a heart surgeon, and me being a cop or a detective."

"Dreams change sometimes, Yasmine. Yours have. You're a lawyer, not a detective."

"Yeah, I guess you're right. Do you enjoy being an ER nurse, even though you have to work so hard? Does it make you happy?"

Naomi nodded. "It does. Really. And you?" she asked, eyeing

Yasmine sideways. "Does being a lawyer instead of a detective make you happy?"

Yasmine smiled. "Yes. And it's not just because of the money. I really do like helping people get what they deserve."

"Good or bad," Naomi said, bumping her shoulder to Yasmine's. "What about the dream you had of marrying Rob and having his babies?" She lowered her tone. "Have you told him about the baby yet?"

Yasmine wrapped her arms around her middle as pangs of excruciating pain ripped through her. Naomi was the only other person who knew about the secret she'd been hiding from Robert. Naomi only knew because she'd found Yasmine's positive pregnancy test strip in the trash. Ever since, her older sister had been harassing her about telling Robert. "Why do you always bring that up? Can't we have a visit without it being a topic of discussion?"

"As soon as you discuss it with Robert, it will stop being a topic of discussion between us. It's not healthy."

"God, I hate you."

"You don't hate me, Yas. You hate that lie simmering inside you for the past four years. You say you didn't have an abortion, but don't be surprised if Rob doesn't see it your way when and if you finally tell him the whole truth."

Taking a deep breath, Yasmine straightened up and, turning slowly, she met her sister's accusing eyes. "You're still in love with Robert."

"Don't be ridiculous, girl. I'm in love with my husband."

"Didn't seem that way when you were fighting in the kitchen yesterday." Forgetting where she was, Yasmine attempted to get up, only to find herself restricted by the iron steel across her middle. She plunked back down in the chair, winded, just as she spotted Peter and Jessica's lift coming toward them from the opposite direction.

Peter was watching them with a worried frown on his face.

"You guys are fighting. Aren't you?" he yelled as their lifts lined up from opposite directions.

"No, we're not," both Yas and Naomi said at the same time.

"Just don't toss each other out of the chairlift, okay? It's a long way down and Jess and I need a ride home. I love you, Mom. I love you, Aunt Yasmine. Play nice."

"Seems like they're the only ones enjoying the view," Yas said, as the kids waved goodbye before pointing to something in the distance that had caught their attention.

"Girl, you know we didn't come here for this tired view."

Yasmine smiled, her irritation dissipated a bit. Nevertheless, she and her sister had some unfinished business. "Admit it!" she said, catching Naomi's gaze.

"Admit what?"

"That you like Rob. That you have a thing for him."

Naomi shrugged. "Yes I like Rob, and I did....*did* have a thing for him back in high school."

"Ah-ha!"

Naomi pursed her lips and rolled her eyes. "Don't 'Ah-ha' me. Every girl in Manchester had a crush on Robert Carter. He was the handsomest, hottest, tallest, sweetest piece of eye candy for miles around."

"Yeah, he was," Yasmine said with a dreamy lilt in her voice.

"I knew you were crushing on him when you were a little girl."

"You knew?"

"Yes, Yas. The way you used to look at him, I knew you felt deeply for him."

"And I thought I was being so careful."

"Not careful enough. I used to find your notebooks with pages and pages where you'd scribbled *Yasmine Marie Reynolds-Carter.*"

Yasmine chuckled. "I think I started writing that when I was five."

"I thought you'd get over him as you got older but you didn't. And that's when I started watching him like a hawk."

"Why?"

"I was your big sister. Robert was quite a bit older than you, and if he'd touched you before you were old enough to understand what was going on, I would have cut his balls off. I stayed close to him to keep an eye on him, not because I wanted him for myself."

Yasmine squeezed her sister's hands. "Oh, Nay."

"Personally, I thought he was too serious for you, but I was wrong. He's not reserved or uptight. He's different in a very good way. You guys belong together."

Yasmine looked off over the tops of the trees at the Star Blaster Ride flying to the top of the tower and then back down, before returning to Naomi. "I tried to seduce him when I was fifteen."

"What? Where?" Naomi grabbed her arm, her mouth and eyes wide with curiosity.

Yas chuckled and then spilled it all to Naomi.

"Oh my God, you little hussy. Mom and Dad would have killed you if they knew." She tilted her head to the side. "Did he?"

"No. He pushed me away and scolded me like I was a little girl. Told me I was too young to understand love. He broke my heart, Nay."

Naomi pulled her close. "So that's why you're afraid to open up to him."

"That, the way Jeremy treated me, and the fact that Rob withdrew from me when I needed him most." Yasmine shuddered. "But, I think—" She paused and shook her head.

"No, I *know* that I'm ready to come clean with Rob. This is the worst thing I've ever done, will ever do in our relationship, and I'm ready to deal with whatever ensues after we talk. If we can get past this, we can make anything work."

Naomi rubbed her hand across Yasmine's back in little circular motion, the way she used to do when Yas was younger and had been curled up with period cramps. "I'm glad you've broken out of your prison. It's time. Robert's a good man and he deserves the truth, all of it. The fact that he pushed you away when you were too young proves how decent he is. Any other man would have taken advantage of you. He didn't. I believe he'll understand when you explain what happened to your baby."

Yasmine narrowed her eyes. "A minute ago, you said he wouldn't."

"I said, *might not.* He'll no doubt be upset, but you'll have to give him time to absorb the information and assess the situation in his mind. I have faith you'll both survive it."

Yasmine laid her head on Naomi's shoulder. As she thought of their lives growing up together as the Reynolds girls, she had to admit that Naomi had been a good big sister to her. Naomi had given her tough love because she didn't want Yasmine to make the kind of mistakes that most of the girls her age had been making. "I love you, big sister." She squeezed her close as their ride came to an end and their feet touched the ground.

"I love you too, little sister. No matter how much we fight, I'll always be in your corner against the world. Just remember that, okay?"

"Okay," Yasmine said, as Peter and Jessica ran over to them.

"Oh, goodie, you made up," Jessica said.

"Of course we made up. We're sisters." Yasmine pulled Naomi close.

"Cool. I was worried Aunt Yasmine would go back to Boston mad and Mom would drive home like a bat out of hell, and we wouldn't be able to see the show, or go visit Grandma and Grandpa and Uncle Luke and Aunt Christine for dinner."

"No. Aunt Yasmine is still here."

"And so is the bat out of hell," Naomi said, ruffling her son's dark curly head.

"Is Daddy meeting us here?" Peter asked about his father who'd opted to work on their new home instead of joining them at the park.

"No," Naomi replied. "Uncle Luke is picking him up and they'll meet us at Grandma and Grandpa's. Come on, the show is about to begin." She led the way to the theatre.

It was turning out to be a great weekend all around, Yasmine thought as she, Peter, and Jessica followed behind Naomi.

She'd come to Manchester feeling uncertain about her relationship with Robert, but she was returning to Boston with a strong determination to secure her future with the man of her dreams. She didn't want to end up like Mary Jane Paul from the hit TV show *Being Mary Jane*: successful career, beautiful home, but no man, and no babies.

She and Rob would have to clear a few hurdles before they would be able to walk hand-in-hand into Happily Ever After, but she wasn't afraid anymore.

Happily Ever After. Yasmine couldn't believe the elation she felt at the thought of saying "Yes" the next time Robert asked her to marry him.

She'd been so caught up in feeling inadequate, of being afraid of getting hurt, that she'd almost missed out on being loved.

As she entered the theatre, Yasmine's mind raced with a crazy mixture of hope and fear. What if Robert never asked her to marry him again? Suppose she was too late and he was indeed tired of waiting around for her. What if that was the reason he hadn't responded to her text?

Lord, she hoped it wasn't too late for them.

§

Yasmine awoke to the smell of bacon, waffles, and eggs cooking, and the sound of muted voices drifting into the spare bedroom next to the kitchen of her parents' condo.

Lifting the lid of one eye, she peeked at the clock on the nightstand. It was eight a.m. *Didn't her parents sleep?* Reaching for the extra pillow on the bed, she placed it over her head. It was comforting to know that her parents still spoke to each other—something a lot of couples their age didn't do anymore—but did it have to be so early in the morning when they knew she was sleeping in the next room?

When the voices still filtered through the feathered pillow over her head, Yasmine rolled over on to her back and stared at the white popcorn ceiling as the events of the previous night surfaced in her mind.

It had been a great family dinner with all the Reynoldses under the same roof, sitting at the same table, and sharing the black-eyed peas soup, pepper rice, curried chicken, and collard greens, topped off with a sweet potato pie that her mother had prepared. It was like old times, the way it used to be before she and her siblings started leaving home one at a time.

They'd always been a close-knit family, and last night had proved that even though the little birdies had left the nest, their filial love was still as strong as when they were growing up and living under the same roof. They had laughed, bickered, and teased, and had made up by the time Naomi and Luke and their families left.

Yasmine had previously planned to spend the night with her

parents, whom she didn't see as often as she wanted. They'd talked and watched TV while snacking on popcorn and cheese—her father's favorite snack—until around midnight when she'd kissed them good night. She'd had a fun, but exhausting day yesterday at Canobie Lake, and then last night with her family, so no wonder she'd fallen into a deep sound sleep the minute her head hit the pillow.

Seeing it was Sunday, Yasmine had hoped to remain in slumber land until at least mid-morning before she had to think about her dreaded and impending conversation with Robert. She just hoped it wouldn't be the last conversation they would have. She prayed her sister was right that Robert would forgive her for keeping the secret of her pregnancy from him.

She still hadn't had time to strategize how she would start the conversation. How does one start such a conversation? *Um, Robert.* No. Rob. Rob would be better. It was more intimate and hopeful. *Rob, can we talk? I have something to tell you. I've been keeping a secret from you and I hope you don't hate me. But first, let me say that I love you…*

Yasmine trembled on a deep breath as she remembered the text she'd sent Robert two nights ago. Maybe she should have waited until after the conversation to tell him so the rejection wouldn't be as horrific if he turned away from her, if he couldn't forgive her. But then again, maybe it was good that she'd sent it ahead of time. She'd sent the text because she'd finally felt confident and liberated enough to trust him with her heart. There was no need for her to psychoanalyze her actions. Robert had her love in writing, and for that she was making no apologies.

And then there was the concern about the location. Where should they have that conversation? Where did she want those memories to take up residence? His place or hers? If they talked at his place and it ended badly, it wouldn't be fair that he should have to live with those memories echoing from every corner of his home.

Yasmine closed her eyes and swallowed as a host of scenarios, probabilities, contemplations, and thoughts battled for space in her mind—the most prevalent was to say nothing at all, the second runner-up was to only give Robert part of the story. Tell him she was pregnant and that she'd lost it. It wasn't a lie.

No, but it's a half-truth and it's just as bad as a lie, that little voice in her head that had recently begun to make itself heard, said.

"You're right," Yasmine whispered to herself. The Yasmine of yesterday, the one who'd been filled with fear and inadequacies would not tell the whole truth. She wasn't that Yasmine anymore. She wanted the kind of love and commitment her parents and her siblings had for each other, and the only way to know if she could have it was to put her heart on the block.

With her confidence and determination spiraling upward, Yasmine opened her eyes, sat up in bed, and reached for her phone. The first step was to let Robert know that they needed to have a serious conversation about their relationship *today*, and that she wasn't taking *no* for an answer. Once she put it out there that they had to talk, *needed to talk*, she wouldn't be able to take it back.

She frowned as she looked at her phone icon. She'd missed a call. Was it from Robert? He still hadn't responded to her text. Filled with anxiety, she touched her thumb to the *on* button for her fingerprint recognition, and then hit the voicemail button.

It was from Robert. He'd called during her DND hours. Was it deliberate? Did he not want to talk to her? Her heart trembled at the sound of his voice and her worries began to dissolve as she listened to his message. He wanted to see her tonight, at his place.

Well, the stage had been set. At least the decision about the venue had been resolved. All she had to do now was show up and confess. "God, please give Robert the heart to forgive me." With a slight tremor, Yasmine set her phone on the nightstand and got out of bed.

Determined not to worry away her last few hours with her parents, she pulled on her robe over her pajamas, slipped her feet into her slippers, and made her way toward the kitchen. Still pretty full from last night, she doubted she'd be able to eat anything, but she would try since her mother had unnecessarily gone through the trouble. Before turning in last night, Yasmine had told her mother not to make breakfast, especially after she'd spent the better part of yesterday preparing a huge dinner for the entire family. But cooking was her mother's favorite pastimes, and it seemed that old habits were hard to break.

"Hey, my favorite baby girl. Did we wake you?" her father asked, looking up from the table when Yasmine walked into the kitchen, his dark face lighting up into a big grin that made the corners of his kind brown eyes crinkle.

"Don't you people sleep?" Yasmine went over to wrap her hand around his broad shoulders and brush her cheeks against the soft crop of salt-and-pepper hair on his head. He was already showered and dressed in jeans and a red and white striped short-sleeve shirt. The citrusy fragrance of his 4711 aftershave flooded her with pleasant childhood memories. Her daddy had been wearing 4711 all her life. She remembered how she used to hug him in the mornings when the scent was strongest so it would linger on her skin throughout the day, just so everyone would know she was Luke Reynolds's little girl.

She also knew that he whispered his "favorite baby girl" line to Naomi too. But since she was the youngest of the Reynolds children, and a full eight years younger than Naomi, Yasmine felt that it had more significance when he said it to her. She was indeed her daddy's baby girl.

"Hey, sweetie. You sleep okay?"

Giving her father a kiss on the cheek, Yasmine stepped over to the stove where her mom, still in her nightclothes, was stirring scrambled eggs in a huge skillet. Some things just never changed, Yas thought with affection as she kissed her mom and smiled into her smooth oval-shaped face—like her own—and big wide brown eyes. Her mother was an attractive fifty-six-year-old woman with subtle skin, who wore her black-dyed hair in a short natural afro, and who had passed on her good looks and genes to her lucky daughters. Yasmine hoped she herself looked half as good as her mother when she climbed into her fifties.

Yasmine looped her arm around her mother's waist as more childhood memories surfaced in her mind: her mother cooking breakfast in her nightgown and a robe with the lingering fragrance of Oil of Olay night cream on her skin, her father dressed for work, Yasmine and her siblings dressed for school and seated around a small kitchen table waiting for the delicious breakfast they had grown accustomed to over the years. The only differences now were that the kitchen was much bigger and nicer than the one she'd grown up in and it was not in their rundown neighborhood in Manchester.

"Mommy, who're you cooking all this food for?" Yasmine asked, picking up the wooden spoon and stirring a pot of grits on the back burner.

"For you, baby, and your daddy," her mother replied, scraping the eggs onto three plates, and adding some bacon that had been drying out on paper towels.

"You know your mother, Yas," her father said behind them. "Cooking makes her happy."

Yasmine held her breath as her mother turned and gave her father a look that she had never seen before. It wasn't contemptuous or repulsive, but it wasn't favorable either.

"Take these plates to the table," her mother said, grabbing the spoon from Yasmine's hands and piling grits on the plates before Yasmine had the chance to further analyze what she'd just seen.

Balancing the three plates on her arms like she used to do when she worked as a waitress, Yasmine took them to the table. "Here you go, Daddy." She placed the one with the most eggs, bacon, and grits in front of her father, as was customary.

"Thank you, little baby." Her father said. "And thank you, big baby, for preparing breakfast," he added, smiling at his wife who'd brought the coffee pot over to refill his mug, and fill Yasmine's as well. "You're a good wife, Marie, and I do appreciate all you do for our family."

Yasmine glanced at her mother, waiting for her to say something, but all she did was offer both of them half smiles as she took the chair across from Yasmine.

As was customary, her father took the initiative in asking God to bless the food they were about to eat. He thanked Him for his favor and protection on the Reynolds family, and asked for blessings and favor for those who were less fortunate than they.

"So," Yasmine said after they'd eaten in silence for a few minutes, "have you two decided which countries you want to visit on your anniversary trip?"

"That's exactly what we were discussing when you walked in," her father said, before placing a forkful of eggs into his mouth.

"Yasmine, you know we can't afford such an elaborate trip," her mother responded, sending her father that unfavorable look again. "If you want to—"

"Mom, you don't need to afford it. Luke, Naomi, and I are paying for it. It's our gift of love to you."

"That's what we were discussing, baby girl. We love you all for offering to send us around the world for a month, but Naomi and Felix just bought a new house, and they have a kid. They should be putting away that money for Peter's education.

Colleges are expensive, as you know. And Luke and Christine are already paying through the nose to keep her father in that assisted living home. As for you, you need to begin saving for your own future so you don't end up like us, not being able to afford to travel in your middle age."

It broke Yasmine's heart to hear her parents talk like that. Her father was right about Luke and Naomi's financial situations. But what they didn't know was that Yasmine was paying for the entire trip, and had made Luke and Naomi swear they would not tell. She didn't want her parents to think she was more successful than her siblings. They were all equally successful in their careers; hers just happened to generate more money, and she had no one else to support but herself. Luke and Naomi had agreed to play along under one condition: that she set up a college fund for Peter to which they would both contribute a fixed amount each month. It was a win-win for everyone.

"Well," Yasmine said after taking a sip of her black coffee. "It's disappointing that you would take this honor away from us. You have both sacrificed so much for us over the years." She looked at her father. "Daddy, you worked two jobs, sometimes three, just to make sure we had new clothes and coats for school every year, heat every winter, presents under the tree every Christmas, and a huge turkey every Thanksgiving."

Tears stung her eyes as she caught her mom's gaze. "And, Mom, you made sure that we had a hot meal every morning before we left for school, that we were showered, our clothes clean, and that we had a nutritious, bagged lunch, and a home-cooked meal every night. Many of my friends' parents didn't do any of those most basic things for them. This trip is just our way of saying thank you. Thank you for loving us and taking care of us, for being there when we needed you, and even when we didn't. Don't take this away from us. Please, Mom, Dad, take the trip."

"Yasmine," both her parents said at the same time.

Her father placed his hand over hers lying on the table. "Okay, baby girl. If it means that much to you and your brother and sister, we'll take the trip. Right, Marie?" he said to his wife.

Her mother shifted in her chair, a look of dismay in her eyes. "I heard all you said, Yas, and I appreciate that you and Luke and Naomi want to do something special for us, but a trip around the world is too—"

The doorbell chimed.

"That must be Ben," her father said, wiping his mouth with his napkin.

Yasmine had met Benjamin Knox and his wife Sheila who lived next door. "You're going out, Daddy?" Yasmine asked, as he got up. For some reason she felt a dull ache in her gut, the kind she used to feel as a child when he would leave right after dinner to go to his second or third job for the day.

"Yes, baby girl. Ben and I are going down to the clubhouse for a bowling league meeting. I won't be long. I promise to be back before you leave."

"You need a meeting," her mother muttered, rising to take her plate, along with her husband's, to the sink. "You lost the last two tournaments."

"I love you too, Marie," he said, his deep chuckles ringing in the air as he made his way out of the kitchen.

"Mom," Yasmine said as soon as she heard the front door close behind her father. "What's going on?"

"What are you talking about?" Her mother averted her gaze by staring out the window over the sink.

"You know what I'm talking about?" Yasmine said, picking up her plate. She set it in the sink. "I saw those looks you gave Dad earlier. Are you two having problems?"

Her mother looked warily down at her hands wringing in front of her and then back up at Yasmine. "Well, I wasn't going to say anything yet, but since you asked, I need you to represent me."

"In what? Are you in some kind of trouble, Mom? Did you break the law, or something?"

"I'm divorcing your father."

CHAPTER TEN

Yasmine fell against the side of the refrigerator as the words registered in her brain. *No.* She hadn't heard her right. Her mother didn't just tell her that she was divorcing her husband after almost thirty-eight years of marriage. The one marriage Yasmine had thought inviolable since she became a divorce attorney, the one marriage she thought could weather any storm that came upon it was about to be destroyed.

No. No. No! This was not happening, not when she was finally emotionally strong enough to open her heart to Robert. She felt sick. She wrapped her arms around her middle to stop the quaking inside. "You're kidding," she said, staring into her mother's face. "Tell me you're kidding, Mom."

"I wish I was, Yas."

Yasmine stepped away as her mother reached out to touch her. She couldn't be touched right now. If she were touched, she would crumble, and there were just too many questions that needed answers. "Are you cheating on Dad?" It was the first thing she could think to ask. Her mother did look good for her age.

"No. I would never do that."

"Has he cheated on you?" She was sure there were a lot of women out there who would love to attach themselves to a fine, handsome man like Luke Reynolds.

"No."

"Has he hit you?"

"Yas, you know your father is not a violent man. He would never hit me. He never hit you nor your brother and sister when you were kids."

"Has he gotten drunk in public and embarrassed you?"

"Yasmine Marie, you know he's never done any of those things. Your father is a good man."

"Then why in hell are you divorcing him, Mom?"

Her mother took a step back at her tone and her disrespect, but Yasmine was beyond caring. Her mother couldn't drop something this heavy on her and expect her not to react, especially when she dealt with divorces in her career. Or maybe her mother thought it wouldn't faze her because she was used to marriages falling apart. Didn't she understand that she couldn't accept this one falling apart? This was her family, her mommy and her daddy, whom she loved with all her heart. It didn't matter how old a child got, he or she never wanted to hear the D word spoken by either parent.

As a child and even as an adult, Yasmine never ever heard her parents argue and fight the way her friends' parents did. Yeah, there had been disagreements between them and there were times when her mother gave her father the cold shoulder, but Yasmine had never felt threatened that they would break up. And now...

She bit her bottom lip and tried to control the nauseating feeling in her stomach at the thought that her parents were splitting up just when she had finally come to understand the importance of loving someone, of giving her heart to someone else for safekeeping, the meaning of commitment. She opened her eyes. "Why, Mom. Why do you want to leave Daddy?"

"I don't love him."

Her mother's honest and simple response shook Yasmine to the core, but as she gazed at her mother, she realized that it was possible. Her parents were never overly affectionate in front of their children, but she'd thought that it was a result of the age they'd grown up in. Younger couples were a lot more liberal with their feelings in public. Michelle and her billionaire girlfriends were always kissing their husbands in public, but she'd never seen the older generations of those families showing affection for each other. She didn't know if they did or didn't do it in front of their children when they were in the privacy of their homes. Nevertheless…

"You were married to him for almost thirty-eight years, and you're just finding out that you don't love him?" *What if I stop loving Robert? What if he stops loving me? Oh God.* "When did you stop loving him, Mom?"

"I don't think I ever loved him."

"Then why did you marry him?" She felt as if she should have a notepad and pen or her tablet handy.

"I was pregnant with Luke."

"We all know Luke was born six months after you and Daddy got married. Just because we never questioned you about it, it doesn't mean we didn't do the math."

"I didn't know if he belonged to your father."

Yasmine took another minute to let that information sink in, just like she would have done with one of her clients. In a 'no judgment' zone. "You were seeing two men at the same time?"

Her mother shook her head. "I had just broken up with my old boyfriend and things between your father and me moved quickly. I married your father because he was the better choice of the two."

Yasmine pressed a hand to her mouth to keep down the bile. So that's why her mother used to tell her father that he couldn't deny his children, Luke especially. She pressed her back into the cold, stainless steel door of the fridge, feeling more and more detached from her mother. Who was this woman who'd raised her, whom she'd admired all her life? Yasmine's mind drifted to Ned, her client. Her mother was no different from Ned's wife who had married one man when she knew her baby might belong to another. "You married Daddy, knowing that the child you were carrying might not be his." She focused her gaze on the flashing timer on the microwave, not wanting to look at her mother.

"It was disgusting and dishonest of me. I'm not perfect, Yasmine."

The desolation in her mother's voice didn't excuse what she had done as far as Yasmine was concerned.

"But the moment I looked into Luke's little face, I knew he was your father's."

"What if he wasn't? Would you have told Daddy the truth?"

"I don't know, Yasmine. I don't know."

"But you must have felt something for Daddy, right?" Yasmine said, trying to find some purpose for her being born, her own existence. "You stayed with him, and then had Naomi and me."

"I felt obligated, Yasmine. I sacrificed my happiness for my children. Like I said, your father is a good man, and I know he doesn't deserve to be blindsided like this—"

"Wait a minute." Yasmine threw up her hands. "You haven't asked him for a divorce? You haven't discussed it? You haven't even told him that you're unhappy? Of course not," she said, answering her own questions. Her father would not have finally agreed to take a trip around the world with his wife if he knew she wanted a divorce. "That's why you don't want to take the trip with him. It has nothing to do with the cost."

"I don't want to hurt him."

She uttered a skittish laugh. "It will hurt him, Mom. There's no getting around it."

"I'm hurting too, Yas. I'm stuck in a marriage that I don't want. That I haven't wanted for a long time."

"How can you say that? Does Daddy love you?"

"I think he thinks he does, but I don't know."

"How did you meet?" Yasmine asked, just realizing that she'd never heard her parents talk about their youth and falling in love with each other. "Were there sparks?" She flared her hands. "I mean, there had to be some kind of attraction to get things started. Or was he just looking for a piece of tail and you gave it up freely and willingly?" She ignored her mother's gasp at her candidness.

"We met at a mutual friend's house. I was just about to start college. He was older and working as a department store clerk. I got pregnant with Luke on our third date. I had dreams, Yas. I wanted to be a phlebotomist. I thought about an abortion but I couldn't go through with it. I gave up my dreams to be a good wife and mother."

"And you were, Mom. But is there any part of you that could love Daddy? Don't you think you should talk about it? Try. Maybe you guys just missed the boat with the courting stage, you know. Now that your kids are all grown, you can begin again. Get to know each other without the pressure of pregnancy, and bills, and children. You can still pursue your dreams."

Please. I have dreams I need to pursue. And if you and Daddy can't make it work, Robert and I won't be able to, either. Please Mom. "You owe it to yourself and you owe it to Dad," she said out loud, her voice threatening to break.

"It might be too late for us. I don't feel him. My destiny might be out there waiting for me."

"This is your destiny, Mom—Daddy, Luke, Naomi, and me. We are your destiny."

"Yas—"

Yasmine blinked back the tears. "What are you looking for, Mom? There's nothing out there. I'm young and I know that. Many of my clients who thought there was something better, later come to regret going through a divorce when they realize that grass is just *grass*. You have a man who doesn't run around on you, never raised a hand to you, doesn't gamble away his money, who took care of you and your children, and who I'm sure worships the ground you walk on. And you want to leave him because you don't feel him? Do you ever think that he might have had dreams that he had to give up when he married you without even knowing that the child he was sacrificing his dreams for might not even be his? Do you ever think of that, Mom?"

"Look who's giving me advice about love and relationship." Her mother got on the defense. "You've been stringing poor Robert along for five years. Five years, Yas. Are you holding out for something better?"

"No. I've just been afraid."

"Of what? Yas, you have it all together. You have a successful career that you built all by yourself. You made your own dreams come true. You didn't let love, a man, or anything else hold you back. I admire you. I'm proud of you for going after what you want."

"Oh, Mom." Yasmine bit back her moan. "There's nothing to admire. Right now, I'd rather have a man, and my child in my arms."

Yasmine swallowed back the hysteria that rose to her throat and gazed at her mother for long silent moments. Their situations were just too close for comfort. If she and Jeremy had gotten married, this could so easily be them in twenty years after their children had grown, or even her and Robert if he'd known she was pregnant, and had married her out of duty and obligation. Obligation, not happiness would have kept them together for a while, and then she would have ended up like her mother, standing in front of her own daughter, wringing her hands, looking lost and petrified, and wanting a divorce at fifty-something.

Yesterday, Yasmine had asked Naomi if she was happy being an ER nurse, but she'd never asked her mother if she was happy being a housewife. Maybe deep down inside, Yasmine suspected that she wasn't, and that it was that suspicion that had kept Yasmine out of the kitchen, kept her from being a slave to cleaning, doing laundry, and all the other household chores that were associated with women. Maybe she didn't want to become her mother.

From what her mother just told her, being a stay-at-home mom wasn't enough for her. It wasn't enough for Yasmine either. Why couldn't she have seen her mother's unhappiness and dissatisfaction with the choices she'd been forced to make? Perhaps she'd put on blinders to her mother's pain so she herself wouldn't feel guilty about her own choices, and for pursuing a career outside of the kitchen when her own mother had been condemned to it.

Feeling the rumble and the cramping in her belly, Yasmine bolted for the guest bathroom next to the kitchen. Everything she'd just eaten for breakfast and perhaps for dinner last night rolled into a ball of turmoil and rushed up her esophagus, choking, gaging on its way out of her. When the earthquake was over, she flushed the toilet and slumped weakly on the floor with her back pressed against the door, sweat dribbling out of every pore of her skin.

When her mother tapped on the door and asked if she was

okay, Yasmine dropped her head into her hands and began to cry. *Of course she wasn't okay.*

She loved her mother, but Yasmine wished she hadn't just confided in her, not just told her that she didn't love Yasmine's father and that she wanted to divorce him. Not today of all days when Yasmine was about to test the strength of Robert's love for her. What was she supposed to do, now? How was she supposed to believe that she and Rob could make it?

There was no Happily Ever After. It was all a farce. A lie. A house of cards built on a foundation of obligation and duty that could crumble at the slightest wind that came along.

Yasmine had no idea how long she'd been lying on the bathroom floor, but her mother's voice drew her back to consciousness.

"Yas, baby, it's Michelle. She's on the phone. I told her you were in the bathroom but she said she would hold. I'll just leave the phone here by the door when you're ready."

Michelle. Just the mention of her best friend's name eased the burden on Yasmine's heart. She could talk to Michelle. Michelle's marriage to Erik was rock solid. That was one marriage that had been raked over the coals of hell but was now one of the strongest Yas knew, all because Michelle and Erik loved each other. *Love* was the thing that had brought them back together after almost a year of separation. *Love* was keeping them together. She needed to hear about that kind of love.

Yasmine raised herself off the floor and opened the door. She picked up the phone from the floor, headed for her bedroom and locked the door behind her. "Michelle," she cried, dropping down onto the edge of the bed.

"Yas. Girl what's wrong? Why are you crying?"

"I did something awful, and I don't know if Robert will ever forgive me." Yasmine wiped at the fresh tears rolling down her face.

"Yas, what did you do?"

"I can't tell you. But I've been keeping it a secret from him. I finally decided to tell him tonight, but I learned something that makes me wonder if I should. I'm scared he might hate me, Mich."

"If it's one thing I know, Yas, it's that my brother loves you."

"Sometimes love isn't enough. You know that. Look what happened to you and Erik when he found out you'd been lying to him?"

"Yes, my lies tore Erik and me apart, but our love brought us back together. You and Robert have that kind of love, Yas. Nothing you did, or will ever do will stop him from loving you."

"How can you be so sure?"

"Because he has told me so on several occasions." She paused and cleared her throat. "I might as well tell you, so here it goes. Since you keep putting him off, tying up his dreams of marriage and a family, I told Rob to start seeing other women."

Yasmine jumped up from the bed. "You did what? I thought you were my friend, my sister." She began pacing, anger and disappointment taking over her emotions.

"It's because I'm your friend and your sister why I told him that. I wanted to see how devoted he was to you."

"What did he say?" Her heart thumped with anxiety as she came to a halt at the window.

"He said he would rather wait a lifetime for you than live out that dream with another woman. He said no other woman on this planet could make him half as happy as you make him. Now, does that sound like a man who can't forgive you, who will ever stop loving you?"

"No. No." Yasmine shook her head as a hot exultant tear

trickled down her cheek. "But what I have to tell him is so bad, Mich. It will hurt him."

"You're hurting him by keeping it from him, Yas. Just like I hurt Erik by not being truthful. I didn't think he could handle the truth. I emasculated him emotionally."

"Is that what I'm doing to Robert?" *Is that what my mother is doing to my father?* She closed her eyes to fight the sinking anguish in her soul. "Why do we do that, Michelle?" she asked, dropping down onto the windowsill.

"It's human nature to be afraid of losing what we have, but our fears and uncertainties do nothing but keep us prisoners. Yas, once you burst out of that prison, you'll find a whole new and better world, more joy and intense happiness than what you're trying to hold on to. If this *thing* is what's keeping you from committing to Robert, you need to let it go. And no matter the outcome, you can stop beating up yourself, and you both can move on with your lives."

"That's the thing." Yasmine sniffled. "I'm afraid that we might move on separately, and I might lose you, too. Robert's your brother, and—"

"I will still love you, Yas. I will still be here for you, no matter what. Our friendship, our love is not contingent on your relationship with my brother," Michelle offered in an encouraging voice. "We were besties long before you and Robert became lovers." She paused. "But I know my brother. He's already invested for the long haul. You just have to trust his love for you."

Michelle was right. *Love* was what Yasmine needed to believe in, not in Robert's emotions that could change with the situations, but in his love for her and hers for him. His love had been the one constant in their relationship, and that's what she had to believe in. She wasn't talking about the lip-service kind of love, but the real thing, the show-me kind of love that she and

Robert had been demonstrating for each other for the past five years.

Maybe Happily Ever After was just another name for Love, or maybe it was just the path that Love traveled, or a street where Love lived, or simply the end result of Love.

Maybe she already had her Happily Ever After and just didn't know it.

"You good, now?" Michelle asked.

Yasmine smiled. "Yeah, I'm good now," she lied, as fears for her parents' marriage took up residence where fears for her relationship with Robert had recently occupied. She was sure Michelle would have some wise words for that situation as well, but Yas didn't think it was her place to share her parents' issues with Michelle. In fact, she hoped that she would never have to share them with anyone.

"Good. That's what friends are for."

"I'm sure you didn't expect to be hit with something this heavy when you called me."

"With you, Yas, nothing is ever heavy. You're not heavy. You're my sister. You were there for me when I needed you. You played a big part in getting Erik and me back together, and look where we are now."

Yasmine laughed, her spirits already lifting. She pulled her feet up on the cushioned window seat. "Right. I didn't even ask about your honeymoon. How was it?"

Michelle chuckled. "Wicked. And I will tell you all about it when we get together?"

"Not fair, you know."

"What's not?"

"That you feel free to share the details of your sex life with Erik, but I can't tell you about mine with Robert."

"He's my brother. I don't want those images in my head, girl.

When can we get together? I miss you," she said, Yasmine was sure to change the subject.

Yasmine sucked her teeth. "Oh really? I find that hard to swallow now that you have your new girlfriends and all."

"Girl, shut up. You know nobody will ever take your place in my heart. Never ever. You are my girl. We're stuck like glue from here to eternity."

Yasmine laughed out loud. "I don't know whether to be scared or glad…"

CHAPTER ELEVEN

Robert added a dash of olive oil and a pinch of salt to the huge pot of water on his stove, and lit the burner under it. He pulled two kitchen towels from a drawer and spread them on the countertop beside a pair of tongs, before lifting the lid off another pot that was simmering over a low heat.

As he stirred the homemade tomato sauce, he grinned like a kid who'd gotten an early Christmas present—the one he really, really wanted but was too scared to ask for in case he got the usual answer: "You know we can't afford that. Why you even bother to ask?"

That was the response he'd grown used to hearing from Timmy Gleason, that is, when the bastard was in a good mood. When he wasn't, Robert would get a punch in the stomach or a smack in the head for asking. At age nine, he'd stopped asking when Timmy had taken out his anger on Michelle, just for being in the room when Robert made his request.

The fact that he could recall the violent memories of his childhood without tensing up with anger and regrets surprised Robert. It was a sign that he was stepping from the shadows of his past, embracing and appreciating his present, and looking forward to a future with Yasmine, merely because she'd texted the words, *I love YOU*.

A surge of warm feelings seeped through him, causing his heart to tremble and butterflies to flutter in his belly. The sensation wasn't rushed or sexual. It was unhurried, unwavering, and spiritual. He'd been floating in the ether ever since he'd read her text yesterday. Last night, he'd gone to bed feeling giddy, silly, fantastic, and elated, not from being in love with Yasmine, but from being loved by her. *She loved him.* It had taken her four years to admit it, and he looked forward to hearing it in person.

Robert tasted the sauce, his forehead furrowing as he analyzed the flavor. He added another pinch of oregano and a bay leaf and stirred one last time before replacing the lid. Pleased that it would be as good as it smelled, he left it to simmer and collected the ingredients for the massaged kale and mango salad to go along with the lasagna he was making for Yasmine. He washed the kale leaves, shook them out, stacked them one on top of the other, rolled them like a cigar, and began to cut them into thin strips before placing them into a large bowl. He loved cooking for Yasmine, and he loved that she appreciated his culinary skills, especially tonight.

He'd deliberately called her this morning during her DND hours. He'd left instructions for her to come straight to his place when she left Manchester, to be prepared to spend the night, and not to worry since he had a fresh outfit for her to wear to work on Monday. He hadn't even mentioned her text.

There would be time to talk about her love for him all night long, he thought, as he sliced the mushrooms into thin strips. He wanted every night to be like tonight where he would come home early from work to prepare dinner and have it on the table, hot and ready for Yas when she walked in the door. Her career was a lot more stressful than his, and he didn't mind taking care of the house and performing most of the housework once they were married. He would do it just to feel her trembling and moaning under him each night when they finally went to bed. Much like it would be tonight.

Robert added the mushrooms to the kale and reached for the avocado when his doorbell sounded. He set the knife aside, wondering who would be calling. Before the thought was out, the doorbell sounded again, and again, and again.

"Hold on. Hold on," he mumbled, totally annoyed now at the incessant ringing. Who the heck could be that impatient? He set the avocado aside, wiped his hands on his apron, and made his way to the front door. As he passed the dining table romantically set for two with fine china, candles, a vase of fresh roses, a bottle of Pinot Noir, and as love songs streamed from the surround sound stereo, Robert's irritation faded.

He wasn't going to let anything or anyone spoil his mood. Whoever was at the door had two seconds to state his or her claim and bug the hell off. The only person he was entertaining tonight was the love of his life. Taking a deep breath, Robert opened his door to find an elderly woman standing on his step.

At the sight of him, her mouth dropped open, her hand flew to her chest, and she inhaled sharply as if she were in shock.

Well, you rang my doorbell, so don't look so surprised to see me. "Hello." He nonetheless offered her a friendly smile. Maybe she was shy, or maybe she'd come to the wrong house. He hoped for the latter.

"Hello, Robert," she said in a voice that seemed to be holding back a flood of emotions, while her warm brown eyes smiled at him through the lenses of her glasses.

Robert frowned as he stared at her. Something about her seemed familiar, but he couldn't quite put his finger on it. She was of average height and weight, and elegantly dressed in cream-colored slacks and an olive-colored silk blouse. Judging from the sprinkles of dark age spots on her pale, slightly wrinkled, yet attractive face, and her short mop of fashionably styled gray hair, he would guess that she was probably in her late sixties or early seventies. And she was wealthy, he thought, as the blue sapphires and diamonds studding the white gold frame of her spectacles shimmered in the afternoon light.

Was she one of his patients, requesting an emergency call? *No.* His patients never addressed him by his first name. Besides, they didn't know where he lived—well, that was his hope. In any case, they wouldn't be showing up at his private residence in an emergency; they would be calling his crisis hotline.

"Can I help you?" he asked, even as his gut began to tighten and his heart began to race for reasons beyond him. He transferred his gaze to her hand clutching the straps of her autumn green Bvlgari purse. He recognized the brand because his sister had one. *His sister...*

"As a matter of fact, I was wondering if you could help me, Robert."

There she went again, addressing him by his first name as if she knew him. And her accent—it was Southern.

"My name is Margaret. Margaret Montenegro," she said, her lips parting into a wide smile this time, a smile that made Robert take a step back as if he'd wandered into speeding traffic. *That mouth was Michelle's, and that nose...* Robert felt as if his breath was about to solidify in his throat.

"May I come inside?" she asked, taking the opportunity of his inability to speak to step inside his foyer. She even closed his door, walked into the living room, and glanced approvingly around the open concept of his Charles River Square, cul-de-sac townhouse.

Robert's legs felt like melting rubber as he forced them to follow her. He noticed the smile playing at the corners of her thin lips when her gaze wandered past the archway leading into the dining area.

"It smells delicious in here," she said, turning to him. "You must cook." She jutted her chin at his apron, her smile now reaching her eyes.

"Who are you? And what do you want?" Robert ripped out the words harshly. "You can't just walk into my house like this and—"

She removed her glasses and peered up at him. "I'm your grandmother, Robert."

Robert fell back against the staircase banister as shock waves reverberated around inside him. His first thought was that this old Southern white woman had somehow discovered that he was searching his family heritage, and had come to try to bilk him of his money. For all he knew she could be related to that woman who'd identified his father as Timmy Gleason.

But then he remembered he'd only rehired Detective Gilbert yesterday. She couldn't have gotten wind of it and caught a plane to Boston that fast. Besides, she didn't need his money; she obviously had her own, or had she simply dressed the part to run her scam? But God, her eyes.

"I'm sorry, Robert," she said. "I don't—I—I didn't know how else to tell you. I've been searching for you for years."

Robert swallowed, breathed composure into his system, and pushed off the banister. "You've been searching for me for years?" he asked, trying desperately to control the tremor in his voice.

"Well, not for you, directly, but for your father. My son."

Robert closed his eyes and braced his hand against the banister as his head began to spin.

"Robert."

He recoiled at the touch of her hand on his arm.

"I'm sorry," she said, pulling back. "I know it's a shock for you. Forgive me for barging into your home and blurting it out a minute after we met. But it was either this way or turning around and heading back to Atlanta without telling you why I'd come to see you."

So that's where his roots lay—two generations back—in Atlanta, Georgia, his genes nestled in the blood of an old Southern belle. Robert opened his eyes and gazed down at her. "How do you know I'm the person you're looking for?"

"You look like your grandfather. Actually, you're the spitting image of him, except for the eyes. He had black eyes, like your sister's. Like Michelle's," she said, her voice softening at the mention of Michelle's name. "Yours are brown like mine."

"I have my mother's eyes," Robert stated coolly, not ready to accept this woman's claim to be his grandmother. Lots of people resembled folks to whom they weren't related.

She tightened her hands on her purse straps as if she were fighting the urge to reach out and touch him again.

"I thought I was prepared to see you in person," she said, toying with the huge rock of the platinum wedding set on her finger. "But when you opened the door, I was thrown back into the past. I almost called you—" She stopped and swallowed. "Let me show you." She rummaged through her purse and brought out an old photo that looked like it had been folded and unfolded several times over the decades. She glanced at it for a few moments before holding it out to Robert. "Here. Your grandfather's name was Christian. Christian Bradbury."

Robert's entire body was trembling as he reached for the photo. A sharp pang whipped through his gut when his fingers grazed Margaret's. They stared at each other, frozen for a few seconds, before reluctantly pulling away.

Needing to physically distance himself from her, Robert forced his legs across the floor and over to the French doors leading to the balcony off his living room. Taking a deep breath, he held up the picture to the light. He felt that sharp pang again as he stared into the black eyes of the man Margaret

Montenegro had just told him was his grandfather. Robert did look like him, a lot—wide prominent forehead, sharp chin, smooth full lips and bushy brows. And like Margaret had said, Christian Bradbury—his grandfather—had Michelle's eyes, or more accurately, Michelle had his and Dwight's, while Robert's were a combination in shape and color to his mother and this woman who claimed to be his paternal grandmother's. Now he knew where he and Michelle had gotten their Grecian noses, and why their skin was a tad lighter in shade than their mother's.

There was no doubt that he and his sister were related to the young couple posing in front of a statue in a park. They seemed happy and in love.

He turned to find that Margaret had followed him. For an old woman, she was quite stealthy on her feet. She definitely possessed a great deal of strength and dexterity. She was probably a riot in her youth, a bit like Michelle, he thought with tenderness.

She shifted from one foot to the other, and glanced warily at the sofa.

Robert immediately snapped into shape. "I'm sorry. Please have a seat—" He paused, not knowing how to address her. "Mrs. Montenegro." Ignoring the pained look in her eyes at his formality, he indicated the black leather club chairs under a window that overlooked Government Center and downtown Boston.

What, did she think he was going to start calling her Grandma two minutes after he met her? Robert walked over to the sofa and picked up the tablet that governed his entertainment system. He was desperate to learn all about his heritage, but not desperate enough to fall at the feet of the first person who claimed to have the answers he was searching for. He turned off the stereo, and joined Margaret at the window. "So, what's your story, Mrs. Montenegro?" he asked, as he dropped his weight into the matching chair across from her. He was still clutching the picture in his hand, not yet ready to surrender the first link to his ancestry, the first piece of evidence he had to his real past.

She set her purse on the table between them and sat with her back straight and her hands clasped on her lap. "Like I mentioned before, I'd been looking for my son for years. Decades, really."

Robert leaned back and crossed one leg over the knee of the other as he studied her queenly poise. She was not only wealthy, but sophisticated, too. She probably attended a few cotillions in her day. She was no *nouveau riche,* either. No, sir. Margaret Montenegro's wealth was generational. She had class and breeding to prove it. Her name alone shouted royalty. "Why did you have to look for him? Why wasn't he with you?" he asked.

She closed her eyes briefly and her bosom rose and fell on a deep breath. Finally, she raised her lids and pointed at the photo in his hand. "Well, as you realize, your grandfather, Christian, was black."

Was. So he was dead. Robert contained his thoughts and his emotions.

She dropped her head and then almost instantly raised it again. "Look. There's no easy way to say this, but my father, your great-grandfather, was a racist son of a bitch."

Robert's eyes widened. So that's where Michelle got her candid personality. He swallowed back the bubble in his throat.

"I'm not ashamed to say it," Margaret said. "When Daddy found out that Chris and I were seeing each other, he threatened to have him shot if he came near me again."

"But you must have disobeyed him. You made a baby together."

She shook her head and tears welled up into her eyes. "I was already pregnant with your father when Chris was chased off. I was only sixteen, and the only reason Daddy didn't have him thrown into jail was because he didn't want anyone to know that I'd sullied myself with a—a *negro*," she said, her voice and gaze dropping.

Robert was sure she was being polite with her choice of adjective to describe the way her father felt about the man who'd fathered her child.

"I didn't dare go against Daddy's orders. He was a powerful man. He could have shot Chris at point-blank range in a crowded room without provocation, and gotten away with it. I couldn't risk his life."

I probably would have shot him too, not because of his race, but for getting my sixteen-year-old daughter pregnant.

She pressed a hand to her lips as if to stifle a sob. "I loved Chris so much. He was the love of my life, and it broke my heart that I couldn't be with him, that I couldn't share the news of our unborn baby with him."

"So he never knew you were pregnant?"

"No. Daddy chased him out of Atlanta, out of Georgia. A friend later told me that she heard he'd joined the army or some other branch of the military, and had gone overseas. I didn't know I was pregnant until three weeks after he left. Daddy would have made me have an abortion if it wasn't for his religious beliefs. So he sent me to a home in Virginia, under an assumed name, and once the baby was born, it was taken from me."

She inhaled deeply before continuing in a tremulous voice. "I didn't even get a chance to hold my precious son in my arms. He lived and died not knowing who his mother was, or that I loved him, ached for him all my life, that I'm still aching for him." Tears, blackened with mascara, rolled down her cheeks in torrents and splashed off her hands, clasped on her lap. "I should have fought for him. I should have…"

Robert laid the photo on the table next to her purse and sat forward. He had no idea how or why it happened, but the next instant, his hands were covering her trembling ones and his thumbs were massaging the thin wrinkled skin of her wrists. "It's okay. You were just a kid. You were powerless against supremacy and bigotry. You did what you had to do for love, and to survive."

She squeezed his fingers. "Thank you for understanding, Robert." She brought his hand up and pressed his knuckles against her cheek.

Something broke inside Robert as the warmth from her touch seeped under his skin, but he kept his emotions in check and tugged his hands reluctantly from her. "Would you like some water?" he asked as she pulled a white handkerchief from her purse and dabbed at her eyes.

She nodded and smiled.

Questions upon questions were spinning around in Robert's head as he walked unsteadily through his dining room and into his kitchen. He took a glass from the cupboard and filled it from the door in the refrigerator. He wanted to know everything about her relationship with his grandfather—how they met, how long they'd been together, when and how he died, if he had aunts and uncles and cousins—but he had no idea how much she was capable of telling him, wanted to tell him. The memories were obviously still very traumatizing for her, and he...

"There's something boiling over on the stove."

Robert turned around to find her standing behind him. Okay, so she was resilient, not letting anything keep her down—another trait his sister had inherited from her, and their mother.

"You're expecting company," she said matter-of-factly.

"Yes." He handed her the glass of water.

She gulped it down quickly, and instead of giving the empty glass to him, she went and placed it in the sink. She washed her hands, ripped off a sheet of paper towel from the roll on the countertop and dried them.

"Is she special?" she asked, stepping over to the island

where he'd been about to make the salad when his doorbell had rung. She picked up the knife and began slicing up his lemons, and even removing the seeds as if she knew what he was making.

Robert frowned. He didn't know if he should be bothered or relaxed at her level of comfort with him. Perhaps it was easy for her since he looked so much like his grandfather, the love of her life. "Yes."

"That's sweet. What's her name?"

"Yasmine. Yasmine Reynolds."

"Your smile, and the way you say her name say how much she means to you. You love her very deeply. Love is important. It's the one thing we all search our entire lives to find. And once you find it, you should cherish it, forget about convention, and sacrifice to keep it. If I never give you any other advice, Robert, dear, it's that you should hang on to love at all costs. You don't want to end up like me—seventy-six, alone, and living a life of regrets."

Her words touched Robert deeply. It was the best advice he'd gotten in a very long time. Who needed a shrink when he had a grandmother who had the scars to prove that love was worth sacrificing for? He was grateful that Margaret didn't grill him about when he was going to settle down and raise a family, like grandmothers loved to do. He wasn't ready to discuss Yasmine with her yet. Strolling over to the stove, he added the uncooked lasagna to the pot of boiling water and set the timer. He then stirred his tomato sauce as he tried to decide between spending the afternoon learning about his past, or planning his future with Yasmine.

"What kind of salad are you making?"

Robert closed the lid and turned around to find that his unexpected, uninvited guest was watching him. "It's a massaged kale salad," he answered, rubbing at the muscles in his neck.

She rinsed the knife under the faucet and picked up the avocado from among the cluster of ingredients. "Sliced?"

"Roughly chopped."

"Your grandfather used to love cooking, too. His father used to run a soup kitchen for homeless and misplaced families in Atlanta."

Robert's interest level went up a notch at having something in common with his grandfather. "Is that how you met him?" he asked, watching her remove the skin from the avocado.

"Yes, I needed community hours during my junior year in high school, so I signed up to volunteer during my Christmas break. Christian was the main chef. He was only eighteen, but Lord, he could cook up a storm. He was good at baking too." A faint smile parted her lips. "It was instant attraction for both of us. We were inseparable after that." Her smile faded. "Well, until one of Daddy's colleagues told him he'd seen Chris and me together on more than one occasion. I should have been more careful…"

As he listened to her revisit her youth, Robert's thirst for information grew stronger, but so did his anxiety. From what Margaret had told him so far, and from looking at the photo, he believed that he and Michelle were her grandchildren, but until a DNA test proved it, Robert preferred not to get too cozy with her.

Not that he had the luxury of time to entertain her with Yas due to arrive in about forty-five minutes. He and Yasmine's timing had been off for years. He just wanted things to go as planned tonight. Waiting one more day to hear about his past wasn't going to change anything about it, but putting Yas on hold might change everything about his future. He wasn't about to risk that.

"Mrs. Montenegro," he said, in as gentle a voice as possible, "I don't mean to be rude, but—"

"Please, at least call me Margaret. Mrs. Montenegro seems so hopeless, as if we will never get past this point. I realize that I'm forcing you to deter from your plans tonight, but I don't have much time, Robert."

Robert stiffened. "Are you ill?"

"No, I'm not ill, but in case you haven't noticed, I'm not that young. I'm seventy-six years old, and whatever little time I have left, I want to spend it getting to know you and Michelle, and my great-grandchildren. You're all the family I have. I need to connect with you, in any way possible, even if it means helping you with dinner for Yasmine. But if you prefer, I'll leave, and hopefully we can meet again soon, maybe tomorrow, if you have time," she finished with a hopeful shimmer in her eyes.

Robert felt like an unsympathetic jerk. He knew what it was like to need one's family. And as much as he was trying to remain cautious, the more time he spent in Margaret Montenegro's presence, the more his heart melted toward her. In his gut he knew a DNA test wasn't necessary to prove her claim. He'd felt it the moment he gazed into her eyes. *They were family.*

He glanced at the ingredients for the salad that needed to be peeled and chopped. With Margaret helping, he might be able to regain the fifteen minutes he'd lost since she rang his doorbell. "Okay, Margaret," he said, offering her an affectionate smile. "I've already made the filling for the lasagna, so if you insist, you can help me make the salad."

The tense lines on her face relaxed into a wholehearted smile as he explained what needed to be done. "Thank you, Robert. I can use an apron, if you have an extra one. This is one of my favorite blouses, and although I can afford to replace it in value, I don't think I'll be able to find this particular style anywhere. I've had it for years."

Robert grinned privately as he recalled Yasmine's panic at her ruined skirt during their lovemaking session two days ago. He fetched a white apron from a drawer and handed it to Margaret. He watched silently as she looped it around her neck and tied the strings into a bow in the back.

"So you're cooking lasagna," she stated as she began chopping the avocado.

"Yes. It's Yasmine's favorite." He shaved the skin off a large carrot.

"What time is she due home?"

"Soon," he answered, choosing not to tell Margaret that Yas didn't live with him. He wasn't sure yet if he wanted her to leave once Yasmine got here. He could call and ask Yas to come later after he'd had time to visit with Margaret, but he didn't want to spook her. She'd finally felt confident enough to tell him that she loved him, and he didn't want her to think he was withdrawing from her love like he'd done four years ago. Since Yasmine was going to be a part of his future, she might as well meet his past.

CHAPTER TWELVE

"So, how did you find out that Michelle and I are related to you?" Robert asked his grandmother as he diced up the carrot into fine pieces.

"It was the billionaires' wedding in Granite Falls last week." Margaret scooped up the avocado chunks and placed them into a small bowl.

"Were you there?"

She chuckled. "I wish. I watched it on TV."

"I didn't know it was important enough to garner attention as far as Atlanta." Robert scraped the diced carrots into a bowl and began skinning the cloves of garlic as Margaret chopped the handful of baby spinach he'd portioned out. He had to admit that it was nice having her help him in the kitchen while they got to know each other.

"You wouldn't know this, but your great-grandfather was a heart surgeon, as was one of my uncles on my mother's side."

"Oh, that's where my interest in medicine comes from," he said with a chuckle.

"It's in your blood." Her mouth tightened a fraction. "I also married a heart surgeon—not by choice. He was the man Daddy married me off to when I turned eighteen. He was twice my age."

Damn! I'm glad I never knew the tyrant, Robert thought as he peeled the skin off a shallot.

"Ferris, my husband, began following The Erik LaCrosse Doctors Abroad Foundation."

Robert glanced at her from beneath lowered lashes. "I thought you said Michelle and I were the only family you had left?"

"Ferris died last year," she said without much emotion.

"I'm sorry."

"I'm not." She set the chopped spinach aside. "He was as cold and prejudiced as your great-grandfather. But I realize now that if I hadn't married him, and stayed married to him all these years, I might not have found you. God works in mysterious ways." She sighed.

She'd obviously lived an unhappy life. *Poor soul.* While she cut the cherry tomatoes into halves, Robert got a container of ice water and placed the sliced shallots inside it to reduce the pungent raw bite shallots were known to possess. "So, your late husband knew Erik. That's how you found Michelle and me," he prompted softly, giving her a tender smile.

"He knew of him, and I think they'd met briefly at a medical convention in Los Angeles some years ago. Before Erik and Michelle married, maybe even before they met, I think."

"My God, it's a small world. Six degrees of separation has never been more real for me."

"Try three." Her lips twisted wryly. "Apart from the fact that it was his knowledge of Erik that led me to watch the wedding, Ferris knew nothing about my child. Even after my father died fifteen years ago, I still never told him. Even though he never loved me, he was a good husband. He respected me." She nodded as if that was enough. "I didn't want to embarrass him, so I searched for my child secretly for years, mostly through the Internet to protect my identity. After Ferris died, I hired a private investigator and launched an all-out search. I didn't care anymore. There was nobody to embarrass or bring shame upon."

"Why didn't you have more children?"

She took her time halving the last of the tomatoes and placed them into their own bowl before answering. "Ferris had two young children with his late wife. He didn't want any more. He just wanted a mother for the two he already had. Daddy was aware of that when he married me off to him. I'm sure he did it to punish me for carrying on with a black man and having a baby with him. His exact words were, 'I would rather have no grandchildren than have them conceived in the same womb as that little—'" She paused and shivered as if she were locked in that painful moment. "Anyway, like he intended, it was difficult for me to raise another woman's children when I didn't even know where my own child was, if he was dead or alive, happy or sad."

"Your father sounds like a real piece of work. I guess I didn't miss anything not knowing him."

"He was, and you didn't."

"What about your mother? Where was she all this time? And did you have siblings?"

Sadness shadowed her face. "My mother was very frail and sickly. She died from pneumonia complications when I was eleven. She was the very opposite of my father, though, and the only person who wasn't afraid to stand up to him. I was an only child, so I got all of Daddy's attention—the good, the bad, and the ugly."

The kitchen timer went off and without even asking, Margaret walked over to the stove and turned off the burner under the pot of sauce, and then tested the pasta. "Perfect," she said, sliding her hands into his oven mitts.

Robert watched her with a flicker of warmth as she drained the noodles into the colander, ran cold water over them, and laid them on the towels to cool. Then instead of returning to the island, she walked to the kitchen window overlooking a park and gazed thoughtfully down at the late afternoon scene.

"This is a lovely home you've made for yourself, Robert," she said, turning to him.

Robert smiled. "Thank you. I like nice things."

"There's nothing wrong with that." She flashed her pearly whites at him. "If you don't mind, may I use your bathroom?" She removed her apron and hung it over the back of one of the chairs.

"Of course. It's off the living room, next to the window where we sat when you first arrived. Come on, I'll show you."

"I can find it. I promise not to get lost. You continue preparing your dinner."

As she shuffled past him, Robert glanced at the clock on his microwave, and then down at the chopped, peeled, and sliced vegetables in their separate containers. With Margaret's help, he'd managed to make up the time he'd lost. The only thing he needed to do was finish the salad, but since massaged kale salad was best when eaten immediately after preparation, and since he wasn't sure when they would be eating it, he gathered the various containers of ingredients and took them to the fridge.

He glanced at the unshucked oysters on the top shelf and with a dose of regret, he dampened a kitchen towel and placed it over them. Hopefully he and Yas would have the chance to enjoy them tomorrow night—that is if she decided to stay another night with him.

Before closing the fridge, he pulled out a platter laden with an assortment of cheeses, cured meats, stuffed black and green olives, mozzarella balls, grapes, strawberries, and mango slices. *His Jacuzzi feast.* He took it over to the kitchen table, and by the time Margaret returned from the bathroom, the table was set for three with plates, utensils, and sparkling water.

"I thought you might be hungry," he said, pulling out a chair for her.

"You are so sweet."

"I should have offered you something earlier. You must think my manners are quite poor, compared to the way you do things in the south. We all know you're famous for your southern hospitality, if nothing else," he said, sitting down in the chair next to her.

She chuckled. "Don't worry about it. I was the last person you expected to show up on your doorstep today. And we had more important matters on our minds," she said, filling their plates with goodies.

Matters that still needed to be discussed, he thought as they both nibbled at the delicacies in silence and watched children playing in the park below. After a few minutes, Robert gave in to his need for physical contact, and rested his hand over hers lying on the table.

She jumped at the unexpected gesture and immediately placed her other hand over his.

He gave her an easy smile. "How did your search for your son lead you to me?" *Grandma.*

She washed down a slice of mango with some sparkling water before answering. "As I was saying, after Ferris died, I began searching for Christian. I never stopped loving him, and if he still felt the same way, I would have liked for us to be together, even if we only had a few years. But he'd died from a stroke a year before my father died. He'd retired from the navy, had married, had a daughter, and two grandchildren."

"I have an aunt, and cousins?" Robert got a bubbly feeling in his chest.

"Yes." She patted his hand. "They're really nice people. They live in Charlotte, North Carolina. His daughter, Camille, told me that before he died, her father had spoken about me and had told her that I was his first love." Her eyes sparkled with apparent pleasant memories of her youth, perhaps the only happy ones she'd had all her life.

"Camille started helping me search for her brother, but we came up empty. I mean, we knew nothing about him, not his name, what he looked like, where he lived. Nothing. The place where he was born and the people who'd been present at his birth were all gone. And even if I'd found someone, they wouldn't have remembered me, or my baby since Daddy had admitted me under an assumed name. I had resigned myself to going to my grave without finding out what had happened to my son. But then last month, every channel was buzzing about the billionaires' wedding in Granite Falls, so I decided to tune in and watch it because of Ferris's association with Dr. LaCrosse.

"It was a beautiful wedding and all the brides were stunning, to say the least. But for some reason, I couldn't take my eyes off Michelle as she stood in the back of the church waiting to walk down the aisle. There was just something about her that felt familiar." She tightened her hold on his hand, and gazed deeply into his eyes. "But, Robert, when you stepped from behind those curtains and stood next to your sister, I almost fainted. It was like seeing a ghost."

"Like when you saw me today." Robert understood. He did look like his grandfather. He was still shaken up over the eeriness of the resemblance.

She nodded, and pressed her other hand to her chest. "Yes. I thought, oh my God, I have a name. *Carter.*" A bubble of joy spilled from her throat. "I was so excited. I immediately contacted the private detective, and then a few days ago, he called me with the news that my son's name was Dwight Carter."

She stopped, and a cold congested expression chased away the enthusiasm from her face. "He also told me that my son had died in prison five years ago for killing Erik's first wife in a hit-and-run accident. He said Dwight had been a drunk all his life and that he'd abused you and Michelle as children. I'd given birth to a monster," she whispered, as tears welled up in her eyes and rolled down her cheeks. "How could that be when his father was the gentlest, sweetest man I'd ever known?" She shook her head sorrowfully. "He'd turned out to be worse than my own father, the man I loathed more than any other person in this world. I'm sorry, Robert. I'm sorry for the pain you and Michelle suffered at my son's hands."

Robert squeezed her hand. "No," he said in a choked voice. "That man was not your son."

"What?" she asked, an incredulous glaze in her teary eyes. "He wasn't my son? Then—"

"The man who raised Michelle and me was a criminal named Timmy Gleason. He was not our father. Your son died thirty years ago. Gleason stabbed him in an alley in Richmond, Virginia, stole his identity, kidnapped my pregnant mother and me, and brought us to New Hampshire. The man I remember, *my father*, your son, was kind, and sweet, and loving. You would have been proud of him, Grandma." The word slid from his tongue easily, as if he were accustomed to saying it. It felt as natural as the memories of his parents. *She was his grandmother.*

Finally, Robert could admit it, embrace, and revel in the sweet and blessed knowledge that he knew who he was. Even if there were undesirable apples swinging from the branches of his family tree, at least he'd found the tree, and the roots from which he'd sprung.

"Oh, Dwight. My son. My poor darling son." Margaret

dropped her face into her hands and wept as if her heart would break all over again.

Margaret's sorrow over the fate of her son pierced Robert's heart. He pressed his lips together, desperately trying to control the dam of emotions that had been backing up inside him since he opened his door to find her standing on his steps—maybe even before then, like when he'd had his first real memory of his childhood.

But he was powerless to hold it all back and for the first time since he'd learned how his father died, Robert began to moan. Before he knew what was happening, he and his grandmother were holding on to each other with tears streaming down their faces. They wept for the loss of a son and a father they would never have the chance to see, to hold, to express their love to ever again. Their cries of grief resounded around the room as the barriers that had kept them apart for two generation collapsed, and the bridges that would connect their past, their present, and their future finally appeared under their feet. They continued holding each other, even after their sobs had died.

For Robert, hugging his grandmother was equivalent to hugging his father. And he was certain that for Margaret, holding him in her arms was like holding her son, the son she'd been forced to give up almost seven decades ago.

"Robert."

Robert's entire body tensed. He lifted his head from his grandmother's shoulder and opened his eyes. His sweet Yasmine was standing near the island in a pair of white shorts and a white blouse, looking all sexy and angelic at the same time.

"Yas." He eased out of Margaret's arms and walked over to Yasmine, wiping the remnants of tears from his face.

"What's going on? Who's that?" she whispered, glancing over at Margaret, her brows drawn together in a puzzled expression.

Robert pulled her into his arms, picked her up off the floor and, covering her mouth with his, he kissed her hungrily, his tongue swerving into her mouth, searching out hers and inviting it to dance with his. This was one segment of his planned romantic evening his heart refused to give up, and he couldn't care less if his newly found grandmother was watching.

The touch of Robert's lips on hers sent a shock wave through Yasmine's entire body. To say that she was surprised at Robert's unconventional behavior would be a gross understatement. It was so unlike him to be amorous in front of people, especially a strange older woman, but she wasn't about to protest. She'd been dreaming of being in his arms for two long days, and the anxiety she'd felt about his nonresponse to her text melted into the flavorsome aroma of his kitchen. Enticed by his enthusiasm, she locked her arms around his neck, burrowed her fingers into his soft black hair, and gave herself over to the moment as his passionate and urgent kisses sent her stomach into a wild swirl.

"I missed you," he whispered against her lips. "You're my world, Yasmine." He held her tightly, crushing her breasts against the hardness of his chest.

"I missed you too." As their hearts beat as one, Yasmine retuned his kisses with reckless abandon. If each time she walked through the door he was going to greet her with intoxicating kisses and a delicious-smelling dinner cooking on the stove, she was ready to move in. Like yesterday…

The sound of a throat clearing brought them back down to earth. Reluctantly, Yasmine drew back her lips from Rob's and gazed over his shoulder at the gray-haired woman watching them with an affectionate smile of approval.

"This must be Yasmine," she said, rising from the chair with an agility that belied her age.

Yasmine suppressed her groan of pleasure as Robert slid her

slowly down his body, holding her a little bit longer as her softness grazed his erection. He was hard as a rock, and he didn't seem to care, she thought, taking a swift glance at the tent in his apron as he turned to face the woman who'd walked over to them.

Robert pulled her close to his side while her lips burned from the heat of his kiss, and her body trembled from the hard contact of his.

"Yes, this is Yasmine. Yasmine," he said smiling down at her, "this is Margaret Montenegro, my grandmother."

Yasmine's hands flew to her mouth to stifle the squeal of shock. *His grandmother.* When did this happen? She'd left Robert two days ago with the uncertainty of his ancestry still hanging over his head, and now here she was, in his kitchen, standing in front of a woman he claimed to be his grandmother. So that's why they'd been sobbing in each other's arms when she walked in.

Theirs must have been tears of joy at finally finding each other, she thought, trying desperately to constrain the new anguish taking root in her heart. Robert had been searching for his family for five years, and she would not allow the fact that his family was finally coming together when hers was threatening to fall apart diminish her excitement for him. She had to hope that her parents would survive the storm whirling toward them.

"It's a pleasure meeting you, Yasmine." The woman's voice pulled Yasmine back to the joyous and unexpected occasion.

Yasmine shook the hand she presented. Despite her age, she had a strong grip. "It's nice meeting you too, Mrs. Montenegro," she said, offering her a genuine smile that she felt deep in her heart. The woman was adorable and the fact that she was Robert's grandmother played a huge role in Yasmine's readiness to accept her, as he had apparently already done.

"It's Ms. Montenegro. But you can call me Margaret."

Margaret's eyes shifted to Robert's puzzled expression. "Montenegro is my family, *our* family name. My husband was Durant. I reclaimed my maiden name after he died." She focused her gaze on Yasmine again. "You, my dear, are simply gorgeous. I can see why Robert is so in love with you."

"And I with him," Yasmine said, looping her arms around Robert's waist and smiling up at him, knowing that it was his arms around her that was bringing her comfort, calming her troubled spirits. She hoped that after she opened her heart to him later on tonight that he would hold her like this instead of turning away from her.

After her conversation with Michelle, she'd gone in search of her mother to tell her that she was sorry, that she understood, and that she would help her work out the situation with her dad. She had to hope that her parents' almost forty years together wasn't in vain. She had to believe in love for them as much as she believed in it for herself. But her mom had left a note that she'd gone to the store.

Yasmine had waited around for a little while, but the possibility of her father returning home before her mom had sent her packing. She couldn't face him and keep her wits about her knowing that his world, the family he'd sacrificed for might be coming undone.

She'd driven down to Hampton Beach and walked along the shore, trying to figure out the best way to approach Robert. Humbling herself, falling on her knees in front of him, confessing, and then begging his forgiveness as soon as she walked through his door had seemed like the right path to take. Just get it over with before he could say or do anything to distract or dissuade her.

The sounds of sobs coming from the kitchen had suspended —not deterred—her plans, since she was determined to get rid of her secret before the night was out. At first, she'd thought it was Robert and Michelle crying over the loss of somebody close to them, but recalling that she'd spoken to Michelle earlier in the day and that everything was good in her corner of the world, Yasmine had rushed into the kitchen, never guessing for one minute that she would find Robert crying in his grandmother's arms, sharing special moments with her. She hoped that before long, she and Robert would have their own special moment when she gazed into his eyes and told him that she loved him. Until then, she was contented to wrap herself in the warmth of Robert's enthusiastic greeting, and share his joy of finding his grandmother.

"So," she asked, giving Margaret a courteous smile, "Are you Rob's paternal or maternal grandmother?"

"She's my father's mother." Robert gazed affectionately at the old woman. "And she tells me that I'm the spitting image of my grandfather. Actually, she showed me a picture, and I do look like him."

"He cooks like him too. Robert's cooking dinner for you. Lasagna's your favorite, he told me."

Yasmine smiled. *So they'd been talking about her.* "Yeah, he likes to do that. He's an excellent cook, thank God, because I don't. Not because I can't," she added hastily. "I just don't have time with my career and all. I get takeout almost every day."

"So you don't live together?"

"No." *But I hope to soon. If he can forgive me for breaking his heart later.*

"Oh. I assumed a woman lived here because the house is so clean and orderly."

"Robert's very orderly. I have a condo in Charlestown, about fifteen minutes from here." She wasn't about to tell this woman that she was a messy housekeeper, and that Robert seemed to enjoy cleaning up after her.

"You're obviously very independent," Margaret said,

watching her closely. "There's nothing wrong with that. I wish I had been self-sufficient at your age, or at least had possessed the courage to fight for my rights. What do you do?" she added hastily as if to avoid any questions about the lack of bravery and independence in her youth.

"Yasmine is an attorney," Robert said. "She's an associate at one of the most acclaimed family law firms here in Boston. Hayward and Harley. In the three years she's been practicing, she hasn't lost a case." His voice was heavy with pride and admiration.

"I'm impressed." Margaret's eyes lit up approvingly. "It must feel gratifying to have accomplished so much at such a young age. That goes for both of you. I feel honored to know that you came from me," she added, smiling at Robert.

"It wasn't easy for either one of us," Robert said. "But as I always say: you have no control over where you come from, only where you end up."

"A profound axiom." Margaret looked past them into the dining room. "You two have plans, very romantic ones from the looks of that dining table, so I should be going. I promised to stay until you arrived, Yasmine. And well, here you are." Her voice displayed a touch of sadness.

Yasmine glanced up at Robert. How could she deny him this pleasure of spending time with his grandmother? Yes, she wanted him to herself, but judging from what she'd walked in on, she knew they both needed more time to bond. She and Robert would have their time later after she left. Plus she wanted to hear the story about how Margaret had tracked him down.

"No." she said, instinctively reaching out to hold the woman's hands. "You don't have to leave. We would love it if you stayed for dinner. Right, Rob?"

He hesitated, as if giving her time to back out before his mouth split into a big smile. "Yes, please stay, Grandma."

"Thank you, Robert. Thank you both." Her face lit up like a Christmas tree. "It feels so wonderful to be called Grandma after all these years," she said, stepping forward and throwing her arms about them both, squeezing them tightly as if she were afraid to let them go, afraid that they would evaporate into thin air.

Yasmine hugged the dear sweet old woman, her heart warming towards her. She was no mothballs, rubbing alcohol, Bengay-smelling grandmother, either. Nope, Prada was the scent that emanated from Robert's grandmother's skin. Judging from her clothes and her Giuseppe Zanotti peep-toe pumps, she was sophisticated and classy, too. No wonder Robert always acted as if he was too good for the ghetto. All the time she'd thought he was reserved and stuffed shirt, he was just being who he really was: distinguished. Notable. Royal blood ran through his veins.

"I'll tell you what," Margaret said, stepping back. "You two go relax somewhere private in this big house while I finish dinner. I was young once, and from the way you were kissing, I know you're anxious to be alone."

"You don't have to do that," Yasmine spoke up as if she was the woman of the house. Well she was Robert's woman, and this was his house, so... Besides, there was no way in hell she was going to get her freak on with Robert with his grandmother in the house.

"I want to hear all about how you found Robert, or how he found you. He's been researching his past for four years, ever since he found out that the man who raised him wasn't his real father."

"He told me about it just before you walked in. My tears were a mixture of grief at the cruel way my son died, and joy that what I'd heard about him being a drunk, an abusive, negligent father, and a criminal wasn't true."

• • •

Robert buried his face in Yasmine's curls and breathed in her delightful scent. He owed her so much. "We have Yasmine to thank for that," he told his grandmother. "If it weren't for her, I might never have known the truth about that man."

Margaret's forehead crinkled. "Is that how you two met? Yasmine was helping you with the legal case?"

"Oh no," Robert said with a chortle. "Yas and I go way back. We grew up together in the same neighborhood in Manchester. I knew her when she was still pooping and peeing her pants."

Yasmine slugged him playfully. In retaliation, he pulled her in for a slow kiss, and grinned at the flush of embarrassment in her eyes.

Margaret chuckled. "Watching the two of you reminds me so much of my Christian."

"Is that Robert's grandfather?" Yas asked.

Margaret nodded. "He used to make me laugh so hard, I almost peed my pants a few times."

"Dad must have taken after him, then," Robert said, smiling at the memories. "He used to make my mother laugh."

"Then it runs in the family, because Robert is a real comic. You just wait until you get to know him. He'll have you in stitches." Yasmine said.

"I look forward to it."

In the abrupt ensuing silence, Robert could almost hear the questions popping in their minds like corn kernels in the microwave. He was glad that his grandmother and his soon-to-be fiancée had hit it off from the start. It was the way it should be. And it was good to have family—other than his sister who'd grown up with Yas—approve of his choice in a future mate.

"You two go sit and munch on the goodies and catch up while I finish dinner," he said, breaking the silence.

"We can help," Margaret offered.

"Nope. I just have to lay the lasagna and the filling in the pan, stick it in the oven, and finish the salad." He draped his other arm over Margaret's shoulder and led the women to the table, first reseating Margaret, and then Yasmine in the chair on the opposite side of the table. He did it deliberately so he would have the pleasure of watching her face while he worked.

"So you've known Robert all your life," Margaret said, resuming the conversation about his and Yasmine's relationship. "That means you know Michelle."

"Know her?" Robert laughed on his way to the stove. "Those two have been inseparable since first grade."

"Yeah," Yasmine said around a grape. "She's my BFF." She gasped. "Oh my God, she doesn't know yet, does she? I talked with her this morning and I know she would have said something."

"No." Robert sprayed the baking dish.

"You have to call her, Rob." Yasmine jumped up. "She's going to freak out."

"What do you think will happen when I call her?" Robert asked, sending her a meaningful look, hoping she would get his gist. After all, they did have a lot to talk about. He was dying inside to hear Yasmine's declaration of love, but he knew he wouldn't be able to respond in the way he desired without raising questions in his grandmother's mind. As much as he was beginning to like her, to warm to her, she hadn't yet earned the honor of knowing the details of his and Yasmine's relationship. He didn't want anyone judging his girl, or second-guessing her love for him, when he himself didn't.

Yasmine slumped back down in her chair, obviously reading into his thoughts.

"Is there something I'm missing?" Margaret asked, watching them warily.

"If Robert called Michelle, she and the entire LaCrosse gang would be here tonight."

"I get it. You and Robert are already giving up some of your evening to me. As much as I would love to meet Michelle and my great-grandchildren, I can wait one more day. My heart is already half full from spending time with you and Yasmine."

Robert placed the lasagna in the oven and came over to stand behind her chair. "I promise to call Michelle first thing in the morning. Believe me, you need to refuel before the LaCrosse gang descends on you." He squeezed her shoulders affectionately before, moving to the other side to sit beside Yasmine.

His grandmother's smile was a genuinely happy one, the kind Robert hadn't seen since she walked through the door. He gathered Yasmine into his arms, and soaked up the joy of having his grandmother in his life. He was tempted to think his day couldn't get any better, but he knew it would, once Margaret left, and he took Yasmine upstairs to his bed.

"You mentioned that Yasmine was the reason you discovered the man who raised you wasn't your father," Margaret said, reminding Robert that there were still many unanswered questions hanging between them. "How did that come about?"

Robert kissed Yasmine on the forehead, and then for the next half hour, he tried to fill in the sixty-year gap for Margaret, starting with his suppressed, yet happy memories of living in Richmond with his parents before the night his father was killed —the last time he'd heard his voice under his window. He spoke of the long bus trip to Manchester, the day his mother went to the hospital and died while giving birth to Michelle, how he'd had to step up and take care of his baby sister by working as a child to buy food so they didn't starve. He told her about Gleason killing Erik's first wife, how he stole Michelle's money and almost completely destroyed her. He told her how Yasmine's suspicions got him to thinking and about the letter addressed to Timmy Gleason—the way he learned about his father's stabbing death. He spoke about the DNA test that set him free from the

shame and the curse of Timmy Gleason, and he shared the information the detective had given him about his father's cremation.

When he finished, tears were rolling down all their cheeks.

"What a horrible, horrible childhood you had because of that man," Margaret said in a choked voice. "And your poor mother —I can't imagine the pain she must have suffered from watching her husband being murdered in front of her, knowing there was nothing she could do for him. If only I'd had the courage to search for my son earlier. I should have run away from my father, fought to keep my baby and find his father so we could raise him together. If I'd only been strong, I would have spared you and Michelle from the abuse you suffered as children, and my son might still be alive. I failed him. I failed all of you."

Robert rushed around the table, dropped to his knees, and wrapped his arms around his grandmother. He had a truckload of regrets of his own. He should have remembered the details of that night earlier, told the authorities about his suspicions, and protected Michelle from Timmy Gleason. He wished his suppressed memories had been evoked by the time he went to see Timmy in jail. Robert knew without a doubt that he would have choked that man with his bare hands with the entire jail population looking on. And when he did remember the events of that fateful night, Robert knew if Timmy Gleason was still alive, Robert would have gutted him like fish and left him to die in one of Manchester's back alleyways, just like the son of a bitch had killed Dwight Carter.

"I'm sorry, Robert. I'm so sorry for being weak," Margaret sobbed against his shoulder.

"It's okay, Grandma. You did what you needed to do to survive," he said, pushing back the dull ache in his belly. Yas was now crouched down behind him, holding him as he held his grandmother. And as they gave in to the sadness and regrets,

Robert made a conscious decision to dwell on the present and the future, and not the past.

"It's all in the past," he said, voicing his thoughts. "My childhood experiences helped shape me into the man I am today. And," he added, catching Yasmine's fingers between his, "Gleason's actions brought us to New Hampshire. If it weren't for him, I would not have met this amazingly beautiful, gorgeous, intelligent woman whom I love with all my heart and soul." He kissed Yasmine's hand, and his heart rocked against his chest when she smiled down at him through teary eyes.

"And Michelle would not have met Erik, the love of her life," Yasmine said.

"So you see, it all turned out right in the end," Robert said, lifting his grandmother's head from his shoulder and smiling into her eyes. He loved her.

Margaret sniffled. "Well, I guess it does bring me a measure of comfort if you look at it that way."

"There's no other way to look at it," Robert said, rising to his feet and pulling Yasmine up with him.

"What about your mother's family?" Margaret asked. "Have you been able to find them?"

"Not yet. Her past is as mysterious as Daddy's. She also grew up in foster care. I suspect that's how they met."

"I have a slew of detectives at my beck and call, the best in the south, and I will have my personal assistant call every one of them when I get back to my hotel room tonight," Margaret promised. "Do you have a birth certificate or some other form of identity I can use as a launching pad?"

Robert shook his head. "Everything my parents owned up to the night my dad was murdered was left in the apartment. I have no idea what happened to their belongings."

"Not even a picture of Dwight," she asked on a hopeful note.

Robert shook his head. "I'm sorry, Grandma."

Margaret patted his hand. "I'm sure there are photos somewhere. We will find them, and your mother's family. I would like to know more about the woman who captured my son's heart, who loved him, and bore him two beautiful, intelligent children." She kissed the palm of his hand, a contented smile on her face.

The timer went off, and Robert excused himself to put the finishing touches on the salad. Soon they moved into the dining room where he and Yas brought Margaret up to speed about her granddaughter, Michelle, Michelle's husband, Erik, and their kids—Margaret's great-grandchildren. As they talked about his sister's marriage, Robert couldn't wait to begin his with Yasmine.

Each time their eyes collided across the table, he was reminded of the night in Amherst, five years ago, when they couldn't wait for dinner to be over so they could give in to the desires of their flesh. And like that first time, tonight they would be making love all night long.

The only difference would be that tonight they would be giving in to the desires of their hearts and souls, as well as their flesh, and when they made love, Yasmine would be gazing deep into his eyes as she told him over and over again how much she loved him.

Robert's heart trembled from the rush of passion, love, and happiness rolling around inside him. Now, he understood what the billionaires had been talking about all this time, what it meant to be loved by that one special woman out of all other women in the entire universe.

CHAPTER THIRTEEN

"I love her, Robert. I really do. She's a sweet old lady." Yasmine squeezed Robert's hand as they stood at his front door, waving, until the taillights of Margaret's cab disappeared up the street.

Robert pulled her inside and closed the door. He folded her into his arms and gave her that lover-boy look, the kind of look that made Yasmine's flesh melt off her bones. If he weren't holding on to her, she would have slithered to the floor in a helpless pile. The man had too much power over her, a blessing and curse.

"Yes, she is sweet, and I love her too," he said in a deep throaty voice, "but you're sweeter. I love you more." He picked her up and placed her on the cushioned bench in the foyer. Then before Yasmine could protest, he'd pulled her shorts and her panties off her waist and down her legs and had swiped her blouse and bra over her head and tossed them on the floor. She stood naked on the bench in front of him with her shorts and panties at her ankles, her nipples tightening into little dark pebbles, and moisture oozing from between the folds of her womanhood, dampening the dark curls at her groin.

"Hmm," he moaned, his gaze sweeping hungrily over her, as he trailed a finger across her breasts. "So sweet." He dipped his head and licked at her nipples, one at a time, rolling his tongue over each, sending sharp zings of desire racing though Yasmine's system.

Shocked at her own eager response to him so soon after his grandmother's departure, Yasmine tried to talk sense into her own head. *No, No*, her mind screamed. *You need to talk to him about your baby before this, or you won't be able to, and you need to. You have to.*

"Rob, I— Rob, we can't— We have to—" She grabbed his shoulders as her body began to tremble and she became lightheaded. "Talk— Talk…"

"Shhh. Later. We had dinner. Now we have dessert. Then we'll talk. I need my dessert." He stood back and shrugged out of his clothes in record time. "See what you did, sweetness?" he murmured, pointing to his enormous rock-hard cock, smooth and thick with engorged pulsing veins running the length of it. It was lying smack against his six-pack, the broad mushroom tip already oiled and ready for some serious drilling.

Talk. Talk! her mind screamed again.

"I've been dying to do this all during dinner," he said, dropping to his knees in front of her, his face at her groin, his nose sniffing out her scent like an animal in the wild, his hot breath tickling the damp hairs of her Venus mound as he lifted her feet one at a time, freeing her from the restrictions of her clothes. "Reminds me of a night five years ago when we couldn't keep our eyes off each other during dinner, and when our hands were itching to explore all the secret hills and crevices of each other's body," he whispered as his warm hands caressed the tingling skin of her calves before sliding up her legs and thighs on their way to her buttocks. He clasped her in his palms and drew her closer.

"Oh God," Yasmine cried, as she felt his hot tongue slice

through the folds of her sex, the tip making connection with her engorged clitoris. She grabbed his shoulders as her knees buckled.

"Oh Goddess," he whispered, taking another swipe at her with his tongue, fluttering it lightly against the sensitive flesh just inside her folds, the tantalizing movements sending little humming vibrations straight between her legs and deep into her groin, her belly. He angled his head, dipped lower, pressed against the opening of her womanhood, pushed his tongue into her body, back and forth, in and out, twirling it around inside her until she began to buck against his mouth, her stomach heaving and her breath coming out in quick little gasps.

Yasmine dug her nails into Robert's shoulders and screamed out his name as her desire reached fever pitch, but just before her volcano erupted, he dragged his tongue from inside her, lifted her effortlessly up from the bench, dropped his weight onto it and settled her on his lap, her hot pulsing sex pressed into the ridge of his shaft. "Hold me," he whispered.

Overtaken with love and lust, Yasmine obediently wound her arms around his neck and her legs around his waist, as his face lazily inched its way across the charged space between them. His breathing was jagged, his breath hot and heavily scented with her woman's fragrance, turning her on by her own scent. Using the tip of his nose, he grazed her cheeks in a slow teasing motion up one side of her face, his warm smooth lips following in its wake to kiss her cheekbones, the bridge of her nose, her eyelids, her brows, her forehead, and back down the other side to the corner of her trembling mouth, where he hesitated before nibbling, withdrawing, nibbling, withdrawing as if tasting her consistency.

When she opened her mouth in a moan of ecstasy, he slid his tongue inside and strummed her, sucking, and twirling his tongue around hers, as he rocked his hips against her, his passion growing stronger as he aroused hers until the blood pounded in her brain, scattering all thought of the secret she'd been ready to confess.

"Yeah, just like that," he whispered in his deep sexy voice as he released her mouth and trailed his sizzling lips down her neck, across her bare shoulder, nibbling on her burning flesh. "We'll be making love all night, Yas, just like the first night. You remember that, baby, huh? God, I love you."

He reclaimed her mouth, kissing her deeply and devouringly as his hands clasped her buttocks, and he lifted her slightly up enough to angle the tip of his cock to the entrance of her sex. He pushed upward as he pulled her down and instantly began to thrust inside her, pushing with slow, drugging strokes until she began to quiver. When the fire inside her burned too hot to be contained, she threw her head back, thrashing on her man helplessly.

He groaned, gripped her hips and pumped her frantically up and down the length of him, dropped his head to her chest, and sucked her tender swelling breasts, moving from one to the other like a hungry confused man who couldn't make up his mind as to which mound of flesh brought him the most pleasure.

Deeper, higher, hotter, harder, his cock rammed into her. Yasmine gasped and gasped and gasped as the core of her sex began contracting violently around Robert's cock, gripping, sucking, churning the fire inside her, speeding her along to a shuddering ecstasy.

"Oh, Yas. Oh God, I'm coming. I'm here." With one last powerful thrust, Robert locked their sexes together, then just as she felt the hot load of his cum shooting into her womb, a powerful gush of love juices came pouring out of her secret place, drenching every inch of his pulsing cock buried deep inside her.

They clung to each other, shivering as the waves of their orgasm washed over them.

Always the first to relax, Robert cradled her on his lap, stroking her gently until she came down from her high. "I had this evening all planned out," he said huskily. "This was supposed to come later, upstairs in bed. This is how crazy you make me, Yasmine Reynolds. I could spend my entire life making love to you every minute of every day, and it still wouldn't be enough. I get a natural high just knowing I can make you come in a minute."

Even though her body still yearned for the intensity of his passion, Yasmine pressed her chin into the muscles of his shoulder, squeezed her eyes shut, and bit her lips to stifle the cry of guilt and pain creeping up on her. She wanted so badly to revel in the pleasure of her aftermath, even fall asleep like she usually did, but that luxury was not hers to have tonight.

She longed to tell him that she loved him right here, right now, but she knew the minute the words left her mouth, they would end up making love again—all night long—and tomorrow she would leave without telling him, and then as time dragged on and he got more and more enthralled with his grandmother, her fear would return and she would bury her secret again.

The passion they just shared might be their last, but it was a risk she had to take. Their hour of truth was now. It was time she found out if theirs was the kind of love that could weather any storm.

That's what you though of your parents' marriage and look what's happening to them, the insecure voice in her head admonished. *You can keep your secret and still have what you have right now. You heard Michelle. Robert's in it for the long haul. He will wait for you forever. Maybe this is as good as it will get. And face it, girl. It's good. You don't need perfect. Do you want to risk something sure for something that might be better? Your mother...*

No! It would be easy to use her parents' marriage as another excuse not to come clean with Robert, but Yasmine knew it would only serve to push her back into her prison of doubts and fears. She'd busted out, and she wasn't going back. With or without Robert's love, she was determined to hold on to her freedom.

Yasmine lifted her head from Robert's shoulder and tried to smile at him. "Rob, we have to talk."

He kissed her lips, grinning like a schoolboy who'd just kissed his first crush for the first time. "Yes I know, but I think we have to clean up first."

Yasmine glanced down to the apex of their thighs to where their mixture of love juices was oozing from between their joined sexes. "Yeah. Hold still." Yasmine reached toward the nearby table and pulled a box of tissues close. She pulled out a few and handed them to Robert. "I'll disengage. You mop."

"I love this kind of teamwork," he said, laughing.

Yasmine ignored the arousing sensations the echo of his laughter caused to her innards and carefully eased off him, giving him enough space to work. Like a pro, he caught every last drop. She stood to her feet and when he got up to dispose of the tissues, Yasmine hastily pulled on her shorts and shirt, not even bothering with her underwear.

"Wow, that was fast," he said.

"I need buffer against you, Robert. I can't think when our clothes are off."

"We don't need to think tonight," he said, coming to stand way too close to her, the heat from his beautiful naked body doing stuff to her mind again. Yasmine picked up his pants and handed them to him. "Put these on."

"Yes, ma'am," he said with a mischievous twinkle in his eyes, as he pulled them on and reached for his shirt. "Wait here." He disappeared into the dining room, and before she could count to ten, he returned with one hand behind his back.

He took her left hand, got down on his knees in front of her and gazed devotedly at her. "This is the way I was supposed to greet you when you first arrived, but we were sidetracked."

Yasmine's heart started jumping so violently she feared it would leap out of her chest. "What—what are you doing, Robert? Is—is this a proposal?"

His expression of excitement turned to irritation. "Can't you let a brother do anything right, Yasmine? No, it's not a proposal. I've learned not to throw those out lightly," he added, his voice dripping with humor. "When I do propose again, I want it to be the right setting. You know me, I'm a romantic."

Yasmine ran her thumb across his lips. "If it's not a ring, what are you hiding behind your back?"

He brought his hand forward. "It's a rose for my number-one bachelorette." His smile was seductive, laced with the devotion he'd shown her since they began seeing each other. "I choose you, Yasmine Marie Reynolds, because you complete me. You make me feel special, wanted, even though not needed," he added, his lips curling in humor. "I love that you're independent and stubborn even though it makes me mad as hell sometimes. But I realize that the things that make me mad at you are the very things that make me mad about you. Listening to my grandmother speak about my grandfather and how she regretted not going after him, not fighting for their love, I realize that I want you in my life however way I can have you. If this is all we have, then so be it. The thing is, I love you, and I know you love me. We don't need a piece of paper to prove it. All we have to do is look into each other's eyes, to touch each other, and love floods every cell in our bodies and pours out of every pore of our skin. I know our past has been rocky, but I promise that I will do everything in my power to make our future smooth. Wherever our path leads, we'll walk it together.

"This right here," he said, pointing to the bench where they'd just made love, "is what we are about. From now on, every time we enter or leave this house, this little corner right here will remind us what we mean to each other. This is our Love Cove. So, Yasmine Marie Reynolds, please accept this rose as a token of my devotion and commitment to you."

"Oh, Robert." Yasmine placed her hand over her mouth to stop from crying out, but she could do nothing about the tears in her eyes. "You're so sweet. And you deserve so much more than what I've been giving you." She took the rose and pressed the crimson petals to her nose, inhaling the sweet fragrance, willing it to diffuse the nauseous feeling that was quickly taking up the space where passion had been spinning a few minutes ago.

Robert was so used to sacrificing what *he* wanted, just to make others happy. She supposed it was a habit he'd developed at an early age when he had to take care of Michelle. He never had the luxury of being a child. He'd become a man at five years old, the day his mother died and left him and his baby sister at the mercies of a murderer.

He wanted to be the kind of father his real father had been, with a wife who was committed and devoted to him, and children he could love and pamper like his real parents used to pamper him. He wanted that kind of family, and he wanted her to be part of it so much that he was willing to compromise his own principles of having children out of wedlock.

The coward part of Yasmine wanted to hang on to his beautiful words and the ecstasy they just shared, take his hand, and walk into the sunset with him. To let sleeping dogs lie. It wasn't like he would ever find out about their child. But the noble part of her knew it was not the route to take—not anymore. It was time she put on her big girl panties and climbed out of the playpen.

He rubbed his knuckles against her cheek, making her jump. "Hey. Come back."

Drawing in a breath of resolve, Yasmine tugged gently on his hand, bringing him to his feet as she rose to hers. "I have to tell you something, Robert," she said, before she lost her nerve. "But you might want to sit down." She picked up her purse from the table where she'd placed it when she first arrived and had heard the sobs coming from the kitchen.

"Why do I feel like my world is about to come crashing down on me?" he asked, as she led him over to the sofa.

Because it might. It was cruel of her to drop this on him when he was so happy about finding his grandmother. She wanted to let him enjoy his newfound filial connection, but she wasn't going to lie to him any longer.

"Yas." Panic edged his voice as she pushed him down on one end. "We need distance, too?" he asked, when she sat on the other end and placed the rose on the glass-top coffee table.

"If I sit near you, I won't be able to go through with this."

"*This?* What is *this?* Should I be worried?"

"I don't know," she answered honestly. *But I am.*

"Yas." He made an attempt to slide across the sofa.

"First off," she said, raising her hand to stop him. "I need to tell you the name of the other man I slept with. My first."

"I already know," he said, settling his back against the arm of the sofa, and bringing his feet up on to it.

She scowled. "You knew all this time?"

He crossed his arms. "Just since Saturday night. Michelle let it slip during a phone conversation. She said you broke up because he got a promotion in another town or something like that."

Her scowl deepened. "Michelle just upped and slipped, or

were you fishing for information after I refused to give up his name?"

"I was fishing," he said dryly. "Other than your string of messed-up clients, I wanted to know if your ex had done something to hurt you and make you afraid to commit to a relationship. I thought he might be the reason you still can't tell me that you love me."

"He did hurt me and yes he was one of the several reasons I couldn't commit, or open my heart to you."

His face contorted with agony, his eyes sharp with concern. "What did he do to you? You told me you loved him a couple days ago, and when I asked, you didn't deny that you'd stopped."

Yasmine inhaled sharply. "I said I *thought* I loved him. Anyway, when I told him, he dumped me. He moved out of town to get away from me."

"That's just plain mean and immature."

"It was a blessing. I later found out that he'd been cheating on me with the woman he married just six months after he dumped me."

"Jerk." He spat the words out vehemently.

She pulled her legs up under her, and leaned back into the arm of the sofa. "When Jeremy and I first began dating, I overheard a conversation between his parents. They didn't think I was good enough for him. They wanted more for him than the poor, uneducated girl from the ghetto. They were worried I would get pregnant and trap him into an unwanted marriage."

Robert's nostrils flared with fury and his chest rose and fell on a deep breath. "Seriously? They actually said those things about you?"

Yasmine nodded.

He dipped his head to the side, his brown eyes sharp and assessing. "You don't have low self-esteem, Yasmine. You never did. So why'd you stay with Jeremy, knowing how his parents felt about you?"

Yasmine shrugged. "Lots of parents disapprove of their children's love interests. It wasn't about them. It was about me and Jeremy. I wanted to prove them wrong, show them that I could be good enough for their son. I started taking more classes and worked two jobs to afford an apartment. Jeremy began spending more time with me than at home with his parents. I guess that's when I began telling myself that I was in love with him, and he with me. I mean, he was my first, my one and only at the time. I thought that meant something to him. I was the perfect girlfriend. I did everything he wanted, even sacrificing my own needs to make him happy."

A light flickered in his eyes, and Yasmine could almost hear him thinking, *like I'm doing*, but he said nothing.

"Anyway, one night, I planned a romantic evening for us. I cooked a nice dinner, had flowers and candles—the works—and later after we made love, I told him that I loved him." Yasmine shook away the memories with a toss of her head.

"You've always been liberal with your feelings." His tone was without malice, almost apologetic.

Don't I know it? "Jeremy said nothing. He just eased out of my arms, got out of my bed, put on his clothes, looked at me like I was a puppy needing its head rubbed, and walked out the door. He stopped taking my calls, and then two months later, he moved out of Manchester. It was over, just like that, no explanation, no nothing. Then six months later, he was married to someone else."

"Oh, Yas. I'm sorry you were hurt like that."

"Between you and Jeremy, and then what happened between Michelle and Erik, I was just scared of putting my heart out there again, you know?"

He nodded, his lips pressed tightly and his eyes sad and misty with the memory. "You know why I acted that way that night, right? It wasn't because I didn't want you. I did. God help me, I did, but—"

"I know, Rob. I put you in a bad position, and for a long time I was mad at you. But now I understand why you reacted that way. You were looking out for me. You were protecting me, saving me from myself, and I appreciate you not taking advantage of my immaturity."

"Yeah, just so Arsie could hurt you," he said in a harsh, raw voice. His eyes swept her face. "Did you see him in Manchester this weekend? Is this what all this is about?"

"I saw his father. He was visiting Mr. George and practically chased me up Naomi's steps to talk to me. He showed me a picture of Jeremy and his daughter, and hinted that Jeremy and I should get back together after his divorce."

"What did you tell him?" he asked quietly.

"What do you think I told him?"

"Knowing you, I don't have to imagine," he said with a soft smile.

"Robert, for the past six years, I was locked up in this prison of inadequacy and fear of failure. I even thought I wasn't good enough for you. I told Mr. Arsenault off. I gave him a piece of my mind, and when I was done, the bars around my heart just snapped and I was able to breathe. I could see things clearly. I wasn't scared anymore, and that's when I sent you that text. I remembered your warning when I left that you weren't going to wait for me forever—"

"Yas, I was just kidding. I'll wait for you forever if I have to."

Yes, Michelle told me. Yasmine glanced at the rose, a reminder of his devotion and the love they'd just shared. "That's the thing, Rob, you shouldn't have to. I was going to call you, but I didn't want to get into it over the phone. Besides, I want to be gazing into your eyes when I finally say those words out loud to you."

"That's how I envisioned it, too." The warmth of his smile echoed in his voice. "So I'm kind of glad you didn't call me."

"I was all set to get down on my knees and tell you how much you mean to me, and beg your forgiveness for keeping you hanging for so long, but then—" She spread her hands. "Your grandmother was here."

His eyes twinkled in the light from the floor lamp behind the sofa. "I had plans for us too. I was to meet you at the door with the rose, pick you up, carry you upstairs to the Jacuzzi filled with bubbles where we would have sipped wine, nibbled on cheese, strawberries, and raw oysters by candlelight while the lasagna was baking."

Yasmine's heart ached with longing, but she was glad Margaret's presence had waylaid his plans. She couldn't think straight when Robert was lavishing attention on her, and if he'd been able to see his plan through, they wouldn't be having this crucial conversation. The only reason she was able to tell him now was that they hadn't made it up the stairs. What they just did at the door was a hot, raunchy quickie—appetizers, as Robert liked to call those frenzied episodes. But his second courses were long and intoxicating.

"Yas, I don't want you to ever think you're not good enough for anybody, and that includes me." He began to scoot across the sofa toward her.

She raised her hands to stop him. "We're not done yet, Rob."

His brows flickered, and he settled back down, seemingly disappointed that he couldn't hold her after such a heartrending catharsis. "You did say there were several reasons you couldn't tell me you loved me."

Yasmine's stomach knotted and her courage wilted under Robert's scrutinizing stare. The magnitude of her actions had become more poignant as she'd listened to Margaret talk about how she'd been forced to give up her baby, when she herself hadn't wanted hers. In the next few moments, she would know if Robert still meant all those wonderful things he'd said to her when he'd given her the rose.

She reached for her purse, pulled out the envelope she'd stopped at home to pick up before coming here, and without looking at it, she leaned forward and handed it to Robert.

"I've been keeping this from you," she said, and then got off the sofa, crossed her arms around her middle and waited for him to explode.

CHAPTER FOURTEEN

A horde of confusing thoughts and feelings washed over Robert as he took the envelope from Yasmine. He had no idea what to expect. After what she'd told him, he just wanted to gather her into his arms and show her how worthy, how loved she was. And that asshole Arsie was due a punch in the face for the way he'd treated her, and for keeping her from moving forward with her life for five wasted years. He and Yas could have been married already and had a couple kids, kids who would have been bouncing on their great-grandmother's lap today. He was going to find Arsie and teach him a lesson for hurting his girl.

With trembling fingers, Robert opened the envelope and pulled out a thin piece of paper. He gasped as he stared at the photo. Not in a million years would he have been prepared for what he saw. He jumped off the sofa and rushed over, gazing down at her, staring at her arms hugging her stomach as his anxiety turned to excitement. "You're pregnant?"

She shook her head. "No, Rob. I'm not pregnant."

He held up the paper. "Then whose sonogram is this? Why are you showing it to me?"

"It's mine. But it's—it's four years old."

"Four years old?" He stared at the sonogram again. "We were together then."

"Yes, we were," she whispered.

He wasn't going to ask if it was his. Yasmine wasn't the type of woman who would step out on her man, but it blew his mind that she'd waited this long to tell him. "What happened to the baby? Did you have an abortion?" *Please say no.* The thought of his child, a child who was… He glanced at the photo again…ten weeks and four days old being poked in the skull by steel instruments and ripped from its mother's womb was unbearable to even imagine. *Not his child.* "Where's our baby, Yasmine?"

"I lost it. I had a miscarriage."

"You lost it?" He closed his eyes to absorb the information. It wasn't any less comforting than if she'd told him she'd had an abortion. "Why didn't you tell me about it?"

"I wanted to Robert. I wanted to." She sniffled and wiped her nose with the back of her hand. "But you weren't there."

"What do you mean I wasn't there? We were together then."

She shook her head. "Look at the date."

He studied the sonogram. Searing pain tackled his gut and made its way up to his chest, gripping his heart, almost choking him. "I wasn't there," he said in a broken whisper.

She shook her head again. "It was right after Michelle and Erik got married and after Little Erik was born. You'd started seeing Dr. West and she was helping you recall your childhood memories about your real father. You were going through a deep depression."

Tears were pouring down her face and she was rocking back and forth on her heels as if she was stuck in that sad lonely period of her life. "You started pulling away from me. I wanted to be there for you. I wanted to tell you about our baby, but you abandoned me at a time when I needed you most of all. You were spending a lot of time with Lani. I thought the two of you were getting back together. And on top of that, I felt like you were blaming me for evoking your memories and making you relive the night your real father was killed. You broke my heart and my trust and my hope for us all over again."

Robert dropped the photo on the coffee table and pulled her into his arms. "I'm sorry, Yas. I'm sorry," he said, tears rolling off his face and into her hair. He cried for the pain he'd caused her, and the loneliness she must have felt at the most delicate time of her life. He cried for the child they'd created from their love, but for whatever reason hadn't made it into the world.

"I didn't mean to abandon you, Yas. It wasn't my intention at all. The time I was spending with Lani was about expanding my practice. I needed something to distract me from what was really going on in my head."

"What was going on in your head that you couldn't share with me?"

"I was feeling like a failure for not knowing what my mother had been going through, the constant fear she must have been under trying to protect me and her unborn child. I felt like it was her anxiety that killed her in childbed. I blamed myself for not remembering sooner. I never blamed you, darling. I love you for giving me back my memories, but at the same time I felt as if I didn't deserve your love because I was a failure."

She pushed a little away and gazed up at him, her eyes red from her crying. "You forgot in order to protect your mom and your sister."

And here she was standing up for him, defending him when he'd abandoned her at the most difficult time of her life. "I should have remembered after she died. There was no reason to avoid the memory. Timmy couldn't hurt her anymore."

"You were a child, Robert. You'd just lost your mom, and you had a little baby sister to take care of. Timmy Gleason still had the power to hurt you. He'd killed your father. Your mother kept quiet to keep herself and you and Michelle safe and alive. If you'd remembered back then, he would have known, and he would have killed you and maybe Michelle to keep from going to prison. Your loss of memory is what kept you both alive."

"Miserable."

"Alive."

"I should have protected Michelle. She shouldn't have had to endure slaps across her face and her back, or punches in her stomach by that piece of shit. It was my job as the man of the family to protect her after our mother died, but I failed. I felt worthless as a man. It's a man's job to protect the women in his life, the women he loves. I not only failed my mother and Michelle, I failed you, too. I forced you to carry around this burden for four years. Is that why you turned down my proposals?"

She pulled away completely and put distance between them again by walking over to a window and gazing down on the street below. "Kind of. I was afraid to trust you with my heart again, but I really did want to finish school, like I said when you proposed the first time. And the second time, I did want to be established in my career. I wanted all the credit for my success to come to me, so no one could say I wasn't worth it."

"You were still trying to prove the Arsenaults wrong."

"Yes." She looked away briefly. "But mainly, it was because of this secret."

"Honey," he said, closing the distance between them. "I would have understood. You didn't have to bear this burden alone all this time."

She nibbled on her bottom lip and then dropped her gaze. "There's more."

"More?" He cupped her chin, raising her face and her gaze.

"I knew that when I finally came around to telling you that I lost our baby, I would have to explain why and how."

"What are you saying?"

"I didn't want our baby, Robert. I was going to have an abortion."

He dropped his hand and stepped back. "You didn't want our child? You were going to abort it?"

"Yes, but the day before the appointment, I knew I couldn't go through with it, so I called and canceled. But the next morning, I woke up with excruciating stomach cramps. Really hard contractions that sent me running to the bathroom. Our baby was gone, just like that. It left me."

"Mind over matter, Yasmine. You were going to kill it. It saved you the trouble."

"I canceled, Robert. I canceled. I couldn't do it. I wouldn't have done it."

"Thinking about an abortion is bad enough, Yasmine, but going through the trouble to make the appointment takes determination." Ice spread through his stomach. "It must give you peace of mind to sleep at nights."

"I don't have peace about it, Robert. Every time I see a baby or hear one cry, my heart hurts, and I get this empty hollow feeling inside me, especially when I see you with your nieces and nephew. That's why I couldn't be present for any more of Michelle's children's births. My arms constantly ache to hold our child."

Robert closed his eyes briefly and sucked air into his lungs. "Then why didn't you want it, Yasmine? Why?" His voice was unusually calm, even to his own ears. But maybe it wasn't calmness. Maybe it was finality. Maybe this was it for them.

"It wasn't the right time for me. I was in school, and you weren't there. You'd left me. You wouldn't even speak to me. You'd shut me out."

His sister had been pregnant with Erik's child when Erik wasn't there, and never once did she think of aborting her baby. His grandmother had been pregnant with his father, and even though her racist pig of a father chased her baby's father away, she never thought of aborting her child. But he couldn't voice his thoughts to Yasmine. He didn't want her to feel any more horrible than she already felt, but he nevertheless needed time to deal with the fact that she didn't want his child, that she was going to abort it.

He clenched his jaws as he stared at her, the pain in his heart and his gut becoming a sick and fiery gnawing. "I need time, Yasmine. I need time to accept the fact that you didn't want my child, that you were going to kill it. At this point, I don't even know if I, if we—" He stopped. The thought of them being over crushed him to powder. He turned and walked away. It just hurt too much to look at her.

"No. No. Robert. Robert. Rob…"

Robert halted in his tracks, his chest burning as if his lungs had been squashed inside his ribcage. Sudden darkness descended around him, paralyzing him. He'd heard that cry before. That agonizing wail, as if her world had had just come to an end, and she had nothing more to live for. *Where? When?*

"Robert. Robert. Rob…"

He shivered at Yasmine's heartrending sobs behind him. *What was he doing?* Only minutes ago, he'd gotten down on his knees in front of her and told her that she meant everything to him. He'd promised her that he would be there for her, make their path to the future much smoother than the path from their past. He'd taken his grandmother's advice about sacrificing and compromising and fighting for love, holding on to it at all cost.

And at the first hurdle in the road, he was proving himself untrustworthy, just like he'd done four years ago. They'd already wasted five years, and he wasn't about to lose anymore. He wasn't about to let pride keep him from going where his heart needed to be—with Yasmine. He wasn't going to take the chance that another opportunity to love her would come along again. It might not. He had Yasmine now. He was keeping Yasmine. He was loving Yasmine.

Robert turned around to see her huddled on the floor, her face in her hands as she sobbed hysterically. He raced across the room, fell to the floor, and gathered Yasmine into his arms. "I'm here, Yas. I'm here. You don't ever have to feel alone again. I love you, and I will always be here for you. I promise."

"I thought you hated me. I wanted to die. I felt like I'd died when you walked away."

"No, sweetie. Not you. I hate myself for abandoning you and making you think that your only choice was to abort our baby."

"I'm sorry."

"Me, too. Me too." His heart was ripping apart as he thought of the little child he would never know, would never hold, but whom he would love nonetheless. It was a part of him and Yasmine, and that's all that mattered.

"I'm sorry I thought about aborting our baby, Robert," she said after a long while. "I just felt so alone. All I could think about was that conversation I overheard between Mr. and Mrs. Arsenault all those years ago. I didn't want to make you feel trapped with an unwanted child. I didn't have anyone to talk to. Michelle had just gotten married and Naomi and Felix were going through a tough time. I couldn't talk to my parents. My father would…"

"Shhh. Shhh." He slowly brushed his hands up and down her back. "It's all in the past. We're on the road to our future. We're in this together, good or bad, easy or hard. I'm not letting it get between us. We'll make it a part of us, find a way to grieve the loss and honor the memory of our child together. Okay?"

She nodded against his chest then lifted her head. Her

beautiful brown eyes were bright, genuine, compelling, sexy, as she gazed into his. "I love you, Robert. I've loved you all my life. I love you so much my heart aches every time I think of you. I'm sorry it took me so long to say it. I want to marry you and have your babies. However many you want. I'll give up my career, and stay home with them and cook and clean if that's what you want me to do. I want to spend the rest of my life with you, showing you how much you mean to me. I love you. I love you."

She struggled to her knees and held his large hands in her trembling delicate ones as a fresh batch of tears slid from under her lids. "Robert Javier Carter, will you marry me, please?"

"Yes. Yes. I'll marry you, Yasmine Marie Reynolds." His laugh was one of rapture. "Oh Yas. I'm the happiest man alive, and you don't have to give up your career and stay home and cook and clean. We'll work out the details when we cross that bridge. I'm just happy we've finally arrived at this most monumental moment in our relationship. I want to shout it from the top of the John Hancock Tower. Which reminds me," he added, pushing his hand into his back pocket and pulling out a black velvet box and flipping it open with one hand. His heart did a quantum leap to his throat at the euphoria, the surprise, the joy and excitement in her eyes.

"Oh my God, Rob!" she screamed as her eyes widened at the humongous eighteen-carat, princess-cut diamond, shooting slivers of sparkles every which way across the room. "It's even bigger than the previous two." She stared at the ring as if it were the forbidden fruit, beguiling, yet out of reach.

Robert shrugged. "I thought you might be holding out for a bigger one."

"I would have been happy with the first one, and that was ten carats."

Robert began easing his hand behind him. "I'm so glad you

said that, 'cause this cost me a couple fortunes. I still have time to re—"

She snatched his arm. "Gimme that. I'm worth it. You know it," she said, grinning seductively at him, her sadness giving way to joy.

"Yes, I know it, especially when you threatened to quit your career and stay home with our kids."

"Hmmm. I might have to keep my career now. Help you wit de bills, you know I'm sayin'?"

Robert grinned at her comical expression. "I have a rich grandmother, so we're good."

She chuckled, causing him to catch his breath. "When did you buy it?"

"Yesterday. After your text Friday, I knew it was just a matter of time, and I wanted to be prepared. Much sooner than I dreamed." He was grinning so hard, his mouth hurt. He placed the box on the floor and pried the ring from its slot, then turned his palm up for her left hand.

She was trembling so hard when he slipped the ring on her finger, he had to hold her firmly. Or maybe they were both trembling. "Perfect fit," he said, smiling into her eyes as he raised her hand to his mouth and kissed the ring. "I love you."

"I love you."

Robert gathered her close until their hearts beat as one, then he bent his head and covered her mouth in a deep kiss, sealing their love and devotion and commitment to each other. He struggled to his feet without breaking the kiss.

And then Robert Carter, the neat freak who couldn't go to bed until his dinner table was cleared, his dirty dishes stacked in the dishwasher, his counters wiped down, his floor mopped, his entire house immaculately tidied, walked up the stairs carrying Yasmine Reynolds, his most delicate rose, his most cherished diamond to his master suite. He gave no thought to their undergarments scattered on the floor in the foyer, or to the cluttered dining table, or the mess he'd left in the kitchen. At least the leftovers had been placed in the fridge a while ago. But he wouldn't have cared about that either.

Ninety minutes later, after they'd soaked in the Jacuzzi, and the musky fragrance of the bubbles lingered on their skin, Robert lay Yasmine down on his great big king size bed, and by candlelight, he worshipped her, kissing his way up and down her body, taking his time to pleasure every inch of her skin, every soft curve, every hidden crevice. He licked her in forbidden places he'd never licked before, nibbled on newly discovered erogenous zones she didn't even know she had. He played her like a musical note, and smiled as she danced in the candlelight, her caramel body heaving under him, bucking and shivering, drenching his satin sheets, as he awakened the desires in her like they'd never been awakened before, making her cry out his name, sigh out her ecstasy, moan out her pleasure as he lavished her with his love.

She was sopping wet, tightly wound, and bubbling like a volcano when he finally spread her wide, mounted her, and loved her into the night.

"Oh dear God," he cried, throwing back his head in sweet agony as his cock head seemed to disintegrate as it passed through the entrance of her burning inferno.

He never knew a woman could be this hot, this slick and this sweet. Lucky for him, it was his woman, and he was the only man allowed to feast at her table of love.

CHAPTER FIFTEEN

R obert was on cloud nine on Monday when he walked through the door of Carter, Obryan & Levitt Orthodontics in the heart of Government Center.

"Good morning, Barbara," he said to his receptionist sitting behind the long, free-flowing reception desk that separated her from the waiting area.

"Good morning, Dr. Carter." She glanced at the clock on the wall. "You don't have any appointments this morning, or did I miss something?" she added, as she scrambled to open up his schedule on her computer.

"Relax, Barbara." He walked around to her side. It was still too early for the first patients, but Barbara's and the other two receptionists' days began an hour earlier than the first appointment of the day. He was sure Gloria and Troy, Vaughn and Lani's personal receptionists, were already at their desks, or would be soon. He pulled a chair up beside Barbara and motioned for her to continue to his schedule.

"See, your first patient comes in at one," she said, relief hanging off her voice, as she gave his attire a once-over. "I should have known you weren't here to work. You're wearing jeans when you always wear a suit."

"Hmm." Robert squinted at his schedule. "I'll be away today and tomorrow morning, so I need you to divvy up my patients between Dr. Levitt and Dr. Obryan."

She gave him a sidelong stare. "They're pretty full this week, Dr. Carter."

Even though the receptionists were individually assigned, they were aware of each of the doctor's schedules, for reasons such as this. "I already spoke with them, and we are rescheduling patients who can be rescheduled, like these two of mine for later today," he said, pointing to his three and five o'clocks. "We'll keep the four o'clock. I think Dr. Obryan can take her. These two for tomorrow morning can see me on Thursday or when it's convenient for them. I'll see them after hours if necessary. I should be back in time for my twelve thirty tomorrow afternoon and can take it from there." He stood up and returned the chair to its previous location. "I'm not here, so hold my calls and ask Gloria and Troy to hold Dr. Levitt's and Dr. Obryan's for the next twenty minutes or so."

"Yes, Dr. Carter."

"Thanks, Barbara." He gave her a smile and left her to her job while he continued to his office overlooking Boylston Street and the Four Seasons Hotel where his grandmother was staying, and from where he would be picking her up soon.

He'd called Michelle early this morning to tell her about Margaret, and she'd been so shaken, she could hardly speak. As he'd predicted, she was about to pack up her clan and head down to Boston. In the end, they'd decided that if it was okay with Margaret, he would drive her to Granite Falls this morning and she would spend the week getting acquainted with her granddaughter and great-grandchildren. They would have her undivided attention since Erik's parents, Philippe and Felicia, were away on a two-week European cruise. Margaret was elated at the invitation.

Robert sighed as he unlocked his office and walked over to his desk. Before she left last night, Margaret had agreed to a DNA test. His gut told him that they were related, but he'd been living in an altered universe for so long, he just needed to know for sure that the one he was about to step into was the real deal. He hoped he hadn't made a mistake by telling Michelle about Margaret before he knew for sure that she was indeed their grandmother.

He dropped his weight into the chair behind his desk, booted up his computer, and then absentmindedly scanned through the e-mails that had been piling up since Friday when he'd left early to surprise Yasmine. Little did he know then that his entire weekend would turn out to be one big surprise after another.

He'd gone through three major life-changing shocks in three days, and although they were all equally epic, the final was the sweetest—hearing Yasmine say she loved him to his face, slipping that ring on her finger, and then making love to her all night long, and into the morning.

Fire shot through his belly as he recalled thrusting inside her deeply and slowly last night as they lay together in the semi-spoon position while her intoxicating musky arousal filled the air around them. She'd been shivering ceaselessly during a seven-minute orgasm while he sucked on her tasty breasts and massaged her swollen clit and the insides of her soft folds with his fingers.

"Stop, Rob. Oh my God, please stop. My heart—my heart is going to explode. I can't—I can't take—Please," she'd begged.

Robert had dragged his cock out of her, but had kept her locked in his arms, their damp skin melded together. "That's what you get for holding on to your love for me for so long. It's love overload, darling. It *can* kill you," he'd said, proud of himself that he could actually make a woman beg him to stop making love to her. It was a first for him, but he knew it wouldn't be his last.

That's the way lovemaking should be, he thought. Unbearable for the participants. When you left your lover's bed, you should feel as if you'd been raked through and through, but still longing to go back for more.

He'd given her a few minutes to catch her breath, turned her over on to her stomach, placed a pillow under her hips, and mounted her from behind like a stallion mounted his mare. Sweat had been dripping off their bodies, soaking the sheets, as he'd taken her deeply and slowly again, making her feel and relish every inch of his hard cock as it entered and left her, their groans and moans and heavy breathing commingled with the slap of their skin. Each time they collided, he'd come close to teetering on the edge of the ledge of "death by love." So intense was his passion that he'd had to drag his cock out of her again.

"Why'd you stop?" she'd asked in a breathless whisper. "Put him back in. Put King Rob back inside me."

"You're too sweet," he'd groaned, his heart and his lungs so full of love and passion, he'd felt as if they were going to explode. "I'm having a sugar rush, and it's making me dizzy."

"From that look on your face, I'd say you're looking at porn."

Robert started and snapped his head up to see Lani walking into his office, her attractive, cocoa-toned face eyeing him. *Shit.* He pulled his hand away from his crotch, not even realizing he'd been pumping his own cock while he'd been reminiscing on his previous night. "Hey," he said, pressing his thighs together under his desk to ease the ache in his groin.

Lani stood in front of him, grinning. "I know that look, Rob. We were lovers once, remember? So it's either porn on your monitor, or you and Yasmine had a wild night of passion."

Robert chuckled. *Nope,* she'd never seen this look on his face because he'd never had it before, but he'd let her indulge in her own memories of them. "The porn's in my mind," he said, unable to stop the wide grin from bursting. "And yes, things are good between Yas and me." He knew Lani would be elated that they were finally engaged, but he and Yas were keeping quiet until they told their families. "Yes, our night was wild."

Lani placed her hands against her heart, her face lighting up with excitement. She slanted her head, causing her long braids to swing across her shoulders. "There's something different about you. You sure there's nothing else going on?"

Robert tried desperately to keep a straight face. Lani and Vaughn were the closest things he had to friends, and he promised himself that they would be the first people he would tell after the families had been informed. He and Yas owed that first right of discovery to the LaCrosse and the Reynolds family after making them wait five years while he and Yas made up their minds about their future. Finally, he could get Luke Reynolds off his back about stringing his daughter along. If he only knew that it was his daughter who'd been doing the stringing.

"Is Vaughn here yet?" he asked to change the subject.

"He is now," a male voice said.

His hard-on dissipated, Robert got up and stepped from behind his desk. "Hey," he said as his six-foot, blue-eyed blond third partner walked in, carrying a Starbucks coffee cup.

"Sorry I'm late," Vaughn said with his usual cheery smile. "Seemed like everybody was running late or early this morning and decided to stop at the same Starbucks location. Ten minutes I stood in line for this. Hey, Lani. You look smashing as usual. You did something different with your hair?" He gave her an enticing smile over the rim of his coffee cup.

"I'm happily married, Vaughn. Save your line and bait for your next catch of the month," she said with a rascally expression that reminded Robert of Yasmine.

Accepting her swing at his liberal sex life, Vaughn made a mewling sound that made them all laugh. Come to think of it, Robert thought, Lani was a lot like Yasmine, which is probably why out of all the women he'd dated before Yas, Lani was the only one he'd thought of as a possible permanent mate. He was sure that if there were no Yasmine, he and Lani could have made it work.

"So." Vaughn turned his attention to Robert. "You said you had a family emergency in Granite Falls. Are your sister and her family okay?"

"Yes. The LaCrosses are all fine. It's just a family matter Michelle and I need to discuss in person." They had never made public the fact that Timmy Gleason wasn't their father. The frenzy about what Gleason had done to Cassie LaCrosse had just died down, and the last thing Michelle had wanted was to have the media hounding Erik and Precious, and or herself, again.

Outside of his and Yasmine's immediate families, the only other people who knew that piece of shit wasn't his and Michelle's father were his shrink and Detective Gilbert. Since he couldn't share the news of finding his grandmother with Vaughn and Lani without going into a lengthy explanation, Robert had to keep quiet. Once the DNA results came back, he and Michelle would decide how to make the information public.

It might coincide with his and Yasmine's news of becoming engaged. He didn't know. One thing he knew though: it wasn't going to be a long drawn-out engagement. They'd been together and had loved each other a lot longer than most marriages lasted. They'd done the hard and the ugly, and survived them. He would marry her today if it were convenient.

"I appreciate your willingness to rearrange your schedules for the next couple days," Robert said, picking up his tablet from the desk and turning it on.

"We're in this together," Lani said, preceding him and

Vaughn to a sitting area under the glass wall. "Coming on board with you is still the best career decision I've made. I'm here to stay." She sat down in a club chair and folded her legs.

"So am I," Vaughn added, sitting in the chair next to her, while Robert took the one facing them. "I couldn't have asked for a better partner. Not to mention the fact that you made us both millionaires through Carter Dental."

"That, we all did together," Robert said, grinning at them. "I'm just happy I had the insight to snatch you up before some other practice got to you. We make a great team."

"We do," both Lani and Vaughn said, nodding.

"We're not done yet. I have plans to take us even further." He smiled at the sparks of interest in their eyes, especially Lani's. Mitt Romney kept his women in a folder. Robert kept his at the forefront of his practice. His smile deepened at the thought of the two other female partners he was planning to bring on board.

Robert had always thought that women should be treated equally to men in the workplace. His resolve to contribute to that cause was now reinforced after learning about the way his great-grandfather had manipulated his grandmother into giving up her child and forcing her into a loveless marriage. And then there was his own mother who'd been forced into a life of terror and abuse because her only means of financial support had been ripped from her.

Now, Robert understood why Yasmine's independence, her strength, her fearlessness, and determination to succeed attracted him so much. If anything should happen to him, he was comforted to know that she could stand on her own, take care of herself.

She was the perfect woman for him.

"Excuse me. Are you Ms. Yasmine Reynolds?"

Yasmine glanced up from her computer screen to see a man in a blue and white courier's uniform standing at her office door. "Yes. I'm Ms. Reynolds." Her gaze dropped from his face to the medium-size box in the crook of his arm.

"Then this is for you." He walked over to her desk. "Can you sign here, please?"

Yasmine signed her name on the screen of the tablet he presented, and then took the box.

"Have a nice day, Ms. Reynolds."

Yasmine glanced at the box, frowning. She wasn't expecting a package, but many of her clients sent her "Thank You" gifts once in a while. She always returned them with a nice, "Thank You, but…" note because she didn't ever want to feel personally indebted to any of her clients, or give them reason to feel that she owed them anything more than her professional loyalty. Although some of them might be genuine gifts of appreciation, it was better to be safe than regretful.

But it could also be from Robert. He did delight in showering her with gifts. Her heart hammered, and a wide smile cracked her lips as she thought of their previous night of passion that had extended into the early morning hours. He'd left their warm bed this morning only because he had to drive Margaret to Granite Falls.

They'd only been engaged for a few hours, yet it felt as if they'd been married for an eternity. After court this morning, she'd thought about driving to Granite Falls to surprise Robert and Michelle, but then a new client, a Mr. Brad Smith, had asked to meet with Yasmine this afternoon. She'd tried to pawn him off to Armand, but the client had insisted on only working with her. Mr. Smith would be arriving in a few minutes.

Yasmine picked up a pair of scissors from her desk and sliced through the tape on the box. Inside that box was a smaller one wrapped in silver paper with little gold hearts. Yasmine beamed. It had to be from Robert. Eagerly, she placed the smaller box on her desk, unwrapped it, and unfolded the tissue paper. "Oh, Rob," she whispered, running her fingers over the soft material of the skirt, an exact replica of the one they'd ruined on Friday while making love on her living room floor. Biting into her lower lip, she picked up the card lying on the skirt.

This is not an apology, darling. It's an invitation to make a mess of this one too, if you so desire. I love you, Rob.

Yasmine leaned against her desk, her body tingling at the memories of being taken by Robert. They'd been together for five years, and yet the magnetism, the passion between them was as strong and intense as that of new lovers. After yesterday, she knew it would only get better between them.

Yasmine's intercom buzzed. Tucking away her salacious thoughts, she pushed the button on her phone. "Yes."

"Yasmine, Mr. Smith is here," the receptionist at the front office announced.

"Thanks, Debbie. Send him to number four on three," she said, referring to the conference room on the third floor that was closest to the garage elevators.

"Okay. Good luck."

Lifting her skirt and the note from the box, Yasmine placed them into her briefcase, grabbed her purse, and left the office, locking the door behind her. As soon as she was done with Mr. Smith, she was heading to her condo to begin packing. She couldn't wait to move in with Rob.

Yasmine walked into the conference room and stopped short when she spotted her "client" standing at the window. Even though his back was turned to her, she recognized him.

He turned with a lizard-like smile on his face, his gaze scanning her up and down, causing her skin to crawl in disgust. "Hi, Yasmine. It's been a long time."

"Not long enough," she said, calmly. She felt nothing. Nothing at all. Her throat was not dry. There was no palpitation in her chest. She did not break out in a sweat from fear or distress. She would turn around and walk away, but that might make him think he'd upset her, and knowing him, it would give him a sense of power over her.

She didn't even care enough to be upset that he'd deceived his way into seeing her. The only question in Yasmine's head was how long it would take him to say what he'd come to say, so she could get on with her life.

"My father told me he saw you on Friday," he said, leaving the window to walk over to her.

"And?"

"He said you looked good. I have to say I agree." He stopped a few inches in front of her.

Yasmine raised her head and studied him. The azure eyes she once thought soft were really weak, and the permanent curl in his lips she once thought was a smile was nothing but a snobbish smirk. He'd grown thick around the middle, and he'd begun to bald at the temples like his father. Some women might find him attractive, but Yasmine knew his heart and his character were anything but—as he was once again proving by assuming a false name and pretending to be a client just to gain access to her. "What do you want, Jeremy?" she asked, to speed the session along.

He looked at her ring finger just like his father had done.

And as she'd wished then, Yasmine now wished she'd been wearing Robert's ring—the big one he'd given her last night—on her finger instead of on a chain around her neck that was tucked down inside her high-neck blouse. She wished she hadn't agreed to wait to tell their families before she could let the rest of the world know that she belonged to Robert Carter.

"I stopped by your condo Saturday and yesterday, but you weren't home."

"How did you get my address?"

"I'm a cop, Yasmine. I can find anyone I want."

That did make her a little scared, but she held her composure. "I repeat. What do you want?"

"Isn't it obvious? You're still single. I'm about to be single. I thought—"

"You thought what? That I would want to come back to you? Why?" She shrugged.

"I was your first, Yas. That has to mean something."

"Yeah. It does mean something."

"See?" He gave her his lizard-like smile. "I knew you'd understand. We were—"

"You were the first and the biggest mistake of my life, Jeremy."

Wow, Yasmine thought, as she turned to leave. This closure was the quickest and easiest one she'd ever made. She wished all her cases were this…

Six years of anger catapulted through Yasmine when she felt a hand on her shoulder. She turned and swung her briefcase at his face. When he staggered back from the impact of the collision, she stepped forward, grabbed him by the collar, and kneed him in the groin with all her strength.

He dropped to his knees, groaning and clutching his crotch with both hands.

"Don't you ever come near me again, Jeremy Arsenault."

Yasmine walked out of the room and up the hall to the elevators. She hadn't even broken a sweat.

"Are you sure we're doing the right thing?" Yas asked as Robert pulled up into her parents' driveway."

"You mean about us?" He grinned at her.

"No, silly. About tricking our families into getting together. I still don't even know if my mom told my dad that she wants a divorce. It might cause some awkwardness, you know."

"She still refuses to discuss it with you, huh?"

Yasmine looked up at the house, her spirits dipping a little. "Every time I try to bring it up, she tells me that she'll take care of it. It's been almost a week."

"Give her time. I'm sure if she'd told your dad, you would have heard about it already. Maybe she jumped the gun when she poured her heart out to you. Maybe she just feels silly about even mentioning it and things are back to normal now."

"You're full of *maybes*."

"That's all we have for now, baby. Everything will be fine, so stop worrying your pretty little head," he said, leaning over to give her a lingering kiss on her lips before hopping out of his car and walking around to her side.

As Robert helped her from the car, Yasmine hoped he was right. They had concocted two different stories in order to get their families together without spoiling their surprise announcement. The Reynolds gang had been told that they'd been invited to the LaCrosse estate for the weekend, while the LaCrosses had no idea they would be entertaining guests.

To maximize the effects, Robert was driving up alone, supposedly for a business meeting with a Granite Falls dentist he'd met at the wedding two weeks ago, when he was really going to check on their dinner takeout order from Ristorante Andreas, an extremely exclusive restaurant owned by one of Erik's billionaire friends. Yas would follow in a couple hours with her parents and Luke and Christine, while Naomi and her family, who were planning to stay an extra day to do some hiking, would drive up separately.

"Rob," Yas said, gazing up at him as they stood at her parents' door.

"What, baby?"

"I know you hate lies, but thank you for telling these two white ones for me."

He rested his hands on her shoulders. "I will lie for you and with you any day. We just have to keep our stories straight for a little while longer."

"Then you probably shouldn't answer any questions. You're not a very good liar, and you know my father. He needs a reason for everything."

He grinned. "I'll just smile and nod and leave the lying in your capable hands then, Attorney Reynolds." He rang the doorbell and then captured her mouth in a hot kiss before she had a chance to respond to his innocuous dig about lawyers being liars.

Yasmine hardly had time to regain her composure before her father pulled her into the house and enveloped her in a big bear hug. "How's my favorite baby girl?"

"Hey, Daddy." Yasmine held on to him, taking deep breaths of his 4711. His greeting wasn't any different today. Maybe Robert was right and her mother had decided not to tell him that she wanted a divorce. Maybe things were back to normal. She hoped. She prayed.

"You good, baby girl?" her father asked, untangling her hands from around his neck. "You're holding me so tight, I can hardly breathe."

Yasmine smiled and stepped back. *He didn't know. He hadn't been told.* "I'm fine, Daddy. I'm really fine."

"Good. Hey, Rob," he said, turning to Robert who'd been standing by patiently.

Yasmine's smile widened as the two most important men in her life hugged each other.

"When are you going to make an honest woman out of my daughter?" her father started with his usual badgering. "It's been five years. I thought you'd be married with a couple kids by now."

"Well…" Robert's voice trailed off as he glanced over her father's shoulder at her.

"See, that's why we don't come by often," Yasmine said in defense of her man. "You need to stop badgering him. I'm the one who's holding out."

"For what?" her father frowned at her. "The man is rich, handsome, and decent as they come. You think there's something better out there?"

"I know there's nothing better, Daddy, and—"

"Yasmine."

Yasmine turned at her mother's voice, her breath catching in her throat as her mother's arms wrapped about her. Yasmine held her, just as tightly as she'd held her father moments ago.

"I haven't said anything to your father," her mother whispered in her ear, her words drowned out by the louder male voices. "I was being foolish. He's a good man. I love him. I don't want to lose him, but I will talk to him about how I feel. Maybe we can see a marriage counselor or something. In the meantime, I've talked to Naomi about taking some nursing classes. I'll make it work. Sorry, baby. I should have thought it through before upsetting you."

"Thank you, Mommy." Tears stung Yasmine's eyes.

"What are you thanking her for?" Yasmine's father asked, looking at them speculatively.

"I've decided to take that trip," her mother said.

"Well, hallelujah." Her father skipped across the floor and whisked his wife away from Yasmine, and then waltzed her around the room. "We're going to have a darn good time, Marie. I've wanted to do something special like this for you and with you for thirty-eight years. But taking care of you and our children came first."

"And now our children are taking care of us," her mother said as she raised her lips to kiss her husband.

"Come on over here, you two." Her father beckoned her and Robert.

As she hugged her parents and Robert, Yasmine was tempted to say that the day couldn't get any better, but she knew it would. Finally, the hug was over and they sat down in the living room.

"So tell me again," her father said, "what's the occasion for this weekend invitation? Not that I'm complaining, but I'm curious, seeing that we were just up there a couple weeks ago for the wedding. Plus, it's kind of short notice, and you two have been overly insistent that the entire family drive up today and together."

Yasmine felt Robert tense beside her. "It's about Margaret," she blurted, before he prematurely spilled their beans.

"Margaret?" both her parents said at the same time.

"Robert's grandmother. His real father's mother."

"You found her?" Yasmine's mother stared at Robert. "How? When? Where?"

And so for the next few minutes, Yasmine listened as Robert filled her parents in with the short version of how Margaret had tracked him down.

"She's been in Granite Falls all week," Yasmine said. "So the invitation is to welcome her into the family." *That* wasn't a lie.

"Oh my. I feel honored that they thought to invite us. But why? I can understand you being there." She waved her hand at Yasmine. "But why us? You and Robert aren't even engaged, much less married, so—"

"Mom," Yasmine said at Robert's quick intake of breath.

"It's Michelle. She grew up with us. Even though Rob and I aren't—" She paused, unable to say it. "She's always thought of you as family. Just because she's rich now, it doesn't mean she thinks she's better than us."

"Wisely said, baby girl." Her father nodded at Robert. "I'm happy you found your grandmother. Roots are important. Now you can tell my grandchildren where they came from once the two of you decide to settle down and start a family. Luke married a woman way past her childbearing years. Naomi has only given me one so far, but I'd like to have more. You're it."

"You'll have more, Daddy." *Probably sooner than you think.*

Her father tilted his head and tapped a finger against his lips, the way he did when he was in deep thought and when something didn't sit well with him. "Are you sure the two of you aren't hiding something? Robert you look kind of—"

"Dad—"

The front door opened, and Luke and Christine walked in. Yasmine expelled a sigh and jumped up from the sofa. The hugging and greeting began all over again, followed by a beehive of chatter about Rob finding his grandmother, and the invite to the LaCrosse estate for the weekend.

"This is such a treat," Christine said, tucking her long blond hair behind her ears as her green eyes sparkled with excitement.

From the look on her face, you would think she'd been invited to the White House or Buckingham Palace for a garden party. She and Luke had only been to the LaCrosse estate once —two weeks ago when they'd gone to Granite Falls for the big wedding. Luke always made excuses not to accept the few invitations they'd gotten over the years, which didn't surprise Yas since he and Michelle weren't close when they were growing up. Luke wasn't that close to Robert either, because like her father, he thought Robert was stringing his little sister along. She felt guilty about the misguided opinions the men in her family had about Rob, and she hoped all that would change after today.

Luke had only agreed to go to Granite Falls this weekend because Yasmine had threatened to tell Christine, who'd recently announced that they'd become vegetarians to battle their weight, that he was gulping down steaks and hamburgers behind her back. Yas was going to have a good laugh at dinner when he couldn't eat what he really wanted. Or maybe he'd come clean with his wife.

"Do I look okay?" Christine asked, pressing her hands against the soft flowing material of her yellow rayon dress that hugged her ample curves nicely. "I lost five more pounds this week, and bought this dress just for the occasion."

"You look beautiful, Christine," Rob said, smiling at her. "That dress is very flattering."

"Well, thank you, Robert. For that you get a kiss." She kissed him on the cheek.

Blushing, Robert turned to Luke. "So how's business at the bank, brother?"

"Hey you don't get to call me that until you marry my sister." Luke punched him playfully on the arm before asking, "Why, you need a loan?"

"I might," he replied, catching Yasmine's gaze and sending her a mischievous wink.

Yasmine smiled inwardly. It was nice to share secrets with her man, instead of keeping them from him.

"As much as I enjoy this little get-together," Robert said, coming to stand beside her. "I have to leave now if I want to make my meeting."

Luke narrowed his eyes. "Meeting. You have a meeting this morning? Aren't you coming to Granite Falls with us?" He sent Yas a confused look.

"His meeting is in Granite Falls," her father said.

"I would think with finding your grandmother, you'd put all business on hold for now," Yasmine's mother said.

At the uneasy flicker of Robert's brows, Yasmine spoke up. "Robert's killing two birds with one stone. He can't let a good business deal slip through his finger. Don't worry, he'll be done and at Michelle's place by the time we get there."

"We—you're not—Wait a minute. You found your grandmother?" Luke asked, gawking at Robert.

"I'll tell you all about it, Luke. Rob has to leave." She laced her arms around Robert's waist, hurried him out of the house, and to his car. "You were starting to sweat," she said, as he opened his car door.

He laughed. "Thanks for the rescue." His studied her thoughtfully. "I guess your mom changed her mind about divorcing your dad?"

"She said it's foolish to throw away thirty-eight years of marriage without trying to mend the cracks first. But she's going after the dreams she'd set aside to raise us. That's good. She can have it all, like me."

"See, I told you."

"Yeah, you did." She rose up on tiptoe to kiss him. "Now, I can't wait to tell the whole world our news."

"Just a few more hours," he said, sliding behind the wheel. "I love you."

"I love you." Yasmine's heart raced at the sound of those words falling from her lips. She would never get tired of saying them.

As she watched him drive away, she thought of her previous visit to her parents' home, and how disastrously different the outcome could have been, not only for her parents, but for her and Robert, too. That day, she'd learned that she needed to trust in their love and not in the failing relationships around her.

She wasn't a part of those relationships. They had nothing to do with her. She had no control over whether other people stayed together or walked away from each other. And even though she was in a relationship with Robert, she'd realized that she had no control over his decisions either.

She'd had to trust that she was offering the best of herself and hope that Robert would accept her as she was, faults, fears, and all.

And he had.

Thank God he had.

CHAPTER SIXTEEN

Robert was forty minutes out of Yasmine's parents' driveway when he realized she'd left her cell phone in his car. It must have fallen out of her purse, and gotten stuck between the two front seats from where it was now ringing incessantly. He glanced at the clock on his dashboard. He didn't have time to turn around and, deciding to obey New Hampshire's hands-free law, he let it ring, and breathed a sigh of relief when it stopped—probably going to voicemail.

He gritted his teeth when it started ringing again, going to voicemail, and then starting again. "That's it," he muttered, pulling off to the side of the road and reaching down between the seats for it. He must have hit the answer button because the next thing he knew, he was sitting in his car fuming, his hands balling into fists as he listened to the voice on the other end.

"Hey, Yasmine." Silence. "What, you not going to say anything?" Silence. "Well, I understand. Just listen then. I realize that you might be mad at me, you know for showing up at your office like that. But it was the only way to make sure I saw you. I wanted to talk about the way we left things, you know, when we broke up. I was young and stupid. I know now that you're the real deal. I've grown up, girl, and I want to give us another try. That's what I wanted to tell you the other day, but well, you know how that meeting ended. I want you to know that I don't blame you. I deserved it for the way I treated you. Anyway, I want to see you again. Maybe we can meet for…"

Robert ended the call. He was surprised at his own coolness as he called up an address in his GPS, put his car into drive, eased back into the flow of traffic, took the next exit, made a U-turn, and in a few minutes, got off the highway again. Another ten minutes, and he was banging on the Arsenaults' front door.

Robert had begun doing his homework on the Arsenaults ever since Yasmine had told him about them. And a few nights ago when she'd told him about Jeremy showing up at her office, he'd seen red. The only reason he hadn't gotten into his car and made this trip that night was because Yasmine had begged him not to. She was scared that he might kill Jeremy, and end up in jail. And she was right to be scared. Since Yasmine had taken care of him in her own way, Robert had decided to let it go, for now. He was still planning on confronting the jerk, sooner or later. He just didn't know it would be this soon.

"Is your son in?" Robert asked, when Mr. Arsenault opened the door.

"Robert. Robert Carter," he said, a smile beginning to curve his lips. "What brings you to our home?"

"I'm here to see your son. Is he in?" Robert wanted to give the older Arsenault a piece of his mind, but he wasn't worth it. He just wanted to do what he came to do and be on his way.

"Who is it, Dad?"

At the sound of Jeremy's voice, Robert forced his way into the house, almost knocking the older man over.

"It's Robert Carter," Robert answered, inches from Jeremy's face.

"Robert, hey, man. Long time no see. What's up?"

"Yasmine. You are to leave her alone. I don't want you calling her, texting her, or trying to communicate with her through any means, physical or electronic. Do you understand?"

He snickered. "That was you on the other end of the line, wasn't it? You heard my message." He shrugged. "Well, as you probably know, I was Yasmine's first, and the fact that you're here tells me you're jealous." He snickered again. "You scared of a little competition, Carter? You afraid she might come back to me, her first man. You don't have a claim on her. She's free for the ta—"

"Get off of him!"

Robert was unmoved by the screams and the four hands pulling at him. All he knew was that he only stopped punching when Jeremy Arsenault was lying still, his face swollen and bloodied. He delivered one more punch. "This is for stealing my bike when we were kids. You jerk!"

"Are you crazy? You'll pay for this. I'm calling the cops. I'm suing you." Mr. Arsenault shouted.

"He is a cop. A dirty one," Robert said, rising to his feet. "Your son fell down the stairs. That is your story in case he needs medical attention. Any other story, and he will be spending a lot of years in jail for possession and distribution of cocaine, and for statutory rape."

"What are you talking about?" Mrs. Arsenault asked, looking up at him from the floor where she was kneeling next to her son.

"Ask him." Robert glanced at Jeremy, still sprawled on his back. "Stay away from Yasmine or, I swear to God, I will kill you!" He slammed the door, walked down the driveway, got into his car, and before continuing on his journey, he deleted all of Jeremy's calls from Yasmine's phone and blocked him as a caller.

Except for the times he'd fought back against the man who'd raised him, it was the first time Robert had ever felt the need to strike another human being. And just like Timmy Gleason, Jeremy Arsenault had earned his beating.

Robert parked in the courtyard of his sister's home, shut off his engine, and unwrapped the cold pack he'd stopped to pick up from the drug store from around the knuckles on his right hand. He clenched and unclenched his fist. Satisfied that he had no broken bones, he opened his car door.

His feet had hardly hit the pavement when the three oldest LaCrosse children came racing from behind a line of shrubs shouting their customary mantra, "Uncle Robert!" There would be four if Fiona was walking already. He swore they must have put some kind of tracking device on his car to know his comings and goings. As he walked across the lawn, he hoped that his own children would always be as excited to see him as his sister's were. He faltered in his step, as he was reminded of the baby he and Yas had lost. He or she would be a little older than Tiffany.

"Hey, you." He opened his arms wide, and was immediately knocked to the ground as they rushed him and began talking at once. More like shouting to be heard over each other, he thought, grinning from ear to ear.

"Our new Grannie Margaret is cool. And nice. Yeah, wicked cool and nice. I like her a lot. As much as I like Grandma Felicia. And Grandma Hayes. No. I love her. She played tag bunny with us. And hopscotch with me. She made peach cobbler. Almost as good as Grandma Hayes. And she smells nice, really nice. Like the mall. Macy's. Can you stay, Uncle Robert? For a long, long time, like Grannie Margaret? Yeah, can you? You can sleep in my room. We—"

Robert didn't even try to decipher who was saying what. To him, it was all the same. "Okay, okay," he said, forcing in a word in as he struggled to his feet. "I get it. You love your new grannie. I love her too. Where's everybody?" he asked, picking up Little Erik in one arm, and Tiffany in the next, and gazing up at the house.

"They're having brunch on the kitchen balcony." Precious hooked her arm in his. "Where's Aunt Yasmine?"

"She can't make it. She isn't feeling well."

"Bummer. Does that mean I can't visit you next weekend? Mom and Dad already said yes."

Robert felt like a jerk lying to her, but he had to follow the script he and Yasmine had written out for this occasion. "I'm sure she'll be better by then."

"Sweet." Precious pulled him toward the back of the house, up the steps, through the kitchen where chefs and servants were busy preparing breakfast, and then on to the balcony.

Michelle was the first to spot him, and she immediately screamed his name and jumped out of her chair.

He had just enough time to put Little Erik and Tiffany on the floor before his sister was in his arms, hugging him as if she hadn't seen him in ages, when in fact it had only been four days since he left Granite Falls.

"You're as bad as your kids," he told her, laughing at the twinkle in her black eyes.

"Well, we know a good thing when we see it. And we don't see you often enough, so when we do, we go crazy."

"I'm crazy about you, too, little sister," he said, hugging her close again. "I'm crazy about all of you."

"You can never get too much love, Robbie, dear. Take it from someone who's just beginning to understand the meaning of filial attention. See what I mean?" Margaret added, laughing, as Precious hugged her from behind.

"Hello, Grannie." Robert looped his other arm around her and kissed her cheeks. He liked that she'd started calling him

Robbie—like his father used to. The DNA tests had come back positive on Tuesday afternoon, twelve hours after they'd sent in the samples—thanks to Erik's association with one of the leading paternity testing labs in the area. Margaret was indeed Dwight Carter's mother, and his and Michelle's grandmother.

"Twice in one week, Robert, and five times in the past month. I don't know if my poor old weak heart can take so much of you."

Robert grinned at Mrs. Hayes, seated on the other side of the table. "You're counting my visits, Mrs. Hayes?" He went over to hug her. "Your heart might be old, but it is neither poor nor weak. It's one of the most beautiful hearts I know."

"You've always been a charmer," she chided him.

"I'm beginning to realize that, Martha," Margaret said. "He reminds me of my Christian in so many ways."

Robert smiled at the two elderly women who'd become fast friends, solely because the one thing they had in common was their love for him and Michelle.

"Are you hungry?" Michelle asked, leading him to the empty chair on the other side of Margaret.

"I'm starving. I only had a bagel and coffee this morning," he said, hugging Tiffany, who'd climbed up on his lap the minute he sat down. "I can use one of those omelets I love."

"Okay, I—"

"You sit, Mom," Precious said, cutting Michelle off. "Visit with your brother and your grandma. I'll go tell the cook to add Uncle Robert's omelet to the order."

"Oh, no." Mrs. Hayes jumped up from her chair. "I'm making Robert's omelet. Save it," she added when Robert opened his mouth to protest. "Like Precious said, sit and visit with your sister and grandma."

"I'll go let Dad know Uncle Robert is here, then."

"Thanks, baby." Michelle sat down and wrapped her arms around her son, who'd climbed up on her lap.

"Such a darling child," Margaret said after Precious disappeared into the house behind Mrs. Hayes. "I still can't believe she's not your biological daughter. Your love for each other is just beautiful." Margaret squeezed Michelle's hand.

"I'm beautiful, too, right, Grannie?" Tiffany said, leaning across to hug her great-grandma.

"You're all beautiful. I'm just so grateful, happy, overjoyed, blessed that we were able to find each other after all these years." Her voice trembled with affection.

"All because of the billionaire group wedding," Robert said.

"Even before that. It was my late husband's interest in Erik's work, and later in his foundation that started it all. He's the reason I watched the wedding, and recognized you." She touched her hand to Robert's cheek.

Michelle leaned her head on Margaret's shoulder. "Who could have known when Kaya, Shaina, Tashi, and I decided to do the wedding last year, that it would lead to this? God works in mysterious ways."

"He does." Margaret's eyes grew misty. "And because of that wedding, I met Christian's daughter, your Aunt Camille, and her children, Allison and Neil."

"I can't wait to meet them," Michelle said with a catch in her voice.

"From our phone conversation on Tuesday, they can't wait to meet us either." Robert rested his chin on Tiffany's head. His family was growing in leaps and bounds.

"I can die a happy old woman, now." Margaret brushed her freckled hands through her great-grandchildren's hair, smiling with love.

"Nobody else is dying around here anytime soon. Not if I have anything to do with it."

Robert turned as Erik joined them with Fiona, the youngest LaCrosse, in his arms. "I totally agree, Erik." He turned back to his grandmother. "You're not allowed to die, not before Yas and I have children." He saw Michelle's eyes light up with curiosity, and before she could say anything, he sat Tiffany on Margaret's lap and got to his feet. "How's it going, Erik?" He gave his brother-in-law a bear side hug.

"Still reeling from the shock of you and Michelle finding your grandmother, and other relatives."

"We all are." He reached for Fiona, who immediately gave him a one-tooth grin and leaped into his arms. He hugged her close, pressing his cheek against the soft black curls on her little baby head. He couldn't wait to have his own children, to bring them to Granite Falls to visit and play with their cousins.

"Can you say 'Uncle Robert?'" he asked, gazing into her button-black eyes like her mother's, her maternal grandfather's, and, now he knew, her paternal great-grandfather's. Tiffany had inherited brown eyes from both of her grandmothers—Violet and Felicia, and her great-grandmother Margaret, while Little Erik had the piercing gray eyes—sprinkled with golden hues— like his father and paternal grandfather, Philippe.

Robert could only guess that most of his children would have brown eyes since it was the dominant color in his and Yasmine's families.

"I thought Yasmine was coming with you," Margaret said, ruffling Fiona's hair.

Robert took a moment to think before responding. "That was the plan, but she wasn't feeling well this morning. She didn't want to get the kids sick, so she stayed home."

"I hope it's nothing serious," Michelle said, her eyes widening with concern. "You guys still good, right?"

"We're still good," Robert answered. "We're perfect." He knew Yasmine had confided in Michelle about the secret

Yasmine had been hiding from him without getting into detail. "It might just be a little summer cold."

"I should call her."

"No. She might still be sleeping. I told her to call me when she felt up to it," he lied.

Disappointment dulled the enthusiasm in Michelle's eyes. "I hope she's over it soon. Haven't seen my girl since the wedding, and we have so much to catch up on."

Robert smiled as he gazed at Tiffany and Little Erik tossing pieces of bread off the balcony to a flock of birds that had descended from the branches of the trees lining the lawn, that extended to a pond a good distance away.

There was a lot they had to catch up on. Much more than any of them could imagine. Since they were planning on starting a family right away, he and Yasmine had begun looking for a home outside of the city, but close enough to their offices. They wanted a house with a big backyard for their children to play.

They were keeping his Beacon Hill townhouse so they could have a place in the city for days when they didn't feel like fighting traffic, or during inclement weather in the long winter months. He didn't have a mortgage on it, and even if he did, he could afford to maintain two households.

Yasmine had stopped taking the pill, and had seen her gynecologist on Tuesday, just to make sure that the fact she'd had a miscarriage four years ago wouldn't be an issue for conceiving again. It wasn't.

"Breakfast is ready." Mrs. Hayes returned to the balcony, followed by a line of servants carrying stainless steel chafing dishes that they took over to the buffet tables and began setting up. "And here are the omelets and coffee," she said, as another group of servants appeared with smaller serving dishes and coffee carafes.

"Whoa. I'm glad I'm hungry," Robert said, his mouth already watering.

"You and me both, Uncle Robert," Precious said, almost running into the servants, leaving the balcony.

"This food isn't going to eat itself, folks." Mrs. Hayes took Fiona from Robert and buckled her into the high chair between her parents' chairs, while Michelle and Erik gathered Little Erik and Tiffany and helped them into their chairs on the other side of the table next to Precious. "I'll fix the children's plates," Mrs. Hayes added, walking over to the buffet. "You, adults, take care of yourselves."

"Yes, ma'am," Erik said, as they lined up at the buffet table.

"Can you stay until Monday and come to Water Country with us, Uncle Robert?" Precious asked, standing beside him.

Robert's hand trembled, causing him to drop the spatula into the ham and cheese casserole. "Um—"

"Precious, you know Uncle Robert doesn't do amusement parks," Michelle said.

"He doesn't have to go on the rides, Mom. He can just watch from the ground."

"Are you afraid of heights?" Margaret asked, placing a burrito on her plate next to a slice of quiche.

Robert nodded as he felt his lungs begin to constrict in his chest, and that same burning sensation he'd gotten when Yasmine had called out to him a few nights ago spread rapidly through him. He felt himself falling, falling into the darkness…

"Has he always been afraid of heights?" His grandmother's voice pulled him back.

"Ever since he was a kid," Michelle said.

"Do you know why, Robert?"

Robert sucked in his breath, carefully stacked some pancakes on his plate, and poured some of the hot maple syrup over them. "No. I don't." *But I'm sure it has something to do with Timmy Gleason.*

"Can we not talk about this now? Just the thought of it is making me dizzy."

"I'm sorry, Uncle Robert." Precious looped a hand around his waist as they walked back to the table and took their seats. "I really forgot."

"It's okay, Precious. I promise to work on it, so I can join you on those crazy rides you like to talk about." *You, and my own children, one day*, he thought, making a mental note to see Dr. West at her earliest convenient. It was time for him to face the whole truth of his past.

"That would be wicked cool."

Robert hugged her, marveling that he could love her so much when they weren't even blood related. At the same time, it pained him to think that it was Timmy Gleason's criminal actions, starting with the murder of Robert's father, to the murder of Precious' mother, that had led them all to this specific crossroad, brought them all to this very moment where their families were making progress and finding healing from the pain and sadness of the past.

A few hours later, while Mrs. Hayes and the three youngest children napped, and the oldest practiced her piano in the music room next door, Robert's head was exploding as he, Michelle, and Erik sat in the family room, listening to Margaret's stories about her father, and the Montenegro family that had deep roots in the south.

The Montenegro family had owned slaves. Many of their sons had died in the civil war defending the south from the invading Yankees. Generation after generation, they had fought against civil rights and had even been active in enforcing the Jim Crow laws of the south. Since the civil war, they'd maintained their wealth and power by investing in steel and energy. And up until the day he died, Oliver Montenegro, Margaret's father, still flew the Confederate flag on his three-hundred-acre property.

"It's possible that my ancestors used to own Christian's. As a matter of fact," Margaret said with a sigh, "my father alluded to that possibility several times."

"Wow." Michelle took a sip of water. "Our ancestors were something else. Weren't they, Rob?"

Robert nodded. For five years, he'd been dying to know where he came from. Never for one minute did he think he would be ashamed of his ancestral past. "I can't say that I'm sorry to have never known them."

"I'm just thankful things have changed," Margaret said, patting them both on the thigh as they flanked her on the sofa.

"There's still a lot to be done," Erik chimed in from a chair on the other side of the coffee table. "Even with the progress since the civil war, sometimes it feels as if we're taking two steps forward and one step back."

"Erik's right. All you have to do is turn on the news to know that prejudice is still a big issue in this country. I mean look at what's happening—" Robert stopped in mid-sentence as Erik's cell phone rang.

"It's the hospital," he said, rising from his chair and walking toward the door. "I'll be right back."

"What's that?" Michelle asked as Margaret reached behind her and took a large brown envelope from the table and handed it to Robert.

"It's the report from my private investigator."

"So soon?" Robert turned the envelope over in his hand, his heart beating heavily as if he'd already found connection with the contents, even though he had no idea what was inside.

"I told you he was thorough. Plus things moved quickly with your detective working with mine. Since it was delivered yesterday, I've been dying to know what they'd found out, but I wanted to wait until we were all together. Go on, open it," she prompted.

Holding his breath, Robert pried the metal claps open and, lifting the flap, he reached inside and pulled out a stack of papers held together by a rubber band.

"Oh my God. They're pictures." Michelle reached across Margaret, snatched the stack from his hand, and tossed the rubber band to the floor. "That's my father," she whispered. "My dad."

"My son. Oh, my son." Margaret's voice was as tremulous as Michelle's, and tears pooled in their eyes as the two women stared at a picture of Dwight Carter, standing at the door of Motors in Motion, the mechanic shop where he once worked.

"He was so handsome," Margaret whispered as she rubbed her thumb over the image of his face. "So strong, just like his father. Oh…" she tapped her hand against her chest as if to will her heart to be still.

"And look at my mom," Michelle said, holding up a picture of their mother in her yellow waitress uniform. "She was so beautiful, and I do look like her. Mrs. Hayes was so right."

"Yes you do, Michelle." And that was the main reason Robert had moved Michelle out of Gleason's apartment and into their own. He did not like the way that repulsive lump of crap had started looking at his little sister.

"Robert, these are our parents." Michelle pressed a hand to her chest, her face twisting in a mixture of pain and delight.

Robert emitted a deep breath and swiped the back of his hand across his eyes to stay the tears, but they came rushing out nonetheless, as memory upon memory crashed over him like a tidal wave. Michelle had never seen their mother. There was not one picture of her until now. He didn't know if there had ever been any taken of her since they'd arrived in New Hampshire or if Timmy had destroyed them after she died. He'd been too young and too concerned about taking care of his baby sister to worry about preserving pictures of his mother.

"Look, Robert." Michelle held up both pictures to him. "These are our parents," she repeated, as if forgetting, that unlike her, he had once known them, had been hugged and kissed and rocked to sleep by them. "I just wish I'd know them."

"Me, too, dear."

As his sister and grandmother's sobs echoed in his ear, Robert wrapped his arms around them and gave way to his own grief. He was still in a far better position than they. He had his memories, even though vague and few, but pictures were all they had.

Finally, after they'd been holding each other in silence for what seemed like an eternity, Margaret struggled free, and they took their time going through the rest of the pictures, lingering on each one as if to stamp the images in their minds forever.

"Was there anything else in the envelope?" Margaret asked. "When I spoke to Mr. Jenkins on Tuesday, he said he'd found some information about both your parents. He said he would send a report along with the photos."

Robert picked up the envelope that had slithered to the floor when he'd pulled the stack of pictures from inside it. "There's a smaller envelope inside the larger one."

"Open it. I want to know what happed to my son after he was ripped out of my arms. I want to know how he ended up in foster care."

Robert ripped it open.

"What does it say?" Michelle asked, anxiety causing her voice to rise an octave.

Robert began reading. "Dwight was adopted by James and Eleanor Carter of Richmond, Virginia. They were both victims of a fatal shooting during a corner store robbery when he was eight months old. The authorities found Dwight in his stroller in the store, and since no other family member came forward to claim him, he was placed in foster care where he remained until he was eighteen."

"I should have been there for my son. I should have searched for him. I should never have given him up. I should have…" Margaret dropped her face in her hands and sobbed hysterically.

"What about Mom's family?" Michelle asked when Margaret grew quiet and nodded for him to continue.

"Edna White was a single teenage mother who died from a rare form of ovarian cancer when Violet was two. After a year of trying to take care of the baby, her teenage father, Alvin Taylor, gave her to the state. Violet grew up in foster care in Richmond. She and Dwight attended the same high school and apparently that's where they fell in love. They got married on Thanksgiving Day, thirty-six years ago."

"Well, at least the puzzle of our ancestors is solved," Michelle said. "We know our parents loved each other and that they enjoyed a few years of happiness before they were torn apart."

"Yes," Margaret agreed, holding each of their hands and squeezing, a bright smile replacing the sadness she'd been carrying around for decades. "Their love produced two beautiful children. My grandchildren whom I've fallen in love with already. And a grandson-in-law," she added, nodding at Erik, who'd returned to the room and was standing nearby, holding a tray with three glasses of water.

"We are grateful to be united with you, Grannie," Erik said, handing them each a glass.

They gulped down the refreshing water as if they'd walked for miles under a desert sun. They smiled at each other as they placed the empty glasses on the tray. They were all at peace.

"How much did you hear, darling?" Michelle asked, rising to hug her husband.

"Enough." He kissed her lips. "You and Rob can finally move out of the shadows of your past. You know who you are."

Yes. I know who I am, Robert thought as he collected the pictures and the report and returned them to the envelope. And not a moment too soon, he thought as the gong of the doorbell resonated throughout the house.

CHAPTER SEVENTEEN

"Who could that be?" Michelle eyed Erik. "Are you expecting company? Your boys stopping by?"

"No. Are your girls?"

"We don't have plans. But—"

"Why don't we all go check?" Robert interrupted his sister and her husband as they wondered if the three other couples with whom they were best friends had stopped by unannounced. "Come on," he said, leaving his seat, grateful that the family room did not overlook the front of the house. Yasmine had texted him on her mother's phone an hour ago with their ETA, and he'd already alerted Ristorante Andreas to bring the order about half an hour after her arrival—a special request, since it wasn't the kind of restaurant that delivered.

They would never say no to Erik's brother-in-law, though. He'd also instructed the servants to put out the bottles of champagne and sparkling cider he'd asked them to fetch from his car and chill, along with twelve flutes, four glasses and a sippy cup with Fiona's favorite juice. All was supposed to be quietly set up in the family room while they loitered in the foyer with their guests.

"We have company?" Precious asked, trying to beat Robert to the door.

"I have this, honey. Step back," Robert said, opening the door. His heart did a double take as Yasmine smiled at him from the other side. But before he could open his mouth, his sister flew ahead of him.

"Oh my God!" she screamed. "I thought you weren't coming. Rob said you were sick."

"Pff." Yasmine slapped her hands on her hips. "Do I look sick?"

"Ahhhhh!" The air was pierced with shrill screams from Michelle and Yasmine as they flew into each other's arms in the foyer, clutching and kissing each other, and jumping up and down like they used to do when they were children.

Anyone watching would think they'd won the lottery.

"Hey, Peter." Precious pulled Peter from between his parents. "I didn't know you guys were coming."

"Neither did they, obviously," Peter said, frowning at his aunt and her best friend.

"They definitely love each other to death." Margaret touched Robert's arm. "You're a lucky man that the two most important women in your life get along so well."

"I am very lucky, indeed," he responded, taking in the confused expressions on the faces of all the members of the Reynolds family, as they greeted Erik and Precious.

"You don't know the half of it when these two get together, Grannie," Erik said. "They forget anyone else exists."

Margaret chuckled. "Robert told me. He wasn't exaggerating."

"Even I used to be jealous of their relationship," Naomi said. "I mean, Yasmine's my sister and she used to prefer hanging out with Michelle over me."

"Well, they are closer in age," Yasmine's brother chimed in.

"And Michelle didn't shoo her away like an annoying fly messing up her ointment, nor did she tattle on her." Mrs. Reynolds spoke her piece. "We all long for friendships like that."

Catching Mr. Reynold's questioning and impatient stare, Robert stepped toward the tangled women. "Hey, you two," he said, prying Michelle and Yasmine apart. "There are folks here who need to be introduced."

"Sorry," they said in unison, their excitement lingering in their voices, as they held each other's hands.

"We just don't see each other often enough." Yasmine jutted her chin at Erik. "I have you to blame. You stole her away from me."

"In all fairness, I did not steal her. She came willingly," Erik retorted with a smirk.

Robert chuckled as Yasmine dismissed Erik's remark with a swat of her wrist and began introducing her family members to Margaret.

"We only just heard about you today," Marie said to Margaret. "It's such a pleasure meeting you."

"Finally, Robert and Michelle can fill in their family tree with names and faces instead of question marks," Mr. Reynolds added.

"You have a lovely, home, Dr. LaCrosse," Christine said, glancing around the foyer.

"Thank you, but please, no Mister and Misses around here. We're all friends and family. Call me Erik."

Christine nodded on a wide smile.

"I'll give you a tour later," Michelle offered.

"That would be nice." Luke grinned. "I like to see how the rich folks live. Might pick up a few ideas for our pad, baby," he said jokingly to his wife.

"You didn't know we were coming, did you?" Mr. Reynolds spoke to Erik, but his gaze was fixed on Robert and Yasmine.

"Didn't know a thing. We didn't even expect Yas," Michelle said. "Robert said she was sick." Her eyes narrowed as she stared up at her brother. "Why did you lie?"

Robert exchanged a secret look with Yasmine.

Michelle slapped her hand to her mouth. "Oh my God, you got engaged. My brother does not lie, so that's the only reason I can think of. You wanted to surprise us all together." She grabbed Yasmine's left hand, then her lips thinned in disappointment. "I guess not. No ring." She caught Rob's gaze. "Are you asking her in front of all of us so she can't say no?"

"Chill, sis." Robert pulled Yasmine close to his side. "Let's all go back to the family room, and then you'll know why you're all here."

He led the way, hoping that everything was set. *It was.* He breathed a sigh of relief as he stood at the door and let everyone precede him into the room.

"Champagne!" Precious ran over to the table where the servants had made an attractive floral arrangement around the glasses and bottles of champagne.

"Sparkling cider for you, Peter, and your siblings," he told her, tickled at her pout.

Little Erik and Tiffany suddenly raced into the room, and within a few seconds, Mrs. Hayes appeared with Fiona in her arms.

While the Reynolds family flocked around Mrs. Hayes and the children, Robert pulled Yasmine into the hallway. His skin tingled with warmth and love and desire as they prepared themselves for the upcoming announcement. "You ready?" he asked, kissing her ring finger.

She nodded. "Thank you for waiting until my family got here. It's perfect."

"You are perfect." He captured her lips with his, his pulse quickening at having a few stolen moments with her. He longed for night to fall so they could lock themselves into their wing.

"Where'd they go?"

At Michelle's voice, Robert reluctantly lifted his mouth from Yasmine's, and hand in hand, they walked back into the family room.

Robert cleared his throat to get everyone's attention. "First of all," he began, "we want to thank all of you for setting time aside and being here with us. Erik and Michelle, thanks for the unauthorized use of your beautiful home. We apologize for the lies and the deception, but it was the only way to guarantee that all of you would make it here today."

"It's because we love each and every one of you," Yasmine added. She nodded to her parents. "Dad, Mom, thank you for being great examples as to what a marriage should be like. You sacrificed your lives, your needs, and your dreams so Luke, Naomi, and I could have better lives. You showed me what love and commitment is all about. I love you."

Robert caught Mrs. Hayes's gaze. "Thank you, Mrs. Hayes, for taking care of me, and Michelle when we needed you. If it weren't for you, we probably wouldn't be alive today." He felt the pressure building in his chest as he turned to his grandmother. "Grannie, the first time you met me, you told me that love was important, that once I found it, I should not let it go, that I should sacrifice and compromise for it. Thank you for those words—words I needed to hear that very night when Yasmine asked me to marry her."

Gasps of surprise resonated around the room. The tension in the air grew so thick, a jackhammer could not have broken through it. Then Mrs. Reynolds asked, "She proposed?" as if it were the most incredible thing she'd heard in a long time.

"Yes, Yasmine proposed because she'd turned me down twice in the past. Of course I said yes. I'm no idiot."

"Con—"

He raised his right hand to delay the well wishes. "We know you've all been waiting for this for four long years, ever since you found out we were seeing each other. So I'm sure that like us, you would not have wanted a long drawn-out engagement, so…"

"So," Yasmine picked up, "not only did we become engaged on Sunday night, but we got married on Wednesday morning." They held up their left hands, displaying their platinum wedding bands and the huge diamond ring on Yasmine's finger.

They couldn't hold back their families any longer, and for the next fifteen minutes, the room was abuzz with screams, hugs, kisses, slaps on the back, and well wishes, and of course questions about Yasmine turning down Robert's proposals twice before.

During a break, Naomi pulled them into a corner. "I guess you told him everything, Yas."

"I did. He took partial responsibility." Robert's wife smiled sweetly up at him. "And I did see my doctor. I can have as many children as I want."

"That's wonderful news, sis. So I expect some nieces and nephews soon."

"We'll try our best," Robert assured her.

"Welcome to the family, Robert." Luke pushed his sister aside as he and Christine came in for hugs.

"Maybe you'll be nice to me now," Robert joked.

Luke passed his hand over his shaved head. "My apologies. I didn't know she was the one doing the stringing all this time, man. What's wrong with you, girl?" He poked Yasmine in the side.

"I was holding out for this." Yas flashed her ring.

"That's a whopper ring," Christine said. "I should have held out for one like that."

"If you had, we wouldn't be married, darling," Luke said, pulling her out of the way to make room for Michelle.

"I didn't know Robert had proposed a second time," Michelle said. "But at this point, I don't care who asked whom. I'm just happy you're together at last. We're really sisters now," she added, squeezing Yasmine's hands. "One big happy family."

"Like you said the other night, we've always been sisters," Yasmine told her. "We've always been family, and now our children will share the same blood, binding us even closer, and forever."

"We have to find you a house in Granite Falls. You live too far away. With Grannie here now, you should think about moving closer," Michelle said. "Our kids should grow up together like we did. They should be able to see each other more than a few times a year."

"Have you thought about a honeymoon location yet?" Erik asked, joining the group.

"No, not yet," Robert answered.

"The Seychelles islands are beautiful this time of year. You can have the island of Michelle all to yourself."

Robert shook his head. "I don't know if I want to be honeymooning on an island named after my sister."

Yasmine giggled. "Yeah, too weird."

"Just pick a spot anywhere in the world and you'll have a LaCrosse private jet at your disposal. We'll be taking care of everything. Spare no expense. It's our wedding gift to you."

Before Robert or Yasmine could respond, his father-in-law took the initiative and asked the adults to take a glass of champagne, and the children their sparkling cider, and then he called for his wife.

"I'm right here, Luke." Robert's mother-in-law said, going over to stand beside her husband.

Mr. Reynolds took his wife's hand in his. "On behalf of my wife and myself, I want to make the first toast of the evening. To our lovely daughter, Yasmine Marie, and to Robert Javier, a boy we watched grow into a loving, caring, respectable man. "We could not have asked for a better choice for our baby girl," her father continued, obviously unaware of the recent tension between his wife and his daughter.

"Robert, you robbed me of the opportunity to walk my daughter proudly down the aisle. But seeing that we waited four years for this day, and the fact that she turned you down twice, I do understand your haste. I would have also slapped that wedding band on her finger faster than she could wink. She's a fine catch for any man, and you're lucky she bit your line, that she chose you above all other men. You have earned the right to call us Mom and Dad." He raised his glass. "To Robert and Yasmine. May your lives be blessed with love and happiness, and may your home be filled with laughter and children."

"Hear, hear."

While the chatter started up again, Robert turned to Yas. "This is forever. You don't ever have to worry about us splitting up. I will never leave you, and I refuse to let you leave me for any reason."

"Not even when my breasts start to sag, when crows start leaving their footprints in the corners of my eyes, and I lose my teeth?"

"Especially not when you lose your teeth. I'll make you new ones."

"Good answer," she said, with an animated smile.

"Oh, I almost forgot. Michelle and I received news about our parents."

"That's awesome, Rob. Is it good?" she added, her liveliness turning to concern.

"It's very good, but I'll share it with you later," he said, as the doorbell gonged.

"Who could that be now?" Erik asked in the seconds of silence that followed the interruption.

"Dinner," Robert stated. "I hope everyone is hungry because I think I ordered every dish from Ristorante Andreas."

"I guess I should let them in and alert the staff."

"Your staff will let them in, but they don't have to do anything else. I hired some help from the restaurant. They're taking care of everything, the food, the drinks, and the service. They're setting up in the great room. Let's just relax and mingle until they call us in to dinner."

"Why don't we give Christine and Luke a tour while we wait?" Michelle said.

"Sounds like an excellent idea." Mr. Reynolds strolled over to Robert and Yasmine. "Why don't you join the tour, Yas?"

"I've been here several times before, Daddy. I've seen it."

"See it again. I need to talk to my son-in-law." He gave her a stern look, the kind a child dared not disobey, no matter how old she got.

"Sure, Daddy. Good luck," Yasmine whispered to Robert.

Mr. Reynolds placed his hand on Robert's arm and directed him away from the crowd. "I received a call from Carl Arsenault a few hours ago. He said you went to their home and attacked Jeremy."

"Yes, that is correct."

Mr. Reynolds laughed. "Good for you. Naomi told me that Jeremy had cheated on Yasmine when they were together, about what his parents had said about my daughter, and about Yasmine's run-in with Carl at Naomi's place a week ago."

"I guess you don't know that Jeremy also went to Yasmine's office to try to win her back."

"He did what? When?"

Robert gave his father-in-law a snapshot version of Yasmine's confrontation with Jeremy. They shared a hearty laugh when Robert told him how Yasmine had taken care of Jeremy.

"I love that child of mine. She's a little tigress, was even as a child."

You have no idea, sir. Robert cleared his throat to mask the chuckle that threatened to erupt from inside him.

"Jeremy had it coming," Mr. Reynolds said. "As for Carl, I'm canceling all my policies with Arsenault Insurance." He held Robert's gaze. "Did you whoop his ass real good?"

"To a bloody pulp."

He tapped Robert on the back. "My daughter is in good hands. I need not worry about her. Thank you, Robert. Thank you for loving her, and for taking care of her."

"Always, Dad."

"*Dad*. I like that. At the expense of sounding cliché, I didn't lose a daughter; I gained a son." He walked back to his wife, shaking his head and chuckling.

As he watched his family and his in-laws mingle, get acquainted and reacquainted, Robert sent up a silent prayer of gratitude and thanks. Everything was all right with his world.

Well, almost…

CHAPTER EIGHTEEN

"*C*ome back here. Come back here, you bitch. You can't hide from me. I'm goin' gut you and your little brat. You hear me? I'm goin' gut you both. You'll be fish food by morning. Both y'all.*"

It was so dark, he couldn't see the trees lining the dirt road before him. But he knew they were there because sharp pain shot up his legs each time his feet hit the ground, and the branches from the trees lashed at his face, his arms, his legs as the firm hand on his wrist pulled him along. The pain spread to his chest. He couldn't breathe. His throat felt like when he ate dry toast without butter on it, his chest stung like he was covered with bees.

He was falling, falling. His foot banged against something hard and he stumbled, pulling her down with him at the same time his chin slammed into a rock and wave after wave of pain exploded through him. Warm sticky liquid dripped down his throat. He opened his mouth to scream from the pain, but she clamped her hand over his mouth.

"Come on, baby. Come on," she whispered. And then, picking him up, she clutched him to her chest and began running again as the mean man shouted behind them, his footsteps, his voice getting closer and closer.

And then she stopped suddenly. He opened his eyes and watched her petrified face as she stood under the bright lamppost, her breath coming out loud and hard, her heart going rumpa pum pum in his ears pressed to her chest.

"Ah, gotcha. You ain't got nowhere to go now. Do ya? Huh, do yah? Gimme that."

Two big strong hands wrapped around his arms, and with one powerful tug, ripped him from his mother's breast.

"No! No!" He kicked at the man, trying to free himself as he hauled him over to a flight of wooden stairs and began climbing. Up and up and up, the man dragged him while splinters ripped into the flesh of his legs, his arms, his belly, and back.

"Robert! Robert! Robert," his mother cried, scrambling up the stairs after the man, trying to grab Robert's legs and pull him down. All she got were his shoes and his socks and he watched in panic as they bounced off the steps and fell over the side into the river below.

"Mommy! Mommy! Daddy! Daddy!" he screamed at the top of his lungs, as she stumbled and almost followed his socks and shoes through the railing.

"Your daddy can't hear you, you little shit," the man said, as he reached the top of the stairs and stood on a concrete landing.

He began to tremble as he heard the sound of the waterfall crashing furiously against the rocks below. His heart beat fast as his mother lurched toward them, hitting the man in the face, and on his chest. "Give me back my son. Give me back my son!"

"You bitch!" He slammed his fist into her face, sending her flying to the concrete, blood dripping from her mouth.

Anger boiled in Robert at the sight of his mother crouched on the ground in pain, moaning and wailing like a wild animal that had been caught in a trap. He'd never heard his mother cry like that before. He'd never heard his mother cry until the night she came home with this man. Where was his daddy? Why had he left them with this mean man?

Robert's rage at its peak, he sank his teeth into the man's arm, biting hard until he tasted blood, kicking and lashing out at him with all his strength. Then the next instant, he felt a massive blow on one side of his *head, followed by an even harder one on the other side. As he stood reeling from the pain, the man picked him up, turned him upside down, held him by his ankles, and hoisted him over the bridge.*

"You can run, you can bite, you can kick, now let's see if you can fly."

Robert swallowed hard to keep from choking as all the fluids inside his body rushed to his head, and the blood from the cut on his chin trickled over his lips and into his nose while the cold sprays from the force of the waterfall whipped his skin. He thrashed about like a fish that had been caught in a net as he fought off dizziness.

"No! No!" his mother screamed behind them. "Please, don't hurt my son. Don't hurt him."

"Bitch, I told you to keep your fucking mouth shut. I saw you. I saw you talking to that woman at the bus stop. You told her to call the cops. Didn't you? Didn't you?"

"I'm sorry. I'm sorry."

"Too late for that. I'm going to toss your little brat in the river. You're going to watch him die, and then I'm tossing you over after him."

"No, please. Not my baby. Not my baby. Robert!" she screamed above the rushing water below.

"Mommy! Mommy! Help me!" he cried, flailing his arms around in the air, as the man swung him back and forth, taunting her, laughing, as she wailed hysterically.

"Please, Timmy. Please don't kill my son. He's all I have."

"You goin' tell anybody what happened?"

"No."

"You goin' try to call the cops?"

"No. No. I promise. I will never tell anyone what you did. I promise." She was on her knees at the man's feet, clutching his legs and pleading, her face so close to Robert's in his upside-down position, he could almost smell the fear in her throat.

"And you'll do everything I tell you?"

"Yes. Yes." She reached through the steel railing as if to catch him, but Timmy swung him to the other side, out of her reach.

"You'll be nice to me? Real nice?"

"Yes. Yes. I'll do whatever you want. Please just give me back my son."

"Next time, I'm goin' drop him." The man pulled Robert back over the railing and tossed him onto the concrete as if he were a sack of flour.

Every bone in his body hurt as his mother picked him up and cradled him close to her heart, her sobs echoing through the night and her salty tears dripping into the cut on his chin, stinging his flesh. He wound his hands around her waist, never wanting to let her go.

"Just remember what you promised. Now stop all that cryin' and come on. We gotta find some place to sleep tonight."

"Robert. Robert. Wake up. Wake up, baby. You're having a bad dream."

Robert snapped awake, his heart racing and his body covered in perspiration. Harsh tremors shook his body, but he drew comfort from the hands holding him, Yasmine cradling his head to her breasts, whispering that everything was okay.

"He tried to kill me, Yas. He dangled me over the bridge upside down and threatened to drop me. And he hit her. He hit my mom. He made her cry, and he made her bleed."

"I know, baby. But he can't hurt you anymore. You're not a helpless little boy anymore, Robert. You're big now, and strong, the strongest man I know. And Timmy Gleason is dead. He can't hurt you or Michelle or your mom again."

"No. Don't leave," he said, when she tried to pry his arms from around him.

"I'm just getting you some water, baby. That's all."

Yasmine's sorrow for him was so severe, it was causing physical pain in every cell of her body. Pushing back the sob in her throat, she reached over toward her nightstand, and by the light of the moon streaming into their bedroom, she poured her husband a glass of water from a pitcher she'd prepared before they went to bed.

"Here, you are baby," she said, holding it to his lips as he leaned back against the cushioned headboard. She bit into her lips when his fingers wrapped around hers, guiding her as she fed him the water.

It had been two weeks since they'd gotten married, and a little over a week since Robert had been having flashbacks about the night Timmy Gleason tried to kill him. His nightmares had begun in Granite Falls after he'd received the report about his parents' lives and seen pictures of them in their youth—some as far back as their high school years, some before Robert was born, and a few of him and his parents before Timmy Gleason had ripped their family apart.

A neighbor who was still living in the apartment next to the one where they used to live had found the envelope with the pictures in the stairwell thirty years ago. She'd knocked on their door to return them, but a woman—probably the one claiming to be Timmy's common-law wife and who'd warned Timmy not to return to Virginia—had answered the door and had told the neighbor that the Carters had moved out of state in a hurry and that she was subletting the apartment. It was her ploy to deflect suspicion.

When the private investigators had questioned the neighbor, she'd said she just felt like she was supposed to hold on to the pictures. Robert had assumed that his mother must have grabbed the envelope when they'd been forced from their home and had dropped it, either intentionally or accidentally, as Timmy had hurried them down the stairs. They would never know.

"Thanks, babe."

Yasmine started at the sound of Robert's voice. She returned the empty glass to the nightstand, and put her arms around her husband's naked torso, still covered with sweat. But at least his tremors had ceased.

"Feeling better?" she asked, nuzzling her nose against his

cheek and chin, the stubble from his beard causing little shivers to ripple under her skin.

"Just hold me," he said, wrapping his arms around her as they scooted back down the bed and nestled under the covers, belly to belly. "It was vivid tonight. It's almost as if I was there again."

"Well, you are there in your mind each time you remember. Did Dr. West hypnotize you again tonight?" He'd done his first hypnotic session about that night upon their return from Granite Falls. "Is that why it was so vivid?"

"No. We just talked, mostly about the few months leading up to my mom's death. He shuddered. "I'm glad you're here with me, now." His hand caressed her back.

She rested her hand against his chest, loving the steady beat of his heart under her palm. "We're in this together. Through the good, the bad, and the ugly. You shared my ugliness, now it's time I shared yours."

Pulling his left hand from between them, he clasped hers, their rings clinking, reminding them of their official pledge of commitment. "I don't know what I would have done if I'd remembered before we got married and were still living apart. I can't imagine waking up in the middle of the night and not having you here to hold me. You make me feel safe, Yas. The safest place in the world for me is in your arms."

"And I with you, Rob."

"I'm sorry I'm such a little boy."

"You've earned that right, sweetie." Yasmine pressed her lips to his forehead and then settled his head on her chest as if he were that little boy of four years who'd been scared out of his mind. He'd grown up that night thirty years ago when he'd seen his mother beaten by a brute, simply because she was trying to protect her son. He'd had to be strong for her, show her that she didn't have to worry about him, thus placing herself and her unborn child—his little sister—in harm's way.

No wonder he'd forgotten everything. He couldn't afford to be soft or weak. He couldn't allow the terror of that night to control him. He'd had to stay in control of his emotions and the only way he knew how to do that was to be on the offense, always. The aloof persona he'd portrayed all his life had been his coping mechanism, his way of fooling the world into believing that he wasn't afraid, that he couldn't be scared when all the time that timid, frightened little boy had been crouching in the dark shadows of his soul.

That little boy had finally emerged, seeking love, comfort, understanding, a warm hand to soothe him—all the things a child needed to feel safe. There was no way in hell Yasmine was going to let him feel ashamed and weak for needing those things, not after all the pain and suffering he'd had to endure in silence.

"I love you, Robert, and I'm here for you for whatever you need. I'll hold you when you wake up crying in the night. I'll always take care of you. I'll always be here for you."

"Yas," he whispered, his voice ripe with admiration, appreciation, affection, gratitude, and love. "My strong, beautiful Yas, you're already everything and more than I need. I love you more than I thought it possible to love anyone. Always and forever," he said, lifting his head, and covering her mouth with his.

It was a sensual kiss, one of appreciation and love, and the joy of knowing that they could share intimacies as husband and wife while holding back their sexual desires for each other. Robert didn't need a lover tonight. He needed a comforter. She was his comforter. Sorrow had carved a deep well into his soul, but Yasmine swore in her heart to fill that well with happiness, and joy, and love, much more than he would be able to contain.

This kind of connection, this togetherness and sharing of

one's heart, mind, and soul, this acceptance of each other without judgment, doubt, and criticism, was new for both of them. They'd been best friends, long before they were lovers. Now, they were best friends in love. They were good. Solid. Built to last for this lifetime and all the others that would follow.

CHAPTER NINETEEN

T he weeks had flown by quickly, Yasmine thought as she followed the hostess to the lounge area in an upscale restaurant and bar near her office. She'd stayed later than usual to prep a client for court on Monday, and was on her way home from dinner at her favorite Thai restaurant when Armand had called and asked her to meet him for drinks to discuss something important.

She'd only agreed to meet him because Robert wasn't home. He'd left for New York yesterday for a conference with some new investors for Carter Dental, and wasn't due home until tomorrow. The conference had been previously scheduled to take place around the time Margaret had come into his life, so of course he'd had to postpone it while he bonded with his grandmother.

Their lives had been crazy busy since their engagement, quickie marriage, Robert dealing with his memories of the night he almost died, selling her condo, moving into Beacon Hill, traveling to North Carolina with the LaCrosse family to meet Robert's Aunt Camille and her children: twenty-three-year-old

Allison and twenty-one-year-old Neil. And then their honeymoon.

Yasmine felt a powerful contraction between her thighs as she thought of the two weeks she and Robert had spent on *Baia Degli Amanti*—the private Caribbean island, jointly owned by Erik and his billionaire friends.

She and Robert were settling in nicely to married life, and enjoying it to the max, making Yasmine wish she'd accepted his first proposal. Voicing her regrets, Robert had told her that nothing happened before its time. He was a broken man when he'd asked her to marry him the first time, and she needed to find herself, become Yasmine Reynolds before she could be Yasmine Carter. That way, she would have no regrets.

"Would you like to see the menu?" the hostess asked, stopping under a window overlooking Fenway Park.

Yas sat down in a chair, facing the window. "No. Just a club soda on the rocks, thanks."

"Would you like a slice of lime or lemon?"

"No. No lime nor lemon."

"I'll send it right over."

Yasmine set her purse on the low table and looked around at the early Thursday evening patrons in the dining area on her left, and those crowding the bar on her right. The food was excellent here, and she knew a line would be forming outside as the evening rolled on. Hopefully by then, she and Armand would have completed their business and she could be home for her prescheduled video chat date with her husband.

Her husband. Yasmine smiled as she glanced down at the rings on her finger. She had been a married woman for a little over two months. And even though she and Rob had been together for five years, it felt new to her. Maybe it was due to the fact that for the first time in their relationship, they were living under the same roof.

Every night, they fell asleep in each other's arms and every morning they awoke that way, except for the times when he was away on business. And their sex life was off the chain, every single time. Damn, she never realized Rob was so romantic and that he practiced Tantric and Taoist sex. He was proving to be the quintessential husband, friend, and lover.

Robert came home early most days, and had dinner cooking and a bubble bath drawn for her, and depending on how dinner was progressing, they would go upstairs and take a bath or shower together. Sometimes they never made it back downstairs.

Two nights ago, Yasmine had come home to a dinner of roasted duck, mashed red potatoes, and grilled asparagus. As usual, Robert had a bath ready for her, and had requested that she wear only her robe to dinner. Yasmine's mind had been reeling with curiosity, and her body had been twitching with anticipation as she'd joined him in the dining room. He too was wearing a robe, and from the lingering aroma of his body wash, she knew he'd taken a shower in one of the other bathrooms while she'd been taking her bath. She'd also been surprised to find a black silk pillow in the center of the table.

Avoiding all her questions, he'd seated her, and then explained that they would be feeding each other while they gazed into each other's eyes. They were to study the expression on each other's faces, and the changes in their pupils as they reacted to the different tastes.

Yasmine had never experienced anything so erotic. As she'd watched Robert's mouth open slightly to receive the food she fed him, the motion of his lips closing over the fork, and her pulling it very slowly from his mouth, her body had begun to heat up and the inner walls of her vagina had quivered uncontrollably. Visions of lying naked on her back, with her thighs spread wide and her soft wet woman's sex opening up for Robert's hard shaft and clasping around him just like his lips clasped the fork, of him withdrawing slowly from her heated sex as she pulled the fork from his mouth, only to thrust back in again, were all driving Yasmine insane with lust. After the first few bites, she'd wanted to rip their robes off and pull Robert down on top of her on the floor, but he'd displayed amazing control.

Once dinner was over, Robert had silently stood up, coaxed her from her chair, removed her robe, placed the pillow on the edge of the table, lifted her up, and laid her on her back on the table with her buttock on the pillow. And while she'd lain there, her body hot and tight with yearning and moisture dripping from inside her on to the pillow, he'd dropped his robe, exposing his erection.

He'd pressed her legs together, and raised them straight up into the air, her soles parallel with the ceiling. He'd stepped closer, and she'd gasped with ecstasy as he pressed the back of her thighs and calves into his stomach and chest, and held them tight. While she gazed into his sexy brown eyes, shimmering with lust, he'd reached down and dragged the tip of his erection, along the length of her hot cavern, starting at her swollen clit and down, down, down, millimeter by millimeter, until he lodged against her taut opening.

Yasmine had opened her mouth on a long scream as he thrust deeply and sturdily into her. She was already tight from anticipation, but the Mermaid position he had her in had rendered her tighter still and had caused the most incredible, mind-blowing friction Yasmine had ever experienced. She'd been on fire, and could do nothing but lie there shivering from the intensity of her pleasure as Robert thrust steadily back and forth inside her, never easing up until he'd collapsed on her, his body jerking spasmodically as he'd flooded her womb with his hot cum.

And then the kitchen timer had gone off, signaling that his crème brulee was done.

"You planned this down to the very second, didn't you?" she'd asked after she'd regained her breath and he lay on top of her, still buried deep inside her. She must have come a dozen times in those forty minutes, or maybe she'd been experiencing one long orgasm for the entire forty minutes. It was all the same. She couldn't walk afterwards.

He'd smiled sensuously. "Hmm. I was conducting an experiment."

"How was it?" she'd asked on a giggle.

"It's not done yet," he'd answered, pulling out of her and snatching a towel from the chair—a towel she didn't even realize was there—and hastily mopping them both up.

"You've been holding out on me," she'd told him, as he'd carried her upstairs. "We've been together for five years. How come you never showed me this side of you before?"

"These are wifely privileges, baby," he'd said, his eyes still drunk with passion as he laid her in the middle of their bed. "I wanted to wait and experience pleasure with my wife that I've never experienced with any other woman."

"You mean I could have been enjoying these unexpected, sensational moments all along?"

"Yep," he'd drawled, slapping her on her ass. "You rest up. I'll be right back with dessert, and then we'll try the G-Force position."

"The G-Force? What's that?"

"That's when I take the reins."

"Sounds freaky."

"Don't worry. You'll love it," he'd said, chuckling as he strode out of the bedroom, his flaccid cock swinging in front of him like a gigantic pendulum, a cock that had been a column of strength and passion just moments before, and which would be again before the night was out.

"I wish I could say that smile on your face is in anticipation of meeting with me."

Yasmine jumped at the sound of Armand's voice. She relaxed her toes inside her heels, never even realizing they'd been curled while she'd been reminiscing about making love with Rob. She squeezed her legs together, trying to stop the tremors happening between her thighs. She could do nothing about the moisture in her panties. Thank goodness it was a leather chair so she needn't worry about a wet spot when she got up.

"Yeah, wish on," she said, as Armand bent down to give her a hug.

"Traffic was horrible out of Dorchester. You've been waiting long?" He dropped his weight into the chair across from her.

"No. Just a few minutes."

"You hungry? I'll pay."

She laughed. "I had dinner, but I ordered a club soda, and here it is," she said, as the waiter approached them.

Armand ordered a mojito and they made small talk about his parents, and his new girlfriend whom Yasmine had met last weekend when they'd double dated with her and Robert. Armand wouldn't keep the new woman for too long.

Yas checked her watch, a dainty gold and sapphire accessory that used to belong to Robert's great-grandmother. She hadn't wanted to take it, thinking that it should go to Michelle. But Margaret had insisted, and Michelle hadn't minded. Like Michelle had said the day she and Rob had announced their marriage, they were one big happy family now.

"You keep looking at your watch. You and Robert have a hot date tonight?" Armand asked around his straw.

"Well, we are newlyweds," she said, grinning. "All our dates are hot." *Even the video ones.*

"Spoken like a woman in love."

She chuckled. "So why'd you want to meet? Does it have

anything to do with your two days of absence from the office this week?"

"It does." He glanced around as if checking to make sure no one could hear him, then leaned closer to her. "A few weeks ago, I was approached by another firm. They want me to join them, as a partner, not an associate."

"You're leaving H and H?" she asked, using the code name they used when they spoke about their firm in public. Yasmine had learned the hard way that the walls did indeed have ears.

"I'm not sure, but I feel that I've risen as far as I can in the seven years I've been with this firm."

"Might be the seven-year-itch."

"Could be. I just know that I want to do more with my life. I want bigger responsibilities and bigger commissions. I'm tired of being an associate. You understand, right? You've talked about hoping to become partner one day."

"I have," Yas said, taking a sip of her club soda to combat the dryness in her throat at the thought of losing the closest friend she had at the firm.

"My parents are getting older, and they want to move to Florida in a few years," Armand said. "I'd like to be able to buy them a nice place, set them up so they can retire in style."

"Is that where the firm is? In Florida?" she asked. "I mean it's not like you have any other ties here in New England." Her voice sounded gloomier than she had realized she was.

"No. It's here in the city."

"Oh, that's good. I was worried that I was losing the one friend I had here. Did you take the offer?"

He shook his head. "No, not yet. I wanted to talk with you first, see if you wanted to join me—"

"You're asking if I want to leave H and H for another firm?" Her eyes narrowed skeptically.

"Not just another firm, Yas. Our firm."

Yasmine gasped.

"We are damned good lawyers, two of the best at H and H, but we have to face the facts."

"We are black and all the other partners are white," she said, a bit uneasy about voicing the facts that had been in her head for a long time.

"Exactly. We would be powerful together." He grinned and carved out a sign in the air. "Picture it: Carter and Hendricks or Reynolds and Hendricks. I'll let you go first because I'm a gentleman," he added on a chuckle.

"So you want us to pull an Alicia and Cary on H and H? Take our clients with us?"

"Families break up all the time. Kids leave home and make their own lives, carve out their own places in the world."

Yasmine wondered why she wasn't feeling as elated as she should be at the prospect of having her name on a ritzy office in Government Center, and not as a partner, but as a proprietor. Maybe it was because her priorities had changed. She was a wife now, and instead of writing briefs and reading law tomes, and preparing opening and closing statements, she was looking forward to reading baby books, learning how to cook gourmet meals, and baby-proofing her home.

Besides, she wasn't enjoying splitting up couples anymore, especially after her mother had asked her to represent her in divorcing her father. That request had been Yasmine's wake-up call. Her career had ceased bringing her satisfaction. Art imitating life was too unsettling. She'd been placed in her clients' children's shoes, and she didn't like it.

Thank God her mom had come to her senses and begun appreciating what she had instead of complaining about what she didn't. Her parents had gone on their anniversary trip and upon their return, they had started working out their issues with the help of a marriage counselor.

"So what are your thoughts?" Armand asked, bringing her back to his idea.

Yasmine took a deep breath. "I don't know, Armand," she said honestly. "The idea is tempting. If you had made the suggestion a couple months ago, I would have jumped at the possibility." She rolled her fingers around her engagement and wedding bands. "Even though I've cut back my caseload, I'm still putting in a lot of hours as an associate. As a partner, especially a start-up one, my responsibilities would increase tremendously."

He sat back in his chair, his shoulders drooping in disappointment. "I understand. It would've been fun though. You and me," he said with a smile.

"Yeah, it would have been, but—"

"But what?" Armand asked, as Yasmine stopped mid sentence.

"Isn't that Sly?" She pointed toward the bar.

His gaze followed hers. "Looks like it. She frequents the joint."

Yasmine narrowed her eyes as Sylvia tried to get up on a stool and stumbled, her clutch falling to the floor. "She looks loaded," Yasmine said, as Sylvia finally made it on to the stool, but left her purse on the floor where it had fallen.

"Or high. Where's the rest of her posse? She never goes clubbing alone."

Yasmine's flesh crawled as an older man snagged the stool next to Sylvia and immediately put his hand on her ass. Yasmine's temper flared when Sylvia knocked it away. "Did you see that?"

"I did. Maybe she's playing hard to get. It's Sylvia. She sleeps around," Armand said, clearly unconcerned. "I've seen her walk out of here with guys she met at the bar."

"He's old enough to be her father."

He huffed. "Like that ever stopped her before."

Yasmine rolled her eyes at him then glanced back to the bar. "Look. She knocked his hand off her ass again, and she's pushing him away. Why isn't the bartender doing something?" Yasmine shot to her feet. If she or anyone she knew was in a similar situation, she hoped someone would look out for them. "Come on, Armand. Man up, or else I will. I have no special love for Sylvia, but she's a woman, and I'm not going to stand by and let some old pervert whose rug looks like he just ripped it off an alley rat hit on her." Impulse propelled her across the floor.

"I got this," Armand said, striding past her to stand beside Sylvia's stool. "You okay, Sly?" he asked, peering into the drunk girl's face.

"Hey, pal," the man said. "Go get your own. This is my stand for the night."

Syl turned and peered up at Armand. "Ar—Armand? Is that you? What you doing here?"

"Yeah, it's me. What are *you* doing here?"

"Drinking." She slammed her hand against the counter. "Bartender, what's a girl have to do for a drink around here?"

Armand stilled her hand. "Syl—"

The man stood up and placed his hand on Armand's arm. "Hey, I said this is mine. You got yours."

"You better take your hands off me," Armand grated through his teeth.

The man dropped his hand, and leered at Yasmine. "On second thought, you want to trade? It's been a while since I had a taste of dark chocolate, and this one here looks extra sweet."

Yasmine jumped back as the man tried to grab her. Then in the next second, he went flying to the floor, knocking over his stool, causing the person next to him to jump out of the way. His rug bounced off his head and landed under a nearby table. The woman at the table kicked it back, and it landed on his chest.

Yasmine swallowed her burst of laughter as a deadly silence enveloped the room and all eyes turned on them.

The bouncer and the manager appeared. "Is there a problem?" the manager asked.

"You bet there is," the man said, looking up from the floor as he rubbed the red area of his jaw where Armand had punched him. "I'm suing the pants off him."

"Sue away. We're both lawyers," Yasmine said, killing the urge to spit on him. She caught the manager's gaze. "This man was hitting on this woman who is clearly in no position to consent to anything. My friend asked him to leave her alone. He tried to grab me and ended up on the floor."

"Is that what happened?" the bouncer asked Sylvia.

Her head flopped as she tried to nod. "He had his hand on my—my ass. I told him to—to stop, but he did it again, but then Armand here—my—my black knight in shining armor, rode up on his steed and rescued me. Go Armand. Hurray."

"You're out of here, pal." The bouncer picked up the man, slapped his rug haphazardly on his head, and escorted him to the door.

"You want some ice for your hand?" the bartender asked Armand.

He shook his head. "I'm fine. He was soft."

"I'm sorry," the manager said. "And thank you for intervening. He did look like a scary character. No telling what could have happened to her if she'd left with him. Your drinks are on the house tonight." He turned to the curious onlookers. "Everything is fine now, ladies and gentlemen. Please enjoy the rest of the evening. The next round of drinks is on us."

"What are we going to do with her?" Yasmine picked up Sylvia's purse from the floor. "We can't leave her here, and she's in no condition to drive, or even take public transportation. We can put her in a cab and pay the driver to take her home. Or—"

she glanced at her watch. If she drove Sylvia to Charlestown, she might have just enough time to get back to Beacon Hill before Robert called her to video chat. If Yasmine were ever in this condition, this is what she would have wanted someone she knew and trusted to do for her. "I'll take her home."

"No. You don't live in Charlestown anymore, Yas. I'll do it. I'll take Syl home."

Yasmine was taken aback at Armand's offer, but before she could react, Sylvia swiveled on her stool, threw her arms around his neck, dropped her head on his chest, and puked all over him. Yasmine stood there watching with her eyes wide and her mouth gaping.

"Shit," Armand hissed under his breath. He tried to remove Sylvia's hands from around his neck and lift her head from his chest. "My brand new Gucci." He glanced down at his tan crocodile loafers covered with vomit.

"Oh crap," Yas said, as the front door of the restaurant opened and Charles Hayward walked in, followed by a mean-looking Hulk Hogan look-alike.

Could it get any worse tonight?

CHAPTER TWENTY

M r. Hayward's eyes scanned the room before zeroing in on them. He strode in their direction, and snapped his fingers at Hulk, who then picked Sylvia up off Armand's chest, tossed her over his shoulder like she was a bale of hay, and carried her outside.

The bartender handed Armand a stack of napkins.

Yasmine watched, still mortified as Armand tried to clean Sylvia's puke off his jacket and shirt. From the disgusted look on his face, she knew it had already seeped past the fabric of his shirt, and into his skin. And it was starting to stink.

"Did you get my niece drunk, Mr. Hendricks?" Mr. Hayward's gray eyes were hard, and held a hint of disappointment as he stared up at Armand.

"Mr. Hayward, I—um—"

"She was already intoxicated when she arrived, Mr. Hayward," Yasmine said. "Another man was hitting on her and Armand punched him out."

Mr. Hayward's eyes lost some of their chill. "I should have known you're not the kind of man who would take advantage of a young girl, Mr. Hendricks. Forgive me."

"I should head home before I start stinking up the place," Armand said, stacking the soiled napkins on the tray the waiter placed in front of him.

Yasmine stepped aside as someone with a bucket and mop appeared and began cleaning the area.

"Can you stay a minute?" Mr. Hayward said, glancing at Yasmine and Armand. "I've been meaning to speak to both of you, and since you're already here, why not?"

Yasmine exchanged a look with Armand. Why would Charles Hayward want to speak with both of them together? Had they screwed up a case? Was a client unhappy with their services? Had he heard about Armand's offer from the other law firm? Had it been a setup to test his loyalty? *Crap.* Had Armand shared his idea of starting a firm with her with someone else, and it had gotten back to Hayward? She wasn't worried about losing her job. Hell, it would probably be a blessing. But Armand…

"Do you have a table?" Mr. Hayward asked.

"We were just having drinks in the lounge," Armand said, exchanging another glance with her over Hayward's head.

Mr. Hayward indicated for Yasmine to lead the way back to their seats, and once they arrived, Armand pulled up another chair for the older man, and reclaimed his chair after Mr. Hayward sat down.

Yasmine held her breath as Hayward unbuttoned his suit jacket and settled down into the chair that seemed to swallow him up. He was a few inches shorter than Yasmine and just as slim, but he projected a sense of authority that couldn't be ignored. What he lacked in stature, he made up in intelligence and his ability to monopolize in the corporate world. He and his twin sister had built Hayward & Harley from the ground up, and once she died, he'd carried on their legacy and worked overtime and double time as if he was making up for her absence.

"Would you like a drink, sir?" Armand asked, breaking the awkward silence.

He raised his hand to stop Armand from calling for the waiter. "First, I want to thank you for what you just did for Sylvia. She's never been one to make good choices, even when she was a child." He smiled with obvious affection for his niece.

"This is hers." Yasmine handed him Syl's Louis Vuitton clutch.

He placed it on his lap and gazed at it for a few seconds before raising his head. "I'm neither blind nor stupid. I know Sylvia sleeps around with the associates at the firm and sometimes with our clients."

Yasmine held her breath and watched Armand's Adam's apple vibrate as he swallowed. They both reached for their drinks and simultaneously took sips, their eyes frozen wide as they stared at each other over the rims of their glasses.

Hayward turned to Armand. "You, Mr. Hendricks, are probably the only single man she hasn't slept with at the firm. And I know it's not for a lack of trying on her part. I'm very grateful to you for not taking advantage of her."

"Thank you, sir," Armand said.

Hayward turned to Yasmine. "I'm certain you've seen the men, including lawyers from the firm going in and out of Sylvia's condo. Yet, I've never heard you talk badly about her, or gossip about what you see."

"I'm not one to gossip about other people, Mr. Hayward. You are my boss, and Sylvia is your niece. I respect that."

"I admire that respect from both of you. You've demonstrated loyal to me and to my family's name. It's the kind of loyalty and commitment Hayward and Harley was founded upon." He paused and ran his palm across, Sylvia's purse, still lying on his lap. "I'm retiring from the practice," he said, his gray eyes intense, as he looked from Armand to Yasmine. "I'm moving out west to be near my children and enjoy my grandchildren. I told Sylvia today. She's been upset. That's probably why she felt the need to become inebriated. She's torn between following me and remaining here in Boston."

"Oh," was all Yasmine could say.

"Which brings me to the reason I wanted to see both of you. I'm offering you the firm."

Shock rippled through Yasmine and her toes curled in her heels as if she were experiencing an orgasm.

"What do you mean you're offering us the firm?" Armand shifted in his chair, causing a whiff of vomit to circulate in their area.

"I evaluated all the associates in the firm and you two stood out because of your outstanding character, but especially you, for being one of the highest producing associates in the firm, Ms. Reynolds." He paused. "It will cost you though."

Yasmine caught Armand's gaze. A firm like Hayward & Harley was worth hundreds of millions. Where did Mr. Hayward think she and Armand would get that kind of money? Her husband was a multimillionaire, but she doubted he'd want to spot her for H & H. She wouldn't dream of asking him. She took the initiative. "How much, sir?"

Mr. Hayward wrinkled his hook-like nose, a smile tipping his mouth. "Hmm. One dollar each."

"A dollar each?" they both exclaimed, staring at each other, then at the old man.

Hayward smiled. "If you accept my offer, you can either keep the name as it is: Hayward and Harley, or you can add Hendricks and Reynolds, or Carter," he added, as he inclined his head toward Yasmine. "It's strictly up to you. Are you interested?"

"I am," Armand said without preamble.

"I have to talk it over with my husband," Yasmine said, her voice trembling. "And he isn't expected home until tomorrow."

"Of course."

Yasmine could only imagine what was going on in Armand's head. A few minutes ago, he was talking about leaving H & H, and taking her with him. And now they'd had the most successful law firm in the area handed to them for two George Washingtons. Yasmine tried hard to contain the cry of excitement bubbling in her chest.

"Regarding Sylvia, if she stays on the east coast, I would appreciate it if you'd look out for her."

"Sure," Yas said.

"Definitely," Armand added.

Mr. Hayward rose to his feet and tucked Syl's purse under his arm. "You have seventy-two hours to think it over and discuss with your families. After that, the offer moves on to the next possible candidates." He glanced at Armand. "Feel free to bill your dry cleaning to the firm, and the replacement of your shoes, if necessary." He tilted his head to both of them. "Enjoy the rest of your evening."

"Holy crap!" Armand held his explosion until the restaurant door closed behind Charles Hayward. "Do you believe that? Hayward and Harley is ours. Ours, Yas."

"Uh-uh," Yas said, as he tried to hug her.

"Oh yeah, Syl's vomit. But I don't even mind."

"It's hard to wrap my head around." Yasmine's grin was so wide, her face hurt. "But, Armand, I'm running from career responsibilities, not toward them."

"Girl, you'll own the firm. You can delegate. You can work from home. You can do whatever you damn well please."

"Yeah, I can. Can't I?" she said, picking up her purse from the table. "But I'll still have to be there."

"Think," Armand said, following her to the door. "In the last few years, how many times have we seen old man Hayward around the office? He usually comes in for the board meetings and to assist if we have problems or questions with a case, but he's not there on a nine-to-nine basis like us. He doesn't need to be. The firm is running smoothly. It's bringing in money."

Yasmine chuckled, her head still spinning with the unbelievable news. "You're right, he has done all the ground work for us."

"Exactly. As long as one of us is there on a daily basis, it will be fine. I'll volunteer to be there every day. You can relax and enjoy Robert and your little Robbies and Yassies that come along in the future."

Yasmine smiled. He had no idea that that future was already upon her. Her heart skipped a beat at the knowledge, even as it ached for the child she'd lost, and would never hold in her arms. Her doctor had said that it was her extreme stress that had caused her to miscarry. It didn't bring Yasmine any comfort since she'd thought of aborting the baby. Even though she knew she would not have gone through with it, the thought that she considered it would haunt her for the rest of her life.

"We have a lot to talk about." Armand's voice broke into her thoughts. "We only have seventy-two hours. Let's make them count before this opportunity moves on to someone else."

Yasmine stepped out onto the sidewalk when Armand opened the door. She pulled her jacket tighter around her chest as the cool evening breeze brushed her skin. "I'll talk to Robert tonight."

"I thought he was out of town."

"He is. But we're video chatting. That's why I need to hurry home."

"Give him my regards."

"I will." *Boy had she been lassoed.* Yasmine thought as Armand helped her into her car and bid her good night. As she drove away from the curb, she felt more liberated about the thought of discussing her professional future with Robert than when she was single and making decisions about her life on her own.

Maybe it was because Robert gave her the freedom to remain independent. He wasn't the kind of man who was threatened by his woman's success, even if it turned out to be bigger than his. He'd allowed her to continue to be *Yasmine*, by taking on the responsibilities of cooking their meals, cleaning their house, and doing their laundry and grocery shopping.

He hadn't turned her into a haggard, frustrated housewife who had to hurry home from the office to cook her husband's dinner, but a completely satisfied one who hurried home from the office to enjoy the delicious gourmet meals her husband prepared for her. Her only requirement as his wife was to be satisfied in his bed, and she was, beyond her wildest imaginations.

And now Mr. Hayward was giving her the chance to be at the top of the corporate ladder—head of her own law firm with a long list of clients, each bringing in millions of dollars a year.

Yasmine had arrived. She had it all. Everything she'd been working for her entire life.

Question was: did she want it all?

Yasmine parked her car in her private space, killed the engine and checked her watch. She had just enough time to take a quick shower before her video call. With her purse and briefcase in hand, she walked up the steps to the porch, turned her key in the lock, opened the door, and stepped onto to a bed of red and white rose petals scattered on the marble floor of the foyer.

If she hadn't known better, Yasmine would have backtracked, thinking she'd entered the wrong house. But she did know better. Her husband had come home early. The elation of his presence flooded her soul as she found herself encased between two rows of vanilla-scented candles, leading from the front door and ending at the spiral stairs. There were twelve in all, six on each side, with vases of red and white roses and baby's breath at their bases. The only light in the downstairs area, the four-feet-high candles flicked softly like a gentle fire in the hearth.

Yasmine's pulse beat like a drum. How did she ever get this lucky? she wondered, heeling the door shut behind her and placing the items in her hands on the table. She stood transfixed, peering through the semidarkness, expecting Robert to appear with a glass of wine or a rose or a wrapped box with a *Because* present inside it.

He loved surprising her with gifts. Sometimes they were exuberantly expensive, like the gold sapphire, emerald and diamond earrings dangling from her earlobes, and sometimes it was a bag or a box of her favorite junk food that cost little more than a dollar. And each time she'd asked him what the occasion was, he would simply say, "Because."

When a few timeless minutes slipped by and Robert hadn't appeared, she took a couple steps forward then halted in mid-stride when Babyface's "When Your Body Gets Weak" floated from the surround sound stereo, followed a few seconds later by Robert's deep voice.

Yasmine had no idea if it was live or prerecorded, but it didn't matter. All that mattered was that Robert's seductive, sexy voice echoed deep in her belly, awakening her cravings for him.

"Good Evening, Mrs. Carter. I am so very honored you can join me tonight. I have been looking forward to this moment. All. Day. Long. I have a delightful evening planned for you, my dear. My only wish, my only desire is to please you. Tonight, I want you to do nothing. Give nothing. Say nothing. Your only command is to receive. All of me. But before we start, I ask that you leave your bags and your clothes at the door. Leave your work, and all your worries, too. Clear your mind, my love. Strip yourself bare before we begin this sensual expedition of lust and love. I will hold you, Mrs. Carter. I

will kiss, and caress you. I will taste every delightful inch of your smooth silky skin, and when your body gets weak, and you lay quivering beneath me, then, and only then will I come inside you. And I will love you. All. Night. Long. So go ahead, Mrs. Carter, take it all off, and then close your eyes. Wait for me… I will be there. I will be there…

Yasmine shuddered as Robert's voice faded out and Babyface took the lead. Her body tightened, her chest heaved, her breasts grew painfully full and tight and her nipples hard, as excitement prickled her skin.

She would never get used to Robert's displays of seduction, never be bored with him. A delicious shudder heated her body at the thought that he might be lurking somewhere in the shadows watching her. She wasn't going to disappoint her husband, not after he'd gone through all this trouble to surprise her.

With Babyface's ballad of love and Robert's alluring promises resounding in her heart, Yasmine toed off her pumps and shoved them to the side, then stood with her body poised like a ballerina about to perform, and her gaze straight ahead as if she were gazing into her lover's eyes. *Ready. Set.*

Swaying flirtatiously to the tempo of the music, she eased her jacket off her shoulders and dropped it on the floor behind her. Free of that first piece of clothing, she rolled her head back, thrust her chest forward, and slowly trailed her fingers up along her thighs and across her hips and stomach. She paused to free her blouse from the waist of her skirt before her hands resumed their leisurely titillating journey north, over her breasts.

Pausing again, she squeezed her tender mounds and gasped from the self-indulgent pleasurable sensations rippling down her belly to the quivering apex of her thighs. Her tongue darted from her mouth to glide sensuously across her dry lips. With unsteady fingers, she began undoing the buttons of her blouse one at a time, and when she reached the bottom, she straightened her arms at her sides and wiggled the blouse off her shoulders. She moaned softly as the silky material brushed her body on its way to the floor, whispering promises like a lover's touch.

As Babyface crooned about getting it on, of turning her on, of no intermissions, of her body growing weak and needing attention, Yasmine unzipped her skirt and, bending forward, she worked it off her hips, over her derriere and down to her ankles. As she stepped out of it and stood, clad in nothing but her black lacy bra and matching panties, Yasmine swore she heard a low groan coming from the vicinity of the living room. *So he was watching her.*

The muscles of her sex contracted vehemently and visions of her husband stroking his huge hard shaft as he watched her undress flashed across her vision. So strong was the image, Yasmine squeezed her thighs together and breathed deeply to fight the dizziness threatening to overtake her. Her dance wasn't over yet, and she knew her curtain would have to fall before the show really began.

Incited by her rising temperature, Yasmine reached behind her and unclasped her bra. Her breasts sprang from the tight restriction and bounced with the simple joy of being free, her nipples growing harder in anticipation of being caressed, of being licked, of being nibbled.

With her body warm and flushed from the heat of the candles, her heart beating with the pulse of the music, the stimulating lyrics, the sultry vocals, and the expectancies of the night, Yasmine eagerly hooked her thumbs into the waist of her thong and pushed the damp strip of silk off her hips, down her thighs and legs, and stepped out of them.

A flood of warm liquid tricked down the insides of her thighs as she removed her earrings and dropped them carefully on her pile of clothes. They would be safe, she thought, dropping her hands to her sides and closing her eyes as the music died and the room grew quiet.

Robert clasped his hand tightly around his shaft as he fought to steady his racing breath. His wife was one hot, wickedly tempting woman, and she hadn't disappointed him. Watching the surprise on her exquisite face when she'd stepped into their love cove had been priceless, and watching her undress had been pleasurably painful. He'd almost come all over himself when she'd removed her bra and her breasts had bounced forth like excited children bursting out of the classroom doors for recess.

Anxious to move the evening along, Robert stepped out of the shadows and allowed his eyes to feast freely on his wife, clad in his favorite outfit—skin. Smooth, soft, silky chocolate skin, drawn tautly and tantalizingly across every provocative curve of her slender body. She was perfection, every man's dream, and every woman's envy.

A hard lump formed in his throat as his gaze rested on the dark-brown mist of her curls cascading from her crown to the delicate curves of her shoulders, shoulders that extended into toned slender arms and delicate hands and fingers that brought him laughter, comfort, warmth, and passion, with just the slightest touch.

He loved the many shades of Yasmine, from the playful girl he'd known as a child, to the poised, intelligent woman and the insatiable nymph she'd grown into. Her beauty was exquisite, fragile, he thought as he took in her dark arched brows, her delicate ears, and long dark lashes fluttering nervously on her cheekbones. He smiled when she wrinkled her nose, jutted her chin forward, and curved her mouth into a frown, probably wondering where he was and what was going on.

Lowering his gaze, Robert took his time admiring the swell of her breasts, firm and full, rising from her chest like two glowing globes of wonder, pleading to be noticed, caressed, molded and shaped. Her erect dark nipples, poking curiously from the center of the puffy knolls of her areolas, were just as enthralling. His mouth watered with the memory of nibbling on her nipples, sucking them into his mouth, tasting the sweet nectar of her woman's essence passing down his throat.

Robert's shaft pulsed against his belly as his gaze caressed the soft flat planes of Yasmine's stomach, fuller at the edges, and tumbling like a gentle rolling hill into the well of her belly button, a place he'd learned to give special attention after discovering it was one of her many erogenous zones.

Inches lower, his gut contracted at the sight of the neatly trimmed dark thatch of hair on her Venus mound, made even more prominent by the flatness of her stomach. And just below that, the glory of her womanhood, the lips swollen and glittering from the juices already seeping from inside her. Robert licked his lips as he recalled the pleasure of licking her feminine softness, the heat of her, and the sensation of being coated with her love sauce.

Reluctantly, his eyes drifted to her thighs that would soon be pressed against the sides of his head while he feasted on her, her shapely legs that would be wrapped around his waist at one point and tossed over his shoulders at another, her delicate heels that would be battering against his buttocks while he slammed into her over and over again, and her dainty toes, another of her erogenous zones, that would be curling inside his mouth while he licked them.

His eyes roved over her one last time from her head to her red-painted toenails, drinking in the wholesome beauty of her smooth chocolate skin glowing in the candlelight. She looked ethereal, unreal in the dim light.

Robert walked toward Yasmine, lust and love running wildly inside him like a swift-flowing river. His heart rippled with longing when he caught a whiff of the female aroma emanating from her body. Like a jungle cat in heat, she was sending out her signals, letting every male in a five-mile radius know that she was ready, willing, and waiting to be taken. Lucky for him, he was the only male in the vicinity, the only male who would be answering her call to mate tonight, and every night for the rest of their lives.

Yasmine felt as if she'd been standing in the dark for an eternity before his shadow fell across her, and the airstream from his body fanned hers as he circled her, moving around her like a phantom before coming to a stop behind her. There were no footsteps, not even the sound of his breathing. "Rob—"

"Shh. No talking yet, my love."

He stood close to her, so close that the heat from his naked body scorched the skin off her back, and her nostrils picked up the natural musky aroma of his body. He smelled of sex. Precum. Mixed with the vanilla fragrance from the burning candles, it was spicy and invigorating. He brushed against her lightly, his body warm and tight, his knees rasping the backs of her thighs, his hairy thighs brushing the hills of her buttocks, his erection, hot and hard, grazing the curve of her back. The shock of him reverberated throughout her entire body, making her tremble, and sending her heart into a frenzied dance.

Would they make love now, here, like they'd done before— with her bent forward, her hands braced against the floor while he entered her from behind? Yasmine's knees went weak at the thought, and she would have collapsed from a combination of excitement and vertigo had he not reached out his hand to steady her. Passion pulsated where he touched her. She whimpered in protest when he withdrew his hand.

Behind her, Robert stifled a groan as his shaft tightened and swelled with need and his fingers itched to caress every inch of her like he'd promised. But he knew that if he touched her intimately, they would end up making love right here and now. And he had much more than a downstairs quickie planned for the night. He hoped she was hungry for him, because, Dear Lord, he was starving for her. Taking a deep breath of control, he pulled a black satin scarf from around his neck, fashioned it into a blindfold, and placed it across her eyes.

She jumped at the initial contact and her hands grabbed his arms. "Rob—"

"Shh. It's okay. Trust me," he whispered, tying the scarf at the back of her head. She'd never been blindfolded before, and he could understand her instant reaction to temporarily losing control of one of her senses. When she relaxed and dropped her hands, he turned her around, his gaze automatically dropping to her open mouth.

Fighting the desire to kiss her, he bent down, hooked his arms at the back of her knees and lifted her.

"Oh," she gasped, her arms instantly going around his neck. "Rob—"

"I said no talking, Mrs. Carter. Do I have to muzzle you too, my love?"

She shook her head, her mouth curving into a smile.

"Good, because I do look forward to hearing your groans and moans of ecstasy as I pleasure you tonight." His walk toward the stairs was made difficult with his cock trapped between his stomach and her hip, but since he would soon be rewarded for his patience, he grunted and bore it.

Yasmine rested her cheek against Robert's chest and gave herself over to the motion of floating through the air as he climbed the stairs with her. With her sense of sight temporarily inhibited, all the others in her system were magnified a hundredfold. His heart beat under her ears with a ferocity she'd never heard before, and she swore she could hear the blood rushing through the chambers of his heart like a river of fire cascading toward a deep waterfall. Her hip burned where his erection rubbed up against her at each step he took.

She tightened her arms around him as the soft sounds of jazz graced her ears and the heady aroma of sandalwood tickled her nostrils. Robert wasn't lying. Jazz and sandalwood did wonders for his libido. This was going to be an all-night affair.

Robert walked into their dimly lit bedroom and over to the king-size bed, surrounded by a circle of burning candles. He placed his wife gently down on her back in the middle of the bed. His eyes misted at the erotic image of her brown form nestled in a carpet of red and white rose petals scattered on the white silk sheet. She was his Yasmine, the only woman he'd ever loved.

"I want to see you," she whispered, reaching out her arms. "It's been two days."

"Soon, love." *Soon.* He eased onto the bed next to her feet. "I promised to kiss every inch of your body, and I'm starting right here," he whispered, clasping her ankles. "So lie back, relax, and enjoy the ride, my darling."

Yasmine squeezed her eyes behind the blindfold and sucked air into her lungs when Robert raised her feet straight up into the air and pressed her limbs into his stomach while he massaged her insteps with his thumbs. She sucked in another breath when his hot wet tongue made a sudden and delicious contact with the underside of her little toe, then dragged across them all toward the other side, and over to her other foot.

Blast after blast of tingling sensation whipped down her legs and headed straight into the core of her wet sex as he sucked and licked her toes intermittently. "Robert," she panted, her legs shaking and her toes curling into his mouth as the onslaught of Robert's fingers caressing her buttocks and belly, and the acute sensation of his cock pumping between her thighs sent the flames careening to every nerve in her body.

As the fire consumed her, Yasmine fisted her hands around the sheet. Her head thrashed frantically about on the pillow. Her back arched, her hips drove into Robert's hand now stationed on her stomach while one of his fingers thrust back and forth into her navel like a mini cock loving her there. And then it happened —her first orgasm of the night. She exploded into a trillion fiery pieces just as a river of hot lava gushed from inside her, forced out by the powerful contractions taking place deep inside her womb.

"One." Robert's heart was thumping in his ears and his cock felt like it was on fire as he watched Yasmine writhing on the sheets, rose petals stuck to her damp skin and nestled in her hair, her stomach rolling like a wind-tossed wave beneath his palm, and her mouth frozen open in the rapturous thrill of pleasure. He removed her toes from his mouth and gazed down at the juices dripping down his belly, past his thighs and knees to soak into the mattress. He'd done that to her, turned her into a quivering pot of ecstasy in less than five minutes.

While she moaned and shivered in the aftermath, he eased her legs to the bed and settled down beside her. Her skin was warm and silky under his lips as he kissed the ankles of one foot, before making his way slowly upward with just enough pressure to let her know it wasn't over, but not deep enough to send her over the edge again too soon. He groaned, as he tasted the smear of love juices on her thigh. Her smell, her heat called out his name as he passed his nose and mouth across her groin en route to the other thigh, and then down, kissing his way to the ankles of her other foot.

When she finally lay still, he spread her thighs, settled himself between them, and placed her legs across his shoulders. There was no time for napping tonight. *Divine sweetness*, he thought as his fingers caressed her.

Yasmine moaned deep in her throat as Robert's fingertips grazed, then parted her. She felt his hot breath on her flesh as his head came closer and closer. He moved his head from side to side, grazing the mat of hair on her mound, sending a streak of tiny shivers into her groin and belly. He opened her wider, and then his tongue licked at the insides of her folds, ever so gently, gliding back and forth from one side to the next, avoiding her little knob, the powerhouse of her femininity that had begun to swell and pulse, nonetheless.

And then he flicked it, pulling a series of long groans out of her as he fluttered back and forth over it like a blind butterfly hovering over a petal, unable to latch on to its target. His lips encased it, tugging gently, his tongue rolling over it, inviting her to dance to the music of his magical touch. Soon her pleasure deepened and her body tightened, and she grabbed his head, and thrust her hips into his face, imploring him to ravish her as she trembled on the edge of another euphoric bliss.

His lips moved against her, nibbling her, his thumb replacing his tongue on her clit as he headed south to explore the most intimate landscape of her body, seeking out and then sinking into her tight opening, withdrawing to work a finger inside her, then inserting his tongue again. Over and over he teased her, played with her, his groans echoing deep inside her as he strummed her mercilessly with his finger, his tongue, and his thumb.

Yasmine locked her thighs against his head and beat her heels against his back, screaming out his name as electricity hummed through. And then she burst into flames, shattering once again into a million glowing stars. She collapsed into the mattress, engulfed in a sea of blistering sensations. "Robert…"

Robert eased up as his name tumbled pitifully from Yasmine's lips. This orgasm was powerful, beyond his imagination, and he didn't want to wear her out yet. Her body had been wound so tightly, for a minute it felt like she would rip his tongue out of his mouth. Never had he experienced anything so freaking wild. His entire face was drenched, and so was the mattress.

He lapped the last of her juices from inside her, swallowed it with a satisfied gulp. "Sweet darling," he said, wiping his chin on the soft thatch of hair on her mound. He removed her legs from his shoulders, spread them wide on the mattress and knelt on the damp warm spot between them. He couldn't deny himself anymore. He'd promised to kiss every inch of her body, but the night was still young. But he'd also promised to take her when her body was weak. *It was weak.*

Bending over her, Robert fitted the ridge of his shaft between her slick folds, hissing as the pulsing heat spread through the length of him. Supporting his weight on his knees and elbows, he stretched out on her, his face close to hers. He covered her mouth with his at the same time his hands curved around the swell of her breasts, and his hips began to move sensuously against hers.

She whimpered as if she were being awakened from a drugged sleep, then her lips parted, her tongue came forth to dance with his and her nipples hardened and pushed into his palms. She was feeling him, all of him. His heart rocked in his chest as her arms wrapped around his back and her legs around his waist. He kissed her deeply, strumming the roof of her mouth, the sides of her cheeks and the insides of her lips. His cock was drenched with her love, his skin burning with her affection as their passions for and because of each other began to peak.

She started thrusting against him feverishly, her hands rushing up and down his back, her thighs closing and opening against his hips, inviting him to come inside. Releasing her mouth, his lips trailed over her chin to her neck where he licked at the sensitive skin. As she sighed into the night, he brushed his lips over one heaving breast and drew the nipple into his mouth, sucking and teasing before moving to the other.

When he felt her body quivering beneath him, Robert reached between them and fitted the tip of his cock to the tight opening of Yasmine's sex. He then reached up, removed her blindfold, and tossed it aside. And as he gazed into the enraptured depths of her sweet beguiling eyes, he drove his cock deep, deep inside her.

Her hips arched upward. Her limbs locked around him. She screamed and came all over him. The pure heavenly rhapsody of her orgasm twisted around him and as her body gripped him tight as a fist, he began to thrust into her, riding her deeper into the vortex of her climax.

Yasmine sobbed helplessly as the sweetly agonizing friction from Robert's thrusts sent a blaze of fire ripping through her, churning her blood into a stream of hot flowing lava. His cock felt as if it had been rooted permanently inside her. There was no space to breathe, no room to move. The quivering of her flesh had become so in tune with his that she could not tell where his ended and where hers began.

They moved sensuously against each other, seasoned lovers, the slap of their flesh punctuated by the liquid, slippery sounds of male hardness sliding in and out of woman's wet heat. It was the most intimate, glorious, efficacious sound in the universe.

Robert wrapped his arms around Yasmine's drenched and trembling body. They had been making love for a long time, and she had been writhing in the throes of her orgasm since he'd entered her. He was in no hurry to get anywhere but right where he was. He was just enjoying the ride, the erotic thrill of watching his wife fall to pieces again and again at his hands, grateful that he was the one to make her moan and scream out his name all night long.

But all good things did come to an end, he realized, when the initial twinges, the barest of tingling in his spine indicated the approach of his own release. Flexing his buttocks, he began to pump with more power and strength, watching her head thrash wildly back and forth on the mattress, her curls whipping about her face, tears of pleasure rolling over the rose petals stuck to her cheeks.

The succulent walls of her vagina gripped the entire length of his cock, massaging it in moist heat, shaping itself to every ridge and contour as his cock grew harder and thicker, sending fire and ice whisking along the length of his body.

She mewled in his ears, drummed her heels into his buttocks and raked her nails down his back, spurring him on like a jockey on a galloping horse. Her passion proved too much for Robert. He felt his orgasm sizzle in his toes, surge up his legs into his spine, his back, his heart, his head, then back down to his groin. He rose up over her, stiffened, and exploded inside her with a harsh cry. He felt the squirts of their mixed juices splatter around him. Her muscles clamped down, fluttering and massaging like a tight gripping fist.

He watched in amazement as her eyes rolled back in her head and she exploded again. Calling on the power of his virility one last time, he rode her through her orgasm then collapsed on her, both of them shivering violently, clinging to each other until their spasms stopped and her legs and arms just dropped to the bed, limp.

Their bodies melded together, his world filled with her and hers filled with him.

Robert sighed as he rolled to his side and pulled Yasmine close, their sexes still joined. No intermission. He smiled at the reason he could let go and enjoy his wife to the maximum.

Yasmine didn't know it yet, but yesterday he'd visited the place where his fear of heights had begun. Afterward, he'd gone to Disney World and taken all the wildest rides he could handle. He'd had a damned good time, screaming his head off in excitement and not in fear for the first time in his life. As he'd moved from one ride to the next, all he'd been thinking about was taking his own children to amusement parks when they were old enough.

And tonight for the first time, Robert had experienced the joy of ultimate bonding with his wife in heart, body, spirit, and soul. He knew now that he could go the distance with her, and she with him, all because he'd finally let go of his fears. His heart was open to any and everything. And so was hers for blindly trusting him without question.

"I'm pregnant."

Robert stiffened at the soft whisper. They'd been lying quietly together for a while. Maybe she'd fallen asleep like she usually did, and was dreaming. His thought flew from his head when her hand came out to caress his cheek. Robert raised his head to gaze at her. Her eyes were wide, the pupils still dilated and glittering from their hour-long labor of love.

"I'm pregnant," she said again, as if reading the doubts in his mind. She caught her lower lip between her teeth as she beamed up at him. "We're going to have a baby, Robert. Why do you look so surprised?" she asked, when he continued to look at her, speechlessly. "It isn't like we haven't been trying since we got married."

Robert's heart pounded against his chest, and his throat tightened as his tears spilled from his eyes and fell into her palm. "A baby. We're going to have a baby."

"Yes, baby. Yes. You're going to be a father, Robert. It's the one thing you've wanted more than anything in the world. You'll have it in eight months."

He shook his head from side to side as his thumb caressed her brows, her forehead, the bridge of her nose, her lips. "No, Yas. You are what I've needed more than anything in this world. This, here," he added, his hands dropping to her stomach where his child now lay nestled, "is a beautiful reward, a byproduct, an extension of my love for you. Thank you, Mrs. Carter. I love you, so much."

"I love you too, Mr. Carter."

They kissed for a few minutes as the joyful news of their

impending parenthood fused them together on an entirely different level.

Eventually, Yasmine drew back and smiled at him. "Why'd you blindfold me?"

"Were you scared, bothered by it?"

"No. I liked it. Loved it. It intensified all my other senses. I smelled everything, heard everything, felt everything. It was like we were one, moving in the darkness together."

"That was the idea, for you to feel my love." He would tell her about his trip to Disney World later. "I also want you to know that you can trust me to take care of you. I will be your eyes when you can't see, your ears when you can't hear. I'll be your everything."

"You are." She gave him a smile that rocked his soul. "To me and our children. You'll be the best father in the world, Rob. Our child will be proud to call you *Daddy*."

Daddy. Her smile was magnificently alluring, and her walls contracted around him, reminding him that he'd promised to make love to her all night long. "Are you up to it?" he asked, gazing into her eyes, as he pushed up inside her.

"Yes. I'll never have enough of you," she said, pushing back.

"Then, let's begin the process all over again."

"No water tonight?" she asked, teasing.

"No water. No sleeping." With skillful dexterity, Robert maneuvered their bodies around until she was lying on her stomach, her cheek on the pillow while he straddled her back. They had not separated.

He traced his fingertip across her lips. "You are my water, and this time, I start at your mouth and work my way slowly south."

Leaning across her back, Robert dipped his head and captured Yasmine's mouth in a deep, tantalizing kiss…

EPILOGUE

Ten months later...

On his way to the nursery, Robert stopped on the open landing and gazed down at the blended families of Reynolds, LaCrosses, Bradburys, Montenegros, and Mrs. Hayes enjoying themselves.

The women were seated in various groups, chattering, sipping wine, and nibbling on the desserts that followed the delicious lunch his grandmother and Mrs. Hayes had prepared. Little Erik, Tiffany, and Fiona were running around chasing each other, and occasionally joining a group of adults until they got bored and moved on, while Neil, Precious, and Peter were in the media room playing video games on the wall size TV screen.

They had all assembled in his and Yasmine's new home, situated in a town north of Boston, to help them celebrate a most joyous occasion—the christening of their son, Robert Javier Dwight Carter-Bradbury. The ceremony had taken place this morning at the church where he and Yasmine worshipped.

It was hard to believe that only a year ago, Robert had been oblivious to the existence of his Aunt Camille, his cousins, Allison and Neil, and his grandmother, Margaret, all of whom he'd grown to love dearly, and all of whom were equally elated to know that they weren't alone in the world. For the first time in his life, Robert had a genuine sense of what family was all about.

He had contemplated dropping Carter and adopting his biological grandfather's name, but had finally decided to hyphenate his last names since the Carters had adopted Dwight and had given him a nice home. He might have had a good life if the Carters hadn't been killed.

Robert and Michelle had finally given a press conference late last year to let the world know that the man who'd raised them wasn't their father, but a murderer and an imposter. They'd paid dearly for that announcement in the ensuing days and weeks with news reporters hounding them down for more information. The madness was all over, and the media vultures had moved on to newer stories. At least, their father's name was cleared publicly, and the infamy had been removed from the Carter name permanently.

Robert leaned against the banister and smiled at the cheerful laughter of his grandmother, his aunt, his mother-in-law, Felicia, and Mrs. Hayes, who occupied some chairs near the balcony overlooking an Olympic-sized swimming pool and a forest of trees in the background.

It was nice to see his grandmother fitting in so well and making new friends, probably the best friends she'd had all her life. She had sold the Montenegro estate, given all the proceeds to charity, and moved to New England permanently. She now spent her time between the LaCrosse and the Carter-Bradbury estates.

Her presence in their lives had proved invaluable during the last weeks of Yasmine's pregnancy and directly following Robbie's birth. She'd been a big help and companion to

Yasmine's mom who'd moved in with them for a while. Yasmine had had a hard delivery, so it was nice to have them both here to divide their time and attention between his wife and his son while he was at the office.

Hearing his wife's lively chuckle, Robert transferred his gaze to the other side of the room where Yas, Michelle, Allison, Naomi, and Christine were sprawled on the floor, their heads propped up on cushions as they looked at photographs of Christian Bradbury in one of the many albums Aunt Camille had brought with her.

The men—Erik, Philippe, Daddy Reynolds, Luke, and Felix —were downstairs in Robert's man cave, shooting pool and complaining about their wives. Robert chuckled to himself at their surprise that he'd had nothing to complain about.

"We'll check in with you in another year or two," Erik had said, as Robert had excused himself to take a business call a few minutes ago, and had thought to check in on his son while he was in the vicinity.

Involuntarily, his gaze returned to the mother of his child. He loved her beyond words, beyond comprehension. He never knew it was possible to love a woman more and more with the passing of each day. She had given him the kind of family he'd had for the first four years of his life with his mother and his father. She had given him the opportunity to be the kind of father and husband Dwight had been. She had put him back together even before he knew he was broken. And now he had more family than he'd ever dreamed of having, all because of Yasmine.

There was nothing to complain about. He had everything his heart could ever desire. And so did Yasmine, *he hoped*.

He'd talked her into taking Hayward's offer, and now she was part owner of the most prosperous law firm in Massachusetts: Hayward & Haley, Reynolds & Hendricks. They'd grown so big, they had opened up two other branches, one in Rhode Island,

and one in Manchester, New Hampshire. The lawyers in Manchester were required to continue the pro bono work Yasmine had started four years ago.

She continued to practice law, not because she *needed* to, but because she *wanted* to. Robert had set up an office for her in one of the two cottages on their ten-acre estate. And so, like Alicia Florrick on *The Good Wife*, Yasmine entertained selective clients at home.

She was a wife and mother, yet she didn't have to concern herself with cooking, cleaning, and all the other important things women worried about. She had servants at her beck and call. Being pleased by her husband in bed and nurturing their son were her only "womanly" duties, the only two things she had to concentrate on. Not a bad life. Not a bad life at all.

Robert tensed as his son's cry came through the hallway monitor. He was awake. He headed down the corridor to the other end of the second floor where the master suite and the nursery were located. Unaccustomed to so much noise, Robbie had found it impossible to sleep in the basinet they kept on the first floor. Robert hoped he would grow out of it since he planned to throw and attend many more family gatherings like this one.

"Hey you." Robert reached into the crib and lifted his son into his arms. Robbie stared at him through a pair of wide, intelligent, brilliant brown eyes—his mother's eyes—and then his cute little mouth opened wide in a toothless yawn. He was beautiful, perfect, his button of a nose a tiny replica of Robert's, his little chin already showing signs of strength and stubbornness.

"Oh, you need a change, don't you?" He placed Robbie on the changing table and in less than a minute, Robbie's little bottom was wiped, powdered, and sporting a fresh dry diaper. Robert picked him up, pressed his lips against his forehead for a few priceless moments before holding him close to his heart, his entire body shaking with joy and pride and love as he felt his son's little heart beating against his own.

Cradling Robbie in the crook of his arm, he walked to a window overlooking a pond. As he stood there, gazing into his son's eyes, he was overcome with an intense sense of protection, the kind his own father must have felt as he'd held an infant Robert in his arms. He so wished his parents were here to see their grandchild.

Robert brushed his knuckles against his son's cheeks. "I love you, Robbie. I will always love you. I promise to protect you, son. With my life, if it comes down to that. I will never let anyone hurt you. Or your mom. You can trust me, okay? I got you, my boy. Daddy's got you." The love in Robert's heart was so fierce, so full that it overflowed, choking him, pushing tears from his eyes, and sending them rolling off his cheeks on to Robbie's face.

In response, his son squirmed in his arms and began to fuss. And when he shoved his tiny fist into his mouth and began sucking on it, Robert chuckled. "Oh, I get it. You're trying to tell your old man to shut up and feed you. Well, let's go see if we can find you something warm and soft—"

"Talking about me?"

Robert turned, and his heart did a jig of love at the sight of his tantalizing wife, wearing an attractive coral silk dress that buttoned down the front. She'd lost all her baby-weight, but her curves had matured stunningly. "Always," he said, grinning, as she closed the nursery door and walked over to them.

"Oh, my little boo is hungry, huh?" she crooned, kissing their son's cheeks and running her hand over the soft mat of curly black hair on his head. "It's just as well, 'cause I'm about to have a letdown." She pressed her hands against her breasts and sat down in the rocking chair under the window.

Robert placed their son on her lap and knelt in front of them. "Does that mean you have enough for both of us?" he asked, unbuttoning the top half of her dress, and helping her slide the silky material off her shoulders. He bunched it around her waist, away from Robbie's face.

"Always." Her eyes twinkled with passion as she smiled at him. "Why'd you think I closed the door?" She caressed his cheeks with one hand, while holding their son securely with the other. "Gotta feed my men."

"God bless you." Robert unclasped her nursing bra, and groaned when her beautiful brown, full-to-bursting breasts sprang from their damp cotton prison and into his hands. "You did have a little letdown." He molded her gently, watching the play of emotions in her eyes, and loving the soft sighs escaping her slightly parted lips as he rubbed his palms over the wide expanse of her dark moist nipples—an endless source of pleasure for him and nourishment for their hungry son—who was now whining and kicking his legs and arms about in a frenzy.

"Impatient, aren't you?" Robert smiled at his son.

"Just like his daddy. Can't get enough of Mommy," Yasmine whispered on a chuckle.

"Never." Robert lifted her left breast and aimed the protruding nipple to Robbie's little mouth. He smiled as the baby's lips immediately latched on to it, and he began making suckling sounds like he'd been starving for a whole day.

Butterflies fluttered in his belly as he watched his son, his second child nurse from his mother as she gently squeezed her breast, pumping the milk into his mouth. Love and devotion were painted on both their faces as they gazed into each other's eyes. It were as if they were cocooned in their own world, totally enthralled with each other, in their own magical sacred space where only a mother and her child could inhabit.

This is what genuine, ultimate happiness feels like, Robert thought, as he gazed at his little family—a family he hoped would grow and thrive in time.

An intense feeling of peace and contentment washed over him, even as his mind wandered to the baby they'd lost. But instead of being filled with regrets and grief, he was filled with curiosity and wonder about what that child would be like today. He saw, felt, and heard the spirit of that child everywhere: in the rustle of the tree leaves outside the window, in the clouds drifting aimlessly in a clear blue sky, in the sound of an ocean wave breaking on the shore. He or she was an angel, a ubiquitous mystery that would live on in his mind forever.

He brushed his fingers across Yasmine's cheeks. She started and then inhaled sharply on a smile as their eyes locked in love. "I love you, Yasmine," he said, his voice trembling with overpowering emotions. "Thank you for giving me a son, for making me a father."

"I love you, too, Robert." Her voice broke as she smiled through her tears of happiness. "Thank *you* for giving me another chance to become a mother. It's the most wonderful feeling in the world. Our son is so blessed to have you as a father."

"He's doubly blessed with you as a mother, Yas." Robert put his arms around them, an amalgamation of filial love flowing copiously from the depths of his soul—fatherly love for his son, and desire and passion for his wife.

Their postpartum sex life had been extended because Yasmine needed extra time to heal. Robbie had entered the world at a whopping ten pounds and six ounces, causing Yasmine's doctor to perform an episiotomy on her. They'd been pleasuring each other orally for the past few weeks, but enough was enough. "How much longer do we have to wait before we can make love? Real love?"

"Just a few more days. I see Dr. Blair on Thursday. I think she'll give us the go-ahead then."

Robert groaned. "It might as well be a few more years. I'm

burning up for you. As much as King Rob loves the attention your enticing mouth has been lavishing on him, he misses *you*."

"I know, baby. I miss him too."

"And speaking of mouths…" Robert leaned in and captured Yasmine's sweet succulent lips with his. Electricity sizzled between them as he kissed her softly and gently, their tongues dancing intimately around each other, making promises of the unbridled passion that was soon to come.

Reluctantly releasing her mouth, he trailed hot kisses over her chin, down her neck, to her heaving chest and the pulsing fullness of her right breast. Their sighs of pleasure echoed in the nursery as his mouth closed over her nipple and he sucked the hot honeyed essence from inside her.

"Robert," she whispered on a shudder. Her hand clasped around his head, holding him close to her breast.

As he reveled in the abundance of blessings that had been bestowed upon him, Robert's heart sang with the sheer delight that came from Loving Yasmine.

THE END

Dear Reader,

I hope you enjoyed following Robert and Yasmine on their journey to *Happily Ever After* in **Loving Yasmine,** the first book in my ***Beyond Granite Falls*** series.

I wish you all the best in your search for that one special "Someone", and if you've already found him/her, then continue to revel in happiness.

Blessings,

Ana

❦

Visit me: www.anaeross.com

Email me: ana@anaeross.com